AN INFI

RESETTING DESTINY

LIV MACY

ALSO BY LIV MACY

The Infinite Universe novels are a set of interconnected, stand-alones. There is no required reading order.

Recommended order:

The Infinites Universe Novels
Becoming Justice
Resetting Destiny

Content/Trigger Warnings: Death, violence, sex, strong language

Copyright 2023 Liv Macy and Write To Read Publishing, LLC

Thank you for buying this book and for complying with copyright laws by not reproducing, scanning, or distributing any part of it in any form without permission. All rights reserved. No part of this publication may be used or reproduced without express permission of the author.

ISBN: 979-8-9872661-2-0

Printed in the United States of America

This is a work of fiction. Names, characters, places, incidents either are the product of the author's imagination or are used fictitiously, and any resemblance to actual persons, living or dead, business establishments, events or locales is entirely coincidental.

Contents

Chapter One	1
Chapter Two	7
Chapter Three	13
Chapter Four	25
Chapter Five	31
Chapter Six	39
Chapter Seven	49
Chapter Eight	59
Chapter Nine	65
Chapter Ten	77
Chapter Eleven	81
Chapter Twelve	89
Chapter Thirteen	99
Chapter Fourteen	107
Chapter Fifteen	113
Chapter Sixteen	123
Chapter Seventeen	131
Chapter Eighteen	139
Chapter Nineteen	145
Chapter Twenty	151
Chapter Twenty-One	159
Chapter Twenty-Two	169
Chapter Twenty-Three	181
Chapter Twenty-Four	195
Chapter Twenty-Five	209
Chapter Twenty-Six	225
Chapter Twenty-Seven	233
Chapter Twenty-Eight	243
Chapter Twenty-Nine	257
Chapter Thirty	271
Chapter Thirty-One	281

Chapter Thirty-Two	297
Chapter Thirty-Three	307
Chapter Thirty-Four	319
Acknowledgments	327
About the Author	329

"They say soul mates will find each other—and that may be true—but they don't tell you about the pain you feel without them. Some will wander, numbing their body until they can function day to day. Some will forget, oblivious to the underlying torment that batters them. And some will burn through their emotions, tearing down everything in their path until they find the other. All of them searching for what makes them whole."

Chapter One

DELANEY

A moan slips from between my lips when the buttery, creamy flavor of a spinach- and cheese-covered oyster explodes on my tongue.

"Do you know you're sexy as hell when you eat like that?"

The whisper flutters through my mind as surely as if Ty had spoken it, and I squeeze my eyes shut.

"Do you know they say oysters are an aphrodisiac?"

My response then had been threaded with sultry tones and flirty innuendo.

"Madame. Are you ready for the next course?"

Though quiet, the voice breaks through my reverie and my eyes pop open, heat rushing through my cheeks. The waiter side-eyes me, looking slightly embarrassed. I shouldn't have come here, thinking the memories wouldn't hit hard. Even after all this time.

"No, I won't be staying after all. Just the check please."

Outside, I wait for the valet in the crisp and breezy evening, a typical mid-Atlantic spring night. The clatter of daylight has slowly drifted to the hum of twilight, and buildings shine with a million lights reflecting from streetlamps.

Stewart's Creek may sound like a town of green grass country, but the only thing the city's farming is glass and pavement. It never sleeps, just snoozes a bit, and the scene is so close to my last visit that a band tightens around my chest.

We had just celebrated our one-year wedding anniversary... and I had let spill the secret I'd been guarding all day.

We were going to have a baby.

I close my eyes, willing myself to see nothing behind the lids. No more memories tonight. Tyson's been gone for five years, and I thought that enough time had passed that I could enjoy dinner at my favorite restaurant. I'd felt drawn to it tonight, but never again.

A black van pulls up to the curb, its once-shiny patina molded by age and reckless drivers, beaten into a defeated version of itself. There's something sinister about it, and my stomach clenches. I step back, gasping, as the door slides open.

A vortex of black nothingness swirls the air.

Bodies in black from head to toe, only their eyes exposed, spill out of the doorway. I swivel, taking them all in. Who are they? Why are they here? I can't tell if they're male or female. Ominous weaponry hangs by various methods on arms, legs, and backs.

Suddenly, self-preservation kicks in and I turn and run, hampered by my heels. I don't want to be around for whatever they're here for. The sting of something cuts into my shoulder, and I run harder, knowing better than to turn around to see how close someone might be.

A patch of uneven sidewalk trips me, and everything slows. My purse sails through the air and lands on the concrete, the contents vomited out in a drunken purge. As my head bangs into and ricochets off the stone curb, pain lances through me and my vision blurs.

Someone leaps onto my back, a knee digging in, grinding the bones of my hips into unyielding concrete. A hand viciously fists my hair, pulling back hard and exposing my throat. I struggle to drag in oxygen.

"Finally." What sounds like a woman's voice hisses in my ear. "Destiny is at an end."

What? They're after me? Why?

I wildly track a curved knife in my peripheral, swinging down. This is it. My blood will spill out and my life will end.

Katrina, my beautiful baby girl. I squirm, but there's very little else I can do, and tears leak out the corner of my eyes. Tires scream through the air, and the smell of rubber burning forces my eyes up.

Is that my car?

POP!

My head's quickly released, and I gasp in glorious air. The dead weight of my would-be assassin falls onto my back, liquid soaking my shirt, the warmth weirdly comforting.

I remain on the ground, staring wide-eyed at the hand that drapes over my shoulder in a macabre embrace. My body begins shaking, stones digging into my cheek, and a ball of energy builds in my stomach. I should get up.

I blink quickly, focusing on the open passenger window of my car and down the barrel of a silencer. The other end of the gun is connected to a hand. My eyes follow the path of corded muscle on an arm that's attached to a body. The face is gorgeous and rugged. Dark stubble and dark hair flopping over an eyebrow—and vaguely familiar.

"Delaney, you have to get moving, get your purse—leave nothing behind—and get in the car."

His voice floats out, husky and warm, soothing my body. I want to curl into a ball and purr. A sense of calm eases the pain on my face, and I close my eyes. I'm so tired, and his voice...a blanket cocoon on a rainy day. I shiver, goose bumps breaking out. Contentment wraps itself around me.

"Delaney!"

The soothing voice is insistent. I frown. How does he know my name?

"Delaney!" the voice shouts again.

"What?" I grudgingly answer. I don't want him to stop talking. It makes me feel...like I haven't in a long time. Safe.

"Get up."

The weight pinning me seems heavier, but I can't do anything about it. My arms aren't moving. Shouldn't they be pushing me up?

"Shit! Two more of the assassins are coming! Move your ass!"

The voice sounds closer with an urgency that stirs something in me. I should do as he says. Why can't I?

The weight's gone and cold air hits my back, snapping me into reality. The body. The blood. My heart stutters in increased tempo and my body temperature plummets. I'm so cold. I shakily push myself onto my hands and knees, intending to stand, but vomit burns through my throat and I throw up my dinner.

POP! Thud.

POP! Thud.

My stomach heaves, but there's nothing left. The chill increases until there must be ice in my veins. This can't be good.

"Move."

I'd like to but my limbs won't obey. Steel-like arms band around my stomach and lift me, flipping me into a cradle hold so quickly that my head spins. Warmth seeps into every fiber of my body, and it's as if I'm made of a hot, viscous fluid. I cling limply to him.

He lowers me into the passenger side, and I'm no longer warm but terrifyingly cold and numb again.

Come back! Give me more of whatever I'm feeling.

I move my head slowly in time to see an assassin through

the side mirror. The door of the van slams shut, and a gloved hand appears out their passenger window, a gun pointing toward us. I should warn my rescuer, but the words take more effort than they should.

I whimper, "They're coming."

The strange man, my savior, hops into the driver's side of my car. "I see them. Stay down."

The screen of the backup camera lights up, and we run over the bodies on the concrete. Bile rises in my throat as the car bucks and bounces. I lean my head back, trying to force air into my lungs—make my body function right—but dark spots dance in front of my eyes.

"My daughter..."

The words are garbled and barely coherent, even to me.

What's wrong with me?

My arms are heavy, and I can't lift them. The spots dance faster, and there are more of them. Closer and closer together until they converge into one big, ominous mass.

Katrina!

Buzzing begins inside my head and drowns out all sound until the darkness swallows me whole.

Chapter Two

DREW

Finally, Delaney's body succumbs to the shock of the evening. I don't know how much longer I can drive without searching her for a tracking device. The Hunters always use them, in case their prey slips their net. They're nothing if not efficient. I pull into the nearest parking garage and into a spot hopefully hidden enough from the prying eyes of nosy humans. Urgency floods me with adrenaline.

I search the vehicle first, using my phone to upload the scanning link. Once it has a connection, I wave the cell like a wand, sweeping over the car in meticulous rows, hoping I'm not leaving any inch unchecked. Lying on the ground, I stretch my arm as far under the car as I can reach. It's torturously slow, but I resist the urge to hurry. This is no time for deadly mistakes.

I open the passenger door of her car and adjust the seat to a reclining position, careful to be gentle. I'm not sure of the extent of any injuries, and I won't until I can get her home. For my sake, I hope she remains unconscious. Touching her for more than a moment, conscious or not, is physically gratifying to me, just as it is for her. There'll be no hiding it.

I ignore the sparks that fly through me. The heat that glides through our veins. It's obvious she didn't pick up on it earlier, even as a part of me reveled in it when I carried her. It's better she remains oblivious. For now. The phone's quiet as I slowly move it over her legs and upper torso but then beeps softly when it registers a tracker.

Shit.

It's embedded in her shoulder. Rage flashes through me, until a crack appears in the screen and I loosen my grip. Those bastards shot her when she was running away. In the back, like a fucking pack of wild animals.

I'll have to dig the damn thing out. Right now. Even though I want to let them come so they can get a taste of my fury. A small whimper rumbles in her throat, bringing my attention to her pale face and the shadows under her eyes. I drag in a few deep breaths, forcing my blood pressure down. All in due time.

A quick glance through the trunk assures me there's no first aid kit. What kind of mother is she?

Thank the Fates I keep my pocketknife clean and razor sharp.

Turning her slightly onto her side, I press a knee to her ribs, using enough force to stabilize her body, in case she regains consciousness. I brush aside her hair, desperate to linger in the tresses, and pay no attention to the way my heart races.

The knife slices through her skin. There it is. I only need to lever the tip under the tracker to pop it out.

"What are you doing to me? Get off! Help!" She screams, thrashing and bucking her body.

I press her down harder, slapping my hand over her mouth. "Be quiet. For fuck's sake. I'm not going to hurt you."

Her eyes roll wildly to the knife in my hand, and I move it behind my back to ease her fear.

"The guys chasing you? They shot you with a tracker. I have to dig it out or they will find you."

Recollection burns off some of the terror lurking in her eyes. She nods, her eyes still huge in her face.

"I'm going to remove my hand. Don't scream."

I wait a heartbeat for the nod, pretending the heat pouring through me at the skin-on-skin contact isn't there.

"Is everything all right here?" The thick southern accent drawls somewhere behind me.

My shoulders drop. Fuck. Of course, he must see the knife I'm holding behind my back. There's no way this doesn't look exactly what it looks like. Delaney sits up and pops her head between me and the car.

"I don't know who he is, and I'm scared. Please help me."

Ah, shit. I always forget that she won't remember me.

I step back and turn, eying the man standing in front of me. Jeans. Flannel shirt with rolled sleeves. And wearing a cowboy hat and boots, no less. Great. Country farm boys are the worst. They love their women in distress. This man isn't going to walk away. I put my hands up and step forward.

"Drop the knife."

I contemplate his request and release it, the clattering reverberating through the garage. The yokel holds his hand out, beckoning Delaney, and the cuff of his sleeve rises higher on the bicep, flashing a sliver of a tattoo—a peculiar motto in Latin on the butt of a shotgun.

I shove Delaney back into her seat. "Grab the knife! He's one of them, and they've tracked you here!"

I spring toward the Hunter, bending over and ramming my shoulder into the flesh under his rib cage. The hard bone meets the softness of his liver and kidney, and we both fly through the air. The crunch of his skull means he won't ever be able to harm her. I groan, getting to my feet. Even landing mostly on top of his body, I'm going to be hurting tomorrow. Concrete impact sucks.

I spin around and my heart momentarily stops before picking up its rhythm, sweat sliding down my back. Fury ripples through me, adding to my previous rage, and I forget the ache rolling through me. I forget the heat that had soothed me. My fists clench with the need for violence.

A second Hunter's arm is wrapped around her chest, and there's a knife at her throat. Delaney's face seems paler. Blood rushes through my veins.

"If you want your death to be painless, you'll take your fucking hands off her."

The knife shakes at her throat, and I inhale quickly. The man's going to cut her instead of pissing his pants in fear. This is getting tiresome. My hands move up in mock surrender, and the knife stabilizes and maintains a small distance from her skin. I exhale slowly. The idiot just cemented my mercy.

"You Protectors are so predictable."

I narrow my eyes at his bravado, but Delaney's snap open, confusion and chagrin written all over her face. Satisfaction curls in my gut. See? I'm not the bad guy. And where's the damn knife I dropped earlier? Did she pick it up? I search her face, willing her to understand my unspoken question. There's the slightest movement and the end of the handle peeps out of her fist. The blade must be pressed against her forearm, just like it should. Does she remember this time? My soul does a little dance, but first things first.

"And you Hunters are fucking stupid, always jumping in unprepared."

It irritates me to resort to schoolyard tactics, but there's nothing they like more than extolling their own virtues. The man's arm suddenly tightens around Delaney's chest, and red tinges my vision. The man's ego is bigger than his will to survive.

"And yet you're standing over there, and I'm over here with a weapon and the target. I think stupid isn't the right adjective you're looking for."

"The *target* you're holding isn't defenseless."

"Oh yeah, that's rich. What's she going to do, beg me to death? Talk me to death? This little lady going to do that all by herself?"

I'd be pissed at his disrespect if it wasn't exactly what I'm aiming for. Interesting though that they don't know just who and what they're hunting. The man's laughing so hard at his own joke that he doesn't notice Delaney stiffening. True to form, the insult is all it takes to give her a nudge toward violence.

"Because a woman can't possibly do you harm?"

She pivots and jams the knife into his side, miscalculating, which I expect without recent training. She loses momentum, falling hard to the ground on her knees. The gasp of pain echoes through my head, and I rush forward, ramming my shoulder against another set of liver and kidneys. I brake hard, planting my feet to the ground and willing myself not to move any farther. The Hunter flies backward and slams to a standstill against the concrete wall.

I reach down to help Delaney but think better of it, reaching instead for my pocketknife.

"Well, this is definitely dirtier than it was when I started."

"Who are you?"

The question comes out in a whisper, soft and barely distinguishable. Her face pales even further and her eyes roll back.

I dive for her, knees sliding across the pavement, and manage to catch the back of her neck, cradling her scalp in my palms just as her eyes flutter shut. Her skin is damp to the touch, and I roar my frustration.

Fuck!

I don't know how many more times I can lose her to Death.

Chapter Three

DELANEY

Sterile antiseptic. The whir and hum of machines, punctuated by beeps. My heart races, driving the beeping higher, and my stomach clenches. I hate hospitals. Have ever since they wouldn't let me in to see Tyson when he had his accident at work. I didn't care how disfiguring electrocution could be, but by the time I won the argument, Ty was dead.

What happened? My eyes pop open as everything floods back. The attackers. The Hunters. The man who saved me. Katrina!

I jerk up in the bed and gasp as pain radiates through my body and centralizes in my shoulder.

"You're okay, I promise." That voice. The cashmere soft quality of it wraps itself around me.

"My daughter. I need to get my daughter." I clear my throat and swallow, but it still feels dry.

A glass of water appears in front of me. "Here."

I gulp quickly and then peer into the cup slowly. It hadn't been tasteless. "What was in this?"

"Electrolytes."

The rugged voice suddenly isn't so innocent, no matter how my body responds to it. Why am I drinking nutrients when I'm in the hospital? There's no IV in my arm. Fear, sharp and rancid, rolls through me. The machine beeps quickly in response to my racing heart.

"Who are you and where am I?"

"The name's Drew. And I'm...a friend." He saved me. But is he though? A memory tugs at me, but I don't know why or what. It's gone before I can focus on it. "And you're in my home."

Not a hospital? I glance quickly around the room. There are no windows. But there are medical cabinets and medical machinery everywhere. I swallow hard. I've never been one for horror movies, but this seems like it would be pulled right from the plot of one.

Drew stands up from the chair again, and I press into the back of the bed. If I'm in his house, I'm truly at his mercy. He sighs and runs his hands up and through his hair, down the back of his neck, and grips it tightly before dropping them.

"If I was going to hurt you, I already would have."

Except for the murderers who like their victims screaming. His statement does nothing to ease the ball of unease in my belly.

"Your daughter is fine."

Terror crawls through me. He knows where Katrina is? How?

"You can see her whenever you feel up to it." The panic surges through me, and my throat tightens until I can't breathe. He has Katrina here. A cold sweat pops out on my back.

He sighs loudly. "I'm not the bad guy here. I'm helping you." Another sigh. "Would it make you feel better if you had a weapon?"

Do I need a weapon? I nod, not sure if I can speak without squeaking. Drew walks to a cabinet and opens it, revealing a vast array of guns attached to the wall.

My heart continues to pound and the sweat drips down my back. Why would he need all that? He removes one and walks toward me. I shrink back, wishing I wasn't scared and vulnerable. He stops and slowly reaches out, holding it by the barrel. It's pointed at him, leaving the grip free for me to take. I snatch it from him, pulling back the slider, my thumb flicking open the lock. I glance down in confusion.

How the hell did I know how to do that?

And why do I feel infinitely safer? I don't even know how to shoot this thing. I glance back up, eyes wide, raising it and aiming at his forehead. "Start talking."

Drew calmly sits back down and peruses me in silence. Did he not hear what I said? Can he tell I don't know what I'm doing?

"And your explanation better include Katrina and where she is. Why am I here?"

His face flushes red and the muscle in his jaw twitches. He's angry? Why?

"When they shot you with the tracker...it was laced with poison." The words sound as if they're wrenched from his mouth. "Backup plan I guess."

If I could imagine words spitting out, this would be it. He's more than angry, which is at odds with the effect his speech has on my body. Silk sliding across my naked skin. The softest satin nuzzling my cheek. I don't know what to process first.

"I thought I lost you." *Huh?* "And I brought you here because taking you to the hospital would make you a sitting duck. I have everything I need to take care of you, and the poison is now out of your system. You'll be fine. Katrina's right down the hall, downstairs. And I brought her here for her own safety. I assumed that's what you would want me to do?"

Uh, yeah.

He hesitates, obviously fighting something. A weight lifts from my shoulders, knowing Katrina is nearby. We can get out of here. I'll protect her from this man, if I end up needing to. I have a gun now, after all.

He kneads his thigh with one hand for a few seconds and then curls it into a fist, giving himself a quick punch. "Fuck it. You're Destiny. Well, one of the Destinies, to be precise."

Oh, boy. He's delusional. This makes getting myself and Katrina to safety trickier. Can I rationalize with him?

"I'm sorry, but my name is Delaney. You must have the wrong person." I nod. This has all been a giant misunderstanding. Those people attacking me must have also thought I was this Destiny person.

"No, not Destiny the name. Destiny, as in destiny itself, like...fate. But not Fate. That's someone else."

My heart rate increases, but then I laugh. "Did I hit my head?"

Drew frowns. Clearly, he didn't expect laughter. "Yes, why?"

I can't contain a snicker that escapes. I must have eaten too many shellfish. Maybe I'm passed out on the sofa. I lower the gun. It's not useful if it's not real. "That stuff only exists in stories and myths. I must have hit my head pretty hard. That's it. This,"—I look all around the room—"Is all something my brain concocted." I stop laughing. It really isn't funny.

"And aren't stories based on some truth? Humans turning fear or hope into something they can comprehend and use?"

I shake my head and he stands, walking toward me. I'm not afraid of him. This is all some kind of convoluted dream.

"Reallllly?" He drags the word out and pinches my toe.

Hard and fast. The warmth that briefly accompanies his words quickly turns to pain and I yelp.

This can't be. I shake my head. "No, this is ludicrous. This can't be real. Because I asked you for an explanation and this, this destiny thing, is what you're coming up with? Nonsense?" Fine. If it's real, there's something strange going on and I want out. "I want to see my daughter and I want to leave. Right now."

"You can't leave. You've got a target on your back, and I won't put you in danger."

At first, a sinking feeling hits my stomach. Then panic ensues. If this isn't a dream, he's right. Those people, whoever they are, will come after me again. Won't they?

"Why? I mean, why are they after me? Who's after me? Why won't you put me in danger? How did you know to get Katrina? What did you tell her babysitter? Why are you helping me?"

With each question, my breathing gets faster till I think I might hyperventilate. I rub my forehead, the questions cascading through my mind giving me a headache. The incessant beeping of the heart monitor seems overly loud, and my palms are clammy.

Drew's been slowly moving toward the doorway, and I focus on his retreat. Why is he looking like he wants to escape?

"It's a bit complicated. I don't know how much information to give you or how you're going to process all this. I don't know if you're going to lose your shit."

I'm confused. Why can't he just answer my questions? "Lose my shit?"

He finally comes to a standstill and leans against the door.

An escape route? What the hell?

"You know the guys at the garage called me a Protector. They're called Hunters, and they're hunting you."

A shiver runs down my spine at the memory of the cold knife against my skin. "Why?

"Something happened to you fifteen years ago."

"You're telling me that I was destiny of the world only fifteen years ago?" I *really* need to get Kat and get away from this man.

"No. You're part of a long line of Destinies. It's an inherent trait you're born with. There are usually several of you to ensure there's at least one active Destiny at all times. Of course, it's much better if there are more, but when one dies, another Destiny is born, and as you can imagine, aren't up to speed yet."

He may be beyond delusional. Because I can't be a Destiny. I'm a mom. And I already have a job. But something clicks inside my brain. And then whatever it is, it's gone, leaving only an ache behind, and I swipe at the spot, pushing my hair to the side. "This...is all ridiculous in more ways than one."

"No, it's not. You just don't remember any of it. Yet."

The word echoes around the room, loud in an obnoxious way. I don't think the volume of his voice went up...but the word jumps out at me. I swallow hard. Why is he making up such lies? What is the point of this? My hands fist into my sheets, my knuckles grazing the gun I laid down in my lap. I can't deny the comfort, the wisp of memory when I held it. My heart rate increases again and suddenly, I feel warmer. Anger seems like a great choice, and I lock it in.

"Amnesia? That's what you're leading with?" I lace each word with sarcasm so there's no question what I think.

He continues to lean against the doorframe, arms crossed, as if he doesn't have a care in the world.

"What do you know of the meaning of Destiny?"

Katrina. Calm. I need to calm down. "Um, things that are

pre-determined? Like, no matter what you do, it's going to happen?" I just have to keep him talking. Maybe use his own words to help me.

"No. That's closer to Fate. Destiny is what can be. What you're meant for. That's the gist of it, anyway. Destiny shapes the things that are going to happen, predetermines them, if you want to call it that. But it *can* be changed. I can't explain that part since I'm not a Destiny myself."

I rub my forehead harder, trying desperately for any of this to make sense in a way I can use to my advantage. "How is this even possible? How can someone—how can *I* decide the destiny of thousands, millions of people?" He definitely has more than one screw loose in that handsome head of his.

"It's not necessarily that specific. I mean it can, and is in lots of instances, but there are plenty of nobodies too."

"I'm sorry, nobodies? What the hell does that mean?" This is all gibberish.

"Nobodies. You know, people who simply...exist, I guess. They aren't important enough to have destinies."

How can he callously dismiss human beings? Drew shrugs as I stare, incredulous.

"It's not my job to unravel the mysteries of the world. I'm only concerned with one thing. You."

And *I'm* worried about how I'm going to get Kat out of this place and away from Drew. Clearly, he has some issues. But I still don't know how. He told me I can see her, but he hasn't offered. Should I ask again? Should I wait and completely assess the situation? There's something I can't describe growing in the pit of my stomach. My intuition maybe, but last time I listened to it, I ended up at The Coveted Pearl and in an assassination attempt. I can't possibly *need* to be here.

"Katrina—"

"Is sleeping. It's the middle of the night."

My body jerks and my stomach clenches again, a slick of the constant fear weaving through me again. Will he ever let me see her? But no, this makes sense. There are no windows here. I had eaten dinner...hours ago? Still couldn't possibly be daylight. Fine. My intuition wins and we keep going with this unbelievable conversation.

"What happened fifteen years ago?"

"You committed an infraction. You, more or less, killed for your own purposes. And that's not allowed. The Council sent Slayers—exactly how they sound—after you, to take care of you..."

I'm not sure what it says about me that I latch on to one thing. "To kill me?" My voice squeaks. "I would've been ten? Someone sent assassins after a ten-year-old?" Why all the elaborate lies?

"Well, as you can see, they didn't get their target. Also, you weren't ten. You were fourteen." Drew watches me like a hawk. I get the feeling he doesn't miss a thing.

"Are you telling me as a ten-year-old, I managed to escape from trained assassins... Wait. Did you just say fourteen?" He must definitely have the wrong person, but he's no longer nonchalantly propping up the door. He's standing, staring intently, his body tense, a coiled weapon. Why?

"In order for you to understand, you have to know more about what it is you do. You envision what's going to happen, and then, it happens."

"I just envision what happens." I speak slowly, letting the words hang in the air. He nods. I nod, then I shake my head. "Yeah, no. I think of things all the time, and they don't happen."

"It's a different state of mind. You *will* it to happen. There are all kinds of training you go through when you're younger. Classes, learning how to decipher visions of the future, languages, customs, all kinds of things you learn in order to be a Destiny. On top of all that, you have physical training: various martial arts and weapons training."

He rattles this all off as if it's a normal, commonplace occurrence for children to have specialized training.

I close my eyes. "Stop. Why don't I remember any of this? And how was I fourteen, exactly? Last I checked, twenty-five minus fifteen does not equal fourteen." I open my eyes.

Ha. Get out of this.

His jaw clenches. "I'm trying to tell you everything. With the powers you have, you have the ability to make things happen. To shape the future. That's why you were considered a liability to the Guardianship. That's why when you break one of the rules, they kill you. And they do it swiftly and without notice. You could envision world wars, destruction, famines, plagues. And they would happen. You can start it, you can stop it, you can control it. Of course, there's always the chance it changes, but that's usually not the case."

"I absolutely take umbrage at being considered a liability. This is absurd," I scoff. "I've envisioned things before, and it's not happened."

I willed Tyson to not be dead. Pregnant, worried about the future and losing the love of my life to an early death, single parenthood staring me down. I damn well willed it with everything I had, and it hadn't mattered.

My chest tightens and my heart, an aggravated pump, pushes the blood thickly through my veins. It's pounding in my ears, pulsating in my shoulder. None of this can be true.

A machine next to me beeps incessantly now. Drew looks at it swiftly. "It would be really helpful to me right now if you took a few deep breaths."

"Why? What's wrong?"

His eyes keep darting to the screen, and I turn my head.

"Are those numbers accurate?" I squeak. "Because I don't think they're supposed to be that high."

"Yes, and it's why I'm worried about overloading you. You need to calm down."

"I'm trying." Sweat beads down my back. My voice sounds shrill even to me, and I inhale deep gulps of air, but the machine's getting louder, the beeps more frequent. I scrunch my face, concentrating. The pounding in my ears moves into my head. I relax my hands that grip the sheets, but they reflexively bunch back up, clawing into the bed.

Suddenly, Drew is right next to me, and my heart rate increases. How did he get here so fast?

"I'm sorry. Don't get too freaked out." He grips my arm tightly.

Suddenly, warmth flows through me and it's as if everything else disappears. My temperature rises and my body relaxes. I sigh gently, my eyes fluttering shut, while my face softens as if the muscles languish under the skin. My blood stops pounding and instead hums through my veins. The machine's beeping slows and quiets. How is this possible? The warmth pools into the pit of my stomach, and it's as if I'm floating in a pool of warm water, caressed by the sun's warm rays. I could stay here forever. I pop open my eyes. Is this for real?

His are closed. The expression on his handsome face can only be described as pure satisfaction. It's uncomfortably close to the expression Ty used to make after a long bout of sex.

"I'd like you to let go of my arm now, please," I say quietly, turning my head away from him.

Please, please let go. I don't understand any of this.

He removes his hand from my arm and the sensations drop away like a curtain dropping at the end of a play. They linger, and in a way, I'm thankful. As the warmth leaves me, the pain returns slower instead of slamming into me like it did earlier.

I still won't look at him, embarrassed by what I felt and by what I saw on his face. And very much afraid the expression on my own face is disgustingly similar to his own.

He clears his throat. "I'm going to get you something to eat from the kitchen. And give you a minute to yourself."

Chapter Four

DREW

I slam my back into the cold walls of the hallway and gulp in the circulated, clean air. Fire. I'm playing with fucking fire every damn time I try to save her. And I'll keep doing it. But I've got to start thinking of gross shit, like maggots crawling over decaying meat. Corpses even. Because I can't keep getting a hard-on every time I brush against her. I can't nearly orgasm from touching her skin. I mean, I'm more than okay with it, but seeing how she doesn't remember me nor has any clue who the fuck I am right now would make it creepy.

But the pure sex that rolled through me when one fingertip rested on the pulse beating madly through the delicate vein at her wrist... A shudder rolls through me. This is not helping. I press the palms of my hands into my eyes. I need to calm down.

The smell of rotisserie chicken wafts from the cart full of food Charlie must've left next to the doorway, and I push off the wall. She must be starving, and her blood sugar's probably dangerously low. The need to protect her, to ensure her well-being does what nothing else has done. Now I can stop looking like a horny teenager.

She lies still on the bed while I push the cart through. Her eyes remain closed, the dark lashes resting on the shadows beneath them. Fury rolls through me again at the thought that the Guardianship sent Hunters. How dare they think they can just eliminate her. Well, fuck them. They underestimated her. They underestimated me. They didn't stop to think about how strong we are together. And apart.

If I didn't know her better, I'd think she was sleeping. Too bad I'm not going to let her just ignore everything going on.

I let the door slam shut. Nothing. She's always been one to dig in her heels.

"Delaney." I pause, giving her a moment to pretend to wake up. "I know you aren't sleeping."

Her body twitches minutely at the comment, but she continues to remain motionless.

"You aren't an ostrich. Sticking your head in the sand isn't going to make all of this disappear. There's no changing it. There's no making it go away. Stop behaving like a child and sit up so you can eat something."

I don't have time for games. "Fine. Don't eat. And later when you faint, you get to feel me touch you as I cart you back into the bed you will inevitably fall out of. I've no problem with that."

Her eyes snap open and she sits up and huffs. "Fine. What am I eating?"

I smirk. She's so true to form I could shout. This Delaney might just be the one. I hand her the plate and a bottle of orange juice. "It's a cold chicken sandwich with lettuce, tomato and cheese. No mayo, but crushed avocado. The OJ will help boost your hemoglobin, which you need after your blood loss."

She looks like she wants to hit me, and I almost tell her to stop acting like a toddler, but I can't. I never know when teasing and pushing will shove her straight over the edge into insanity.

"How the hell do you know when I'm sleeping? Never mind. Where exactly is Katrina?"

Oh good, she's willing to continue. But she hasn't started eating yet. I motion at the sandwich and hand her a napkin. "She's downstairs."

She takes a big bite and chews quickly, surprise crossing her face. Was she not expecting something edible?

"That's not enough. Where is she?"

"She's well-guarded. You don't have to worry." The look on her face says otherwise, but I don't know how to put her at ease. I don't know anything about kids.

"Yeah, mothers don't work like that. I want proof. I want to see her."

This is something I don't have experience in. None of the previous Delaneys had children. The thought of some man touching her, fucking impregnating her, infuriates me to the point everything in the room blurs.

The vision dancing through my brain mocks me like a fucking dripping carcass dangling in front of a winter-starved wolf. I curl my fingers into fists, and it takes everything I've got to ease the red out of my sight. She's *my* soul mate.

"What's the point of waking her in the middle of the night? We have things we need to discuss." Her face hardens, the jawline tightening. This is just what I need—her contrariness at anything that hints of anyone telling her what to do. But I can't risk her taking her kid and running. She thinks I don't know what she's thinking.

She's wrong.

I'm not going to risk her destroying the world because she has a case of the motherhoods, but if I don't let her do what she wants, I risk it all anyway. Rock, fucking hard space.

I quickly text Mark and the reply buzzes in seconds. I hand the phone to Delaney who takes it, careful not to touch me. Regret weaves through me. There was a time she'd have purposely brushed fingers just for the hit.

Her eyes narrow as she glances at the photo. My own quick skim showed a dark-haired, darker-skinned, mini version of her curled up in a bed, clutching a stuffed bear.

"If you don't take me to see her in the morning, I'll find her on my own. I'll call the police. I'll scream for help. I'll do everything in my power to get to her, and if you deny me this, you'll quickly wish you didn't."

The words are soft but determined, backed by the conviction I know she's capable of. But does she? I'm not about to find out. Not if I can help it.

I nod and she slumps back into the bed, relief clearly running through her.

"Thank you. In the meantime, tell me everything else. I promise I'll keep my heart rate down."

"Finish eating and I'll tell you more. But not everything. I don't think overloading you is going to help anything. Plus, you need time to rest."

Understatement of the year. Overloading her won't help her. Or me.

"Deal. Twice now you've mentioned the Guardianship. Want to tell me what that is?"

She picks up the sandwich for another bite. What can I tell her? The Guardianship is a complex living, breathing entity that would take entirely too much time to delve into. Besides, what difference does it make? I'm not going to let them kill her. I swallow past the rage attempting to burn me again.

"The Guardianship is exactly what it sounds like. It's comprised of those of us tasked with guarding the world."

"Guarding the world? From what? And don't tell me aliens. I don't think I can handle that right now."

"From itself, actually. Humans have a way of trying to destroy their own existence." I shrug. "I don't know if aliens exist."

"Yet you say humans as if you aren't one." She grabs the orange juice like it's a lifeline, taking deep gulps.

Her throat moves with the labor of swallowing, and all I want to do is trail kisses down it. I respond without giving the words much thought on how it will affect her.

"I'm not a human. I'm a Guardian. You're a Guardian."

Chapter Five

DELANEY

What is he talking about? I nearly choke on the juice and the bread that now seems lodged in my throat.

"Need me to pound you on the back?"

His voice sounds concerned, but I shake my head and cough hard until the tickle goes away.

"We're not human?"

"I mean, technically we are, but not like normal humans."

Yeah. This just cements that he's not in touch with reality. It would've been easier if he had just taken the alien bait I gave him, but maybe he's trying for plausible. I bite down for another, much smaller, mouthful and motion for him to continue.

"We have abilities normal humans don't."

I nearly snort but catch myself in time. "You said I committed an infraction and the Guardianship wanted to kill me. Did they take away my abilities?"

"No. They aren't capable of taking them away. That's the subtlety to your gift, it's not *on* all of the time. It's when you tap into that part of your brain—that sense—that starts it. Then when you're envisioning things, that's when it occurs."

"How do you know so much?"

"You know the Hunters called me a Protector."

"Yes. I'm guessing you protect people. This Guardianship isn't creative when it comes to titles, is it?" I can't help my snark. You'd think someone capable of creating this entire fabrication would create better names.

"First of all, the Guardianship isn't a company that hands out titles. It's an entity that came into being thousands of years ago. And we Guardians are born with specific abilities and called after them."

I think about that statement. If I were to make things up, I'd do something similar. "That actually makes sense. Like a classification instead of a title."

"Precisely. But my job isn't to protect people." Drew pauses and peers intently, holding my gaze. "It's to protect you."

Hold up. What?

"Me? I'm confused. You said you're born with abilities and that it's just what people are. Why are you supposed to protect me, specifically? Wait. Why now? Where have you been?"

"I'm not *supposed* to protect you, as you put it. I'm not *assigned* to you. It's not a job like that."

He pauses and shoves his hand through his hair again and then trails it down his neck and grips the back of it.

Trepidation curls in my gut, turning the bread sour. No matter what he says, I have to remember it's not real. I take a few experimental breaths. My eyes remain locked on his.

"You've heard of the term soul mates?" he asks quietly.

"You've got to be fucking kidding me!" My voice explodes, and the tempo of the beeping increases frenetically. Of all the things to say!

"No. And unless you want a repeat of earlier, I suggest you calm down."

He points at the monitors, and I close my eyes, but taking deep breaths doesn't seem to be working. Panicking is only helping the escalation.

He thinks he's my soul mate?

Drew's voice interrupts my thoughts. "Empty your mind. I know it's hard, but just picture nothing, like a black space. Now, envision a small bright dot, like a light at the end of a tunnel. Can you see it?"

I barely nod, not trusting myself to speak. I can't let him touch me. As it is, I can barely focus when his voice seems to dip into me—saturate me. I picture a bright, small dot as if my life depends on it.

"Okay. Now picture that light getting bigger, until it surrounds you. All you see is white. When it does, focus on your breathing. Listen to it. Hear the air come into your lungs and hear it come out."

At first, my breathing's shaky. But as I concentrate on inhaling and exhaling, the sound steadies. The pattern becomes rhythmic and controlled. I open my eyes and glance at the monitor. My rates are back to normal if not lower than before.

Neat trick.

I slowly turn to him. "Explain."

"I'm not sure the explanation is one you want to hear right now."

He gets up from the chair he's sitting in and begins pacing. Not necessarily heading for the door this time, just a simple symbol of agitation. Is this something he doesn't want too? I can't believe I'm even considering this mystical crap as reality.

"I'm guessing from your earlier reaction you know the term."

"I do. I also know beyond a *shadow of doubt* my soul mate

was my husband. So, I'm just dying to hear what you have to say."

I cross my arms in front of my chest. It pulls on my shoulder again, and I quickly uncross them. Stupid wound throbs harder.

"The soul mate terminology you think you know and apply to yourself, and your deceased husband is nothing compared to what I'm talking about."

My stomach drops. How does he know Tyson's dead? But more importantly, where does he get off telling me what kind of relationship we had? It was special and wonderful and all the things lovers should be.

"Watch yourself," I growl. "You're getting awfully close to pissing me off."

"I'm trying not to bombard you with information *and* keep you from freaking out. This isn't easy for me."

"Don't talk to me about easy! My daughter's who-knows-where in this house, I'm being hunted, and you're telling me all sorts of wild things, undermining everything I've ever known to be true. And you expect me to believe you and sit placidly by just—just *breathing*, when all I want to do is scream and cry and go the hell home and wake up, realizing this is one of my nightmares!"

"You have nightmares?" Abruptly, he stops pacing and stands in front of the bed, gripping the edge. "What kind?"

I jerk, startled at the change in his tone. "Just vague ones. I don't understand them."

"What are they about?"

His eyes roam over my face. His knuckles are white, his hands squeezing the life out of the metal. I hope he doesn't hurt himself. Or me.

"Usually, it's fragments, like scenes. Sometimes, you're in them." I hate telling him that, but it's got to be pertinent. I finally realized why I thought he was familiar when I *knew* I didn't know him.

"Oh?" His eyebrow wings up.

"Not like that."

His mood changes are lightning quick and just as confusing.

"You can fantasize, you know."

He grins. It transforms the serious, handsome face into something resembling boyish charm. My stomach tightens and I glare at him.

"No. I can't. I mean, I don't. About you. I don't even know you."

Drew smiles, as if he's amused by the possibility of starring in sexual fantasies, but he lets it go. "If you ever want to talk, I might be able to help you decipher them. They may be memories rising to the surface."

I scrutinize his face. "You're serious."

"I *am* sorry what I'm telling you tonight's upsetting you. I'm not very good at finessing things like this, and there are some things I can't smooth over. It's what it is, and no amount of honeyed words will take the sting away."

I accept his apology. He's right. There's probably no way to tell me any of this without me reacting abnormally.

Cause it's not normal. And it isn't true.

"Humans tend to think of soul mates as their true love. Like, their other half, right?"

I don't know where he's going with this. "Yes. That's a super simple explanation though. It's more than that. Like, Tyson and me. We loved each other and couldn't conceive of the idea of not being together. I looked forward to seeing him at the end of the day. He was...my best friend. I shared everything with him. I wanted to be with him and not anyone else." Ever, but that choice was taken away from me.

"If he were alive, would you have shared with him how you feel around me?"

Dammit. I can't deal with hypotheticals. Wait. I narrow my eyes. What does he know about how I feel?

"See? Your notion of soul mates has loopholes. Mine doesn't. Hear me out." He raises his hand, stopping me before I can do more than sputter. "Soul mates in our world is far more drastic and permanent. In our case, two halves of one whole. Traits and characteristics complement each other. What I don't have, you do. Together, we're a perfect combination. Apart, we're only one half of ourselves, our soul crying out for the other, wandering lost—a vital piece missing. You know you felt a connection, a...something.

"Humans try to 'find' their soul mates, but we're drawn to each other—always. Aware of the other at all times, no matter how far apart. Do you understand? Our souls are split in half. You have one half, and I have the other. You wanted to *share* everything with Tyson? You *are* my everything! You're the very essence of my being, and you're not ever replaceable.

"You say you couldn't conceive the idea of being apart from him? We *can't* be permanently apart. If one of us dies, the other will eventually follow. It's so physically painful it leads to actual madness. You cannot live without half of a soul for long.

"So while you *thought* you couldn't live without Tyson, I literally can't live without you."

I search his face. He stills, perhaps sensing my need to judge his honesty. What am I supposed to do with his outburst? His green eyes pierce my own. Burning from under thick black eyebrows and ringed by dark lashes, they're clear but full of worry, wondering how I'm going to process this news, I suppose. His face is covered in stubble, and he looks tired, his tan face pale, but I don't see anything that indicates he's lying.

Fuck.

"I don't know what to say. I believe you believe this to be true. But I don't believe it. I can't be your soul mate. I've never felt this pain you're describing. I *can't* be your soul mate."

I keep repeating myself, but how else can I be clear? He obviously believes what he told me. Whatever I'm feeling is not what he's describing. He's talking about do-or-die stuff, and I'm talking about experiencing relaxation sensations and prickling skin.

We aren't on the same page at all.

Chapter Six

DREW

My beautiful, bullheaded love. I'd show her the truth by planting my lips on hers, ravaging her mouth, but there's no way to know if she'd crack.

"Repeating yourself isn't going to work. In time, you'll know what I'm saying is the truth. I don't have to prove it to you. You will feel it yourself."

"This stuff you're saying. It doesn't make any sense. I've never felt something was missing. I've never missed you. I never even knew you existed until recently."

Her soft-spoken statement suddenly hits me hard, and weariness settles like a blanket over my shoulders. The reminder that she's been without the pain, without the tearing agony I've been living through is double-edged. On one hand, I'm happy she's been spared. On the other, it's not fucking fair. I wince—I'm an asshole—and I plop myself back into the chair.

"I've never died, so you've never felt that pain. Have you never felt like something was... off?"

She shakes her head, and I try to keep my frustration from

my voice. "I don't know. Maybe that was part of your plan. I truly don't know because I wasn't privy to it. I only know you are you. And you're most definitely my soul mate."

I've got to make her believe it. There's no way forward without her cooperation.

"So, you say you're my Protector."

"Being your Protector is my ability. Being your soul mate is my life."

"If you're my Protector, why is it you're protecting me only now? From what? Why are they hunting me? Who's hunting me?" A shiver vibrates her body. "The Guardianship. They're hunting me. Because they didn't kill me the first time?"

I won't let them. I'll tear them apart limb by limb, first. I'll cut down every bastard with the little sense to come after her. Their stupidity in blindly following orders will be their death sentence. My fists already ache with the effort.

"I will not allow them to kill you. You have my promise."

She grimaces, and the urge to reassure her rolls through me. "Please believe me. You're safe here, and they'd have to carry you out over my dead body. I won't lose you again."

"Thank you." Her words are lined with sincerity, and hope fills me. Maybe she's coming around. Maybe she's starting to remember.

"Why did the Guardianship want to kill me the first time?"

And maybe it's just wishful thinking. Damn. I run my hand through my hair and grip the back of my neck, squeezing until the headache that's brewing at the base of my skull recedes. Do I move forward? Isn't that what this is all about? One step in front of the other until we either get where we need to be or until all of this starts over again.

I slap my hands down onto my thighs and the sound echoes. Fuck it. "I'm pretty much out of options at this point." Pushing off the chair, I walk over to the medicine cabinet and remove a prescription bottle marked Penicillin.

"Please take two."

She eyes the label suspiciously, a small frown pulling her mouth down.

"It's an antibiotic. I cleaned out your shoulder pretty well when you passed out, but I needed you to eat before I could have you take that." She's still hesitant, and annoyance flits through me. "Your lack of trust in me sucks. I can't wait for your memory to return. For multiple reasons."

"Honestly, can you blame me?" She sounds bitter. What the fuck does she have to complain about? Has she been on a never-ending, never-resolving, pointless fucking quest while swallowing mind-blowing pain?

I blow out a breath. It's not her fault. I have to remember that. "I can't make you swallow the pills. Without them, your shoulder will get infected. And then you'll have to stay in bed until you get better."

She pops them into her mouth. "I took your pills. Now please tell me what I need to know."

"Just a warning to you. If you do lose your shit, I will hold you down and force you to calm down. Do you understand me?" Anticipation causes my heart rate to increase, and damned if I don't sound out of breath. This is supposed to sound like a threat. Instead, I'm kinda hoping she does freak out. Not enough to burn down the world, but just enough that I get to touch her again. Just enough that gratification punches through the echoes of pain and loss.

"Yeah, I get it. You'll put your hands on me, even though I don't want you to. You know, there are specific words for that."

Sorrow dulls the joy that curled in my gut. Does she really think I'd do anything she didn't want?

"I've known you since I was born. Since you were born."

She inhales sharply. If there was any way that any of this wasn't a shock to her, I'd take it. But how do you tell someone all the things you've lived through with them? The love that binds you together? How do you tell them when they don't remember any of it?

"Soul mates, remember?"

"You're saying we have the same birthday?"

"Yeah. Same soul, same birthday. That's kinda how it works."

Disbelief flies across her expressive face. How can she think I'm lying? Even knowing that she doesn't remember, how can she deny the sensations, the connection our souls have? It's as if someone sucker punches me every time I think about her not aligning with me.

"Not only were we born on the same day, but we've grown up together. Trained together. Schooled together. Played together. Slept together, and no, not in that way. I know you like I know myself."

Delaney makes a choking sound. "That's not possible."

I clench my jaw. What can I say that will prove to her I'm not making any of this up? "You just don't remember. You somehow suppressed your memories."

I ball my hands into tight fists. If only Delaney had left me a note, a guidebook. Any-fucking-thing. I'm running blind, with no idea what I'm supposed to do.

I pace the room again. How much should I divulge? Something's different this time, I know it, but I don't want to break the fragility of her mind. It's too easy for me to lose her.

"There were several incidents when you were a child. Enough that it put you under the Guardianship's scrutiny. There are consequences for your abilities. Particularly if your use of them is personal. There are prices to pay. Nature demands balance. Headaches, nightmares, hallucinations.

Then there are no documented incidents for a couple of years."

"Each one gets documented?"

"Like any entity, the Guardianship needs to be able to track its people, keeping tabs on them and, of course, to rein in the rogue ones. Guardians, like you in particular, have some amazing abilities. Abilities that are powerful. Yes, they're used to protect this world and the people living in it. But they can be used to bring great harm too, and it's the Guardianship's responsibility to prevent that."

With each nugget of information, I scan her face, her body language. Is it too much? Will she break? Her body's stiff, as if she's clenched all of her muscles, but her skin isn't too pale, eyes aren't too wild. A brief memory surfaces of a vengeful Delaney standing on a cliff, hands thrown up in the air like some goddess full of wrath, raining pain upon humanity. I don't want a repeat of that particular version of her. Maybe I should slow down. But damn it, urgency increases in my body daily. Something's coming. I'm not willing to stand around and fucking wait for it.

"Um. I want to know more, but I have to use the bathroom."

Normal body movements. Normal language. Relief that she's still okay floods my body. I'm on the right path.

I point to the far side of the wall beyond the monitors. Delaney's eyes flicker between the gun and the bathroom. What the fuck did I do to deserve this? My soul mate, my reason for living doesn't trust me enough to piss in a toilet without fear of what I might do. I clench my fists and hide them behind me. The last thing I need is her seeing my frustration.

She grasps the weapon, pulls back the sheet, and gasps loudly. Adrenaline shoots through me and I pivot, immediately searching for a cause.

"Whose clothes are these? Did you undress me?"

I whip my head around as the words bring another version of Delaney from my memories. Both of us in bed, naked, fitting together like two pieces of a whole. Soul meeting soul, as close as we can ever be without fusing. The pleasure shutting out the rest of the world. Healing emotions, soothing me.

The pain that ripped into me, the agony of my soul crying for its mate after I lost her again was almost worth it. I swallow hard, attempting to force the instant erection down and focus on Delaney's horrified face. What had she asked? Shit. Undressing her. I will my body to stop giving me away

"I couldn't very well clean and bandage your shoulder through your shirt. Your clothes were completely ruined. I'm not having you lay in them in a sterile bed. But no, you can rest easy, I didn't undress you. Liza's the one that did you and gave you a sponge bath. And the clothes are yours."

She shudders, and I echo the movement, unable to drop the memory of Delaney's lithe body from behind my eyelids. Unfortunately, her current memories aren't the same as my own. I stare at her open mouth, the horror that I may have undressed her while unconscious slowly leaving her face. Irritation briefly replaces need. What kind of asshole does she think I am?

Suddenly, her look of relief pisses me off, no matter how irrational. Dammit, I know she doesn't remember, but it's hard not to take it personal. Doesn't her soul strain toward mine? Doesn't it echo my own's pain at being apart?

Doesn't she need me like I need her?

Delaney swings her legs over the edge of the bed and stands up. And immediately sits back down, closing her eyes.

She needs me.

"Are you okay?" I push out of my chair so fast I have to grab it to stop it from hitting the floor. "I can give you a hand if you want." I strain to keep my lips straight, but I can't stop the wistfulness coloring my voice.

"No, thank you. I just need a second." She inhales deeply a few times and opens her eyes.

I stand back just enough to leap forward if she needs me. I want to touch her. The urge is strong enough that I step back again. She doesn't want me.

She picks up the gun again and slowly heads to the bathroom, closing the door softly. I throw myself back into the chair and rub my temples. I need to focus on what needs to be done. Not what I want. Sex might help us feel a million times better, stronger and faster, but it sure won't help her mind. I learn my lessons quickly.

How do I tell her I love her, that she can trust me without actually saying it? What do I do to uncover her memories?

The door opens and Delaney limps out of the bathroom, holding on to the security of her weaponry. Doesn't she know that I could easily disarm her? She doesn't remember her training. But it helps her feel better, and maybe the feel of it, the familiarity will unlock a door in that tightly sealed brain of hers. But some people need the words rather than the actions.

"I promise you, if I'd meant to harm you, I'd have already done it."

"Honestly, I don't think there's a single thing you can do. This, *all* of this, is so fantastical, it defies my reality. I don't know what's real and what's not."

Fuck. I need her to understand.

"All of it's real. The way you feel when I touch you should prove that to you."

"That doesn't prove anything! That makes this even weirder."

But she feels something.

Yes. Fuck yes.

"What if I told you things you know are real? Things I couldn't possibly know." That's got to convince her.

"Sure, because if you actually made any sense, that would really make my day right now."

"I know you have a scar on your ring finger on your left hand from punching a brick wall when you were mad after losing a training match to me."

Her thumb rolls over the spot. "First, that scar is from catching my hand on a fence when I was younger. Second, you could've seen that when I was passed out." She crosses her arms.

There's nothing I like better than a challenge. "You have a crooked pinky toe on your left foot. You broke it during a wrestling match with me and you never taped it."

"Wrong. I broke it running it into the corner of my bed in the middle of the night one night after getting up with Kat when she was a newborn. And again, something you could have seen."

"You have a scar on your right shoulder in the front, from my blade when we were fencing."

She shakes her head. "From a motorcycle accident. And I'm also seeing a pattern here. You, hurting me."

Another memory surfaces of both of us, much younger, sparring in a training room. Fighting matches ending in laughter. Tickles to ribs, and when we became teenagers and hormones entered the picture, light kisses and nips of the lip. My dick twitches, but I ignore it and laugh. "I can't help it that I've beaten you a few times in our matches. You've left enough of your own marks on me. We're pretty equal, I'd say."

"Still nothing that can't be seen. You're proving nothing."

"You love seafood."

She snorts, crossing her arms and then uncrossing them. "I was leaving a seafood restaurant today when you saved me."

"You have a high metabolism, thanks to your Guardian abilities."

"Lucky guess, I'm pretty slim."

She's smug, thinking I've nothing to give her as proof. But my analytical brain has been miles ahead, setting her up. "You have exactly four grey hairs on your head. No matter how many times you pull them, dye them, or otherwise get rid of them, they always come back in the same exact spot," I counter.

She inhales hard, her face paling.

Boom, baby.

"How the hell did you know that?"

I lean back. There's no way she can deny what I've told her simply because it's the truth.

"Because a strand of your hair turns gray whenever you manipulate events. It's permanent. Four incidents. Four strands of gray hair."

Chapter Seven

DELANEY

The hairs on my neck stand up. I ball my hands into fists to hide the slight tremor. My skin dampens with a film of sweat as my body reacts to his knowledge of my secret. There's absolutely no way for him to have known.

Not even Ty knew, and we lived together. It's always freaked me out. I've plucked those things from my head, only to wake up with them in the morning. It's not normal. I'm not normal.

Shit.

"This is all real? Everything you've said to me? Why can't I recall any of this!" I groan with frustration. My mind whirls with all I've learned tonight and everything that's happened in the last several hours. It's all real? I'm not sure how to process this. The assassins attempt on my life. The incidents Drew speaks about. My ability to create destiny. How is this possible?

Yet, I have four gray hairs on my head that regrow in less than twelve hours if I pluck them. I've tried dying my hair. Those same strands are gray seconds after.

I know they're real. It doesn't matter that I can't explain their existence. Somebody else knows and doesn't think something is wrong with that.

My soul mate? I curl my hands around my stomach, holding myself tight. My world is crumbling around me.

He sinks to the edge of the bed, and I shrink back, not wanting him to touch me—afraid of the strange feelings flowing through me—yet my body yearning for him to do so.

"I know it's a lot to understand. Lesser people have collapsed under the weight of such knowledge." He rubs the back of his neck. "I know all too well. But you're strong enough. You just need some time. You need rest." He drops his hand into his lap.

I reach out, forgetting I don't want to touch him. My hand is almost to his arm when I pull back. "I need to know all of it. I promise I can handle it."

He turns and scrutinizes my face, his eyes roaming over my head. I keep my face still. I'm sure he's seeing the same shell-shocked face I'd seen reflected in the bathroom mirror, dark smudges and wide eyes. He looks...sad. Does he wish I had touched him?

"It seems you might be."

There's a brief flicker in his eyes before he turns his head. He's still sitting on the bed. He laughs once. Really? Is he okay? I'm not sure how to process his mercurial moods. "What's funny?"

"Just thinking about one incident. You were seven." His lips draw up. He looks younger when he smiles.

"Since you have an affinity for toys, this, too, was over a plaything."

"I was seven." I sniff, my chin tilting. "I've since outgrown them, I assure you."

"Have you?" He laughs again, and gestures toward the gun. "I think you just upgrade them."

I scowl. I'm not amused.

He abruptly sobers. "It doesn't matter. I just wanted to explain the progression. You had nightmares for weeks. The greater the output, the greater the consequences. In this incident, you created a pretty drawn-out future. The longer or more complex it is, the toll on your body is longer or more complex in return."

"Do you know what the difference is between the nightmares and stuff and the gray hair?"

"The nightmares, the hallucinations, those are penalties for using your ability for your own personal gain. You always get a gray hair when you change things, regardless. When you're creating a future or constructing a possibility for saving the world, like in your capacity of Guardian, you don't get the penalties. You only get a strand of gray hair for manipulating the future."

"What happens when all of my hair turns gray? Please tell me I don't die."

"No, you don't die, but your ability to create or change paths essentially dies and you begin to age like a normal human again."

"And so the circle of destiny continues," I murmur as my brain pieces together what Drew has said. Fear rolls through me. Does Katrina have the same Destiny traits? Will this Guardianship, whoever they are, come after her too? Will they try to kill her? Instead of increasing in tempo, my heart rate actually slows down and calm replaces panic. My hands have stilled. Steel resolve tightens my spine and my thoughts center on one thing.

Over my dead body.

He nods. "Exactly."

Impatience floats in. I need to know everything. Now. "How bad were the consequences on my third and fourth incidents?"

His hands are once again knotted into fists, the knuckles standing out white against his skin. Tension radiates out of his face. A sense of foreboding washes over me. I know that whatever comes next won't include laughter. I know this incident isn't a funny story about a little girl who was too smart for her own good.

"How bad was it?" I repeat. My own muscles tighten in preparation. I need to know what I'm capable of.

And I need to relearn it.

"It's the catalyst that started this ball rolling. Are you sure you want to know about this incident now? We can wait." His tone indicates I never have to know if I don't want to.

Why stop now? Why the hesitation?

There's a faint hint of tension still around his eyes. It seems both of us are big on focused facial searches. This is the point of no return. It'll be all or nothing. I either accept everything he states as true or I accept none of this is and I've hit my head harder than I thought and am lying in a hospital bed somewhere, conjuring up an alternate reality.

Ha, pun intended.

I frown and twist my fingers in my lap. If this incident is the one that resulted in me forgetting my abilities, forgetting a million different memories, for years, I need to know. I think of what he's already told me, the connection between us, the way contact of any kind, but especially physical, makes me feel. All of it tinged with the blinding clarity of truth. And I won't risk Katrina thinking maybe this is crap when it very well may not be. No. I won't risk her life. I nod, making my decision.

"You were fourteen." His voice sounds flat and angry. Not the anger that vibrates with passion, but the kind that makes you think icicles are warm in comparison. Drew's voice gives monotone a startling depth. Devoid of the vibrancy most people have when speaking, the unconscious inflection of words people use makes his words hard. Lethal, like a weapon on its own. And they're directed toward me. The blood drains out of my face, leaving it colorless.

What kind of monster am I?

Suddenly, the coldness of his voice embraces me, making gooseflesh pop on my arms. I'm not sure I can even imagine what I've done that would create this much anger in someone who claims to be my soul mate.

I only hope it's something I can make up to him or whomever I hurt. By his tone, I imagine it'll be a hard feat. I hope I didn't cause anyone pain. I'm weak at the thought, as if I've been deprived of food for months, and then deprived of oxygen. I see the dreaded black spots dancing in front of me.

"I think I'm going to faint."

"Take a deep breath, put your head between your knees. You won't faint."

As per his usual rapid swings, his voice has lost the coldness and seems back to normal. It once again comforts me. I inhale several times, laying my head on my knees. For the first time tonight, I'm afraid to know.

Afraid of something that happened long ago. Several minutes pass in silence. An awkward tension emanates from Drew. Maybe he wants to comfort me. I think I'd like to be comforted, but I don't know how to say it.

"I'm okay. I can deal with this. I need a moment."

"If there was a different way to all of this, I'd gladly find it."

His voice is low, rough. His assurance does nothing for my dread.

"Just tell me all at once. Get it over with. That way, I can do something about it, fix it. Make it right."

His face grows rigid, and he sits ramrod straight. The tension's back, and he stares at his hands, flexing them open and shut.

"What did I do that was so terrible?" I whisper, barely

managing to get the words out over the lump that seems to have grown in my throat.

He raises his head swiftly, astonished. "You didn't do anything wrong!"

I jerk back. This isn't the reaction I expected.

"*This* incident wasn't your fault." Drew stands and stalks the length of the floor, back and forth, like a caged animal. His hand shoves viciously through his hair, rubbing hard down his neck. He stops. Though all movement from him has ended, the perception of madness is equal in the stillness.

Staring at the hand gripping his neck, my eyes drift down the strong lines of his back. He drops it and turns.

"What you did was completely justified. It should *never* have been documented. And if it had been, it should've been in my file, not yours."

"Then why are you angry?" My voice sounds soft after his explosion.

"If I'd been there to protect you, which is *my* job, this incident wouldn't have happened. You wouldn't have been forced to forget. We'd have had *years* together." Drew's body slants toward mine.

"Tell me already, would you?" My stomach's churning. What if Katrina has to deal with all of this? How can I protect her?

"You were spending the night at a friend's house. You were supposed to be safe, as her parents and the house were checked out before you went over. It's Guardianship protocol, particularly for young Destinies. You have so much power—power that can be easily manipulated by others who seek to harm the world. That translates to anytime you go somewhere, with someone, their background is checked out, the location checked and made sure is secure, undercover guards posted, that kind of stuff. You do understand you're vulnerable as a child?"

I nod. I get the concept of it, and the why, but how creepy.

"Nobody knew her parents planned to drop you both off at the mall and let you wander around on your own. I mean, you were fourteen, anything could happen to you!"

His jaw clenches and unclenches. I'm riveted by the fact that he's so overprotective. Fourteen wasn't too young, and it's almost how I am with Kat. I'd do anything to keep her safe, but she's five and I had been much older.

"You two thought it would be safe to walk outside." He points, his finger inches from my nose. "You knew better! Yet, outside you went! By this time, I, as well as others, were racing to the mall." Drew pauses, perhaps collecting himself before continuing.

"I was frantic, scared and spurred on by the ever-mounting feeling that something was wrong. By the time I reached you, you were already in trouble."

Drew looks away, jaw clenched again. His fists can't get any tighter, fighting against the memory. The rage is visible in every line of his body. It's surreal to me, this story I'm an intricate part of, when I feel nothing. It's as if the story happened to someone else, seen through the eyes of the speaker. I know I should feel something. Guilt at what we did? Rage about what happened?

"There were four men, older boys really, that had cornered you both." Drew's jaw finally releases its steel trap. "You were beautiful even then. And all I saw was red."

Oh shit. No.

He shakes his head at the question that must be all over my face. "I was too late, but not that late. One man had your friend on the ground. His hands were wrapped around her neck, choking her, by the time I got there. She was holding her ground and fighting back."

His voice becomes quieter. "But she didn't make it. If

someone else from the Guardianship had gotten there sooner, she wouldn't have died."

My body tenses. That girl had been a friend and the fact that grief doesn't bombard me makes me nauseous. Why have I forgotten her? Maybe I blocked this all out. Maybe that's why I don't have these memories.

"I couldn't save her. Please understand. My only priority, ever, is you. I *cannot* and *will not* be sorry for that. I'm only sorry she died."

Horror sweeps through me. He didn't try to save her?

"When I came upon the two of you, you were fighting a man, and there was one down on the ground. And so I was going to take on the fourth. As I was running towards him, you knocked the one you were fighting out. I guarantee they never saw that coming." He pauses, pride in his tone. But his tone quickly mutates back.

"You stood there catching your breath, and the one I was going after ran at you. It happened so fast."

He stares off, his eyes unfocused. Uneasy, I know we're coming to a dreaded part of the story, and I'm sorry for him. I'm sorry for the anger and sorrow he's reliving. I've nothing but the curiosity and horror of a bystander. No memory of it. The silence lengthens, and the tension and anger once again rolls off him in waves I can sense, even without his touch. The connection we have is slowly becoming stronger.

Drew suddenly jumps up and walks over to a cabinet across the room. He pulls out a bottle of some alcohol, bourbon maybe, and a glass. He pours himself two fingers and drinks it all in one shot. And repeats the sequence. He raises the bottle in a silent question.

"No...thank you."

"I yelled out to you," Drew whispers as he pours himself more of the amber liquid. "You turned to me then. A momentary distraction." He bites off each fragment as if the words won't come out. "He barreled toward you and backhanded you so hard, I swear you flew twenty feet. You slammed into the concrete and didn't move. I was convinced you were dead. And I'd not let him get away with it. Rage and horror colored every thought I may have had, and I went ballistic on his ass."

Chapter Eight

DREW

The bourbon burns in my gut. The alcohol doesn't have a high enough proof to drown my rage. I slam another shot, just in case this one might be more effective, but it's not. I'm out of the moonshine that is far better at doing its job.

"I was pounding my fists into him over and over. I couldn't see straight, and I couldn't hear anything. I had one objective: to kill him."

And if I had, maybe things would've turned out different. Maybe I'd be more human.

Empathy, the thing I lack the most, crosses Delaney's face. Her eyes soften and they lose a little of the fear.

"You know this isn't your fault, don't you? Just because you yelled had no bearing on anything. I'm sure it wouldn't have turned out any better if you hadn't."

The Fates truly created someone who was my better half. She doesn't know who I am, what we've been through. She has no vivid memories keeping her fueled through the years. Yet she still senses my emotions. Tries to heal them. I don't deserve her, but I can't help but thank them for her.

"The story isn't finished yet. That was my mistake—allowing rage to consume me. I never saw or heard the other two coming. They hauled me off him. At fourteen, though like you I had training, I wasn't ready or prepared for the kind of anger and the desperation of men who have committed a crime. Not to mention all I could see was you laying on the ground." My voice drops and turns raspy. "They beat the living shit out of me."

Bitterness tinges every word. I'm ashamed of myself. Of my inability to reason. To think. Everything I've ever been taught, everything I've ever had has flown away so easily.

And because of my stupidity, I pay the price. Every fucking day.

"I was barely conscious when you finally stood up. I saw you." I close my eyes, but it does nothing to dissipate the image I carry with me. "All I saw was you. Your fury. You stood there, hands in the air, blood trickling down your arms, like some war goddess. You were yelling something, but I couldn't hear with the ringing in my ears. Your hair was wild, whipping in the wind, your eyes hard. Blood was pouring out of a gash on your cheek, and your lips were swollen and puffy. You were fourteen. But you were magnificent. Power, standing on the edge of a storm."

She's done that once again since then, but the chaos and terror she rained on the world was not what it should have been. She wasn't the same. But I loved her then, just as much as I had before all this shit started.

I pace the room, my footsteps moving faster and faster till I'm sure I'm a blur. We've got the speed, and now, it's almost second nature. The good news is she can track me with her eyes. Which means even when she doesn't know the things she can do, her body does. That's got to be a good sign.

"You, you had righteousness on your side. Your friend was dead. Anything you did at that point should've been justified."

I should stop talking. Stop telling her things. I'm close to her. I'm able to reach out and touch her if needed. But she needs to know. *I* need to know. Is this Delaney the right one? Will she try to end the world and take me down with it? Will she finally remember? The thought of living with her, of her knowing it all, of *all of this* ending once and for all spurs me forward. I take a deep breath.

"You had them die. All four of them."

The words, soft on the air, are brutal. There's no turning back. I crouch down at her feet, ready to do whatever needs to be done. Her breathing increases rapidly, but she seems to be holding it together.

"You had no choice. They'd have killed me, as they had killed her, as they'd surely have killed you. They wouldn't have left survivors."

"There are always choices."

She lurches out of the bed and hauls it to the bathroom. The sounds of her vomiting echo through the room. Should I go to her? Would she accept my assistance? Could I hold her hair for her and rub circles into her back? Not without sensations wrapping themselves around us. I don't know if she wants the reminder that life as she knows it is all a sham. She heaves a few more times, and I wince. No one likes getting sick, but I'll stay here in case she needs me. When the whimpers start, I tighten my muscles so I don't rush into the bathroom and gather her in my arms. The need to hit something, anything, creeps up on me. If only it would help. But I can't fight ghosts.

The sound gets louder, and now she's full-on sobbing. Fuck. I can't stay away from her. I stride into the bathroom and my chest aches at the sight of her lying on the floor, arms curled around her knees, hugging herself into a ball. The need to slay for her roars through me. I want to kill everyone in the Guardianship that has brought her to this moment in time.

How dare they cause her pain? Make her take this path years ago? It can't be just the boys she killed. I have to tread even more carefully. Her emotions are running amok, and maybe asking her to be chill about all the things I've revealed is actually the worst thing I can be doing. Dammit.

I slide down the wall and sit beside her. Maybe she doesn't want me near her, but I can stay as long as she needs. I'll be right here for her. Tears continue to pour down her face, and I want to reach out and bring her into my lap so bad I can fucking taste it. Not for the touch, but to soothe her pain. Her tears tear something in me that nothing can fill. I promise I'll make it safe for her again.

She stirs, and I hold my breath when it looks like she'll climb into my lap of her own accord. But at the last second she sits upright and leans against the wall next to me. The heat of her thigh reaches mine, a hairbreadth away. And then she leans her head against my shoulder. It's like an invisible cloth made of the softest material on earth blankets me. The longer she stays here, the more heat rushes through my veins and warms me to my toes. I can't help myself. I slide my arm up and rub small circles into her lower back.

When she sighs languidly, I know without a doubt she feels exactly the same way. Her body melts into me. She'll heal at the prolonged contact, but there's no need to hide anything else. The sound of her deep inhalation, knowing the scent of my body is invading her nostrils, causes my heart to race. My soul strains toward her, and the hairs on my body tremble like individual tuning forks.

"I shouldn't just sit here." She moves to stand, and I get a clear look at her face—guilt written all over it. She's wrong. I reach out, my hand locking onto her wrist, and the warmth shoots through me again. She looks down, and I want to yank her into my lap but don't.

"There's nothing wrong with getting comfort. This

doesn't mean anything. I know, dammit. I know you have a life. A child. I don't ever want you to think because we have this connection that I'd abuse it for my own pleasure or try to change anything you have going on in your personal life. Like, if there's someone."

It doesn't occur to me till right now that she might have a boyfriend. A fiancé. I never stopped to check that she might have some person in her life that she has a relationship with. Sex with. I drop her hand before the anger rushes into me and I break bones in her delicate arm. I want to hit the wall until I plow through the concrete. Fuck. It's not her fault she has a life without me in it.

"There's no one but Katrina right now. But...it doesn't feel...right."

"Oh, it definitely feels right." Joy explodes through my mind and body until I feel like I could fly. Hot damn! She's single!

"See, it's that right there that makes it not right! This is all so...weird! And...and...oh my god. You love me."

She sounds horrified, and suddenly the joy recedes, leaving a bitter aftertaste in my mouth. Does she think I'd force her? How can I make her mine again if she's scared of me?

I stand up. "It doesn't matter what I feel. I'd never do you harm, and that means not ever asking you to love me. That's not how this works. You're my other half. To make you miserable would make me miserable. Take comfort in that. I'll do anything you need, always. But you can't ignore the connection we have. It's there for a reason, we're better because of it."

I don't understand the look on her face. For once, I can't read her. I'm going to end up putting my foot in my mouth or screwing this all up. She walks over to the sink and rests her hands against the rim, her eyes closed as if she's trying to gather herself. I better leave before she tells me to just fuck right off.

Chapter Nine

DELANEY

By the time I look up, Drew's left. Relieved, I brush my teeth using a toothbrush that's still in its package. When I'm done, I walk out of the bathroom into the empty room. I fix the sheets and blanket on the bed and crawl in. I wish I could fall asleep and wake up in my own bed at home and realize this is some vivid nightmare. I don't know how to process this. How do I focus on everything when half of my mind is on Katrina, and the other half is busy replaying all the sensations my body has experienced in the last half hour?

I'm hoping we're done for the night, but then there's a knock and the subsequent opening of the door. I sigh dramatically, hoping Drew takes the hint. I'm done. I've had enough. I don't want to talk anymore. I don't want more information ripping apart my world.

I check the time pointedly. I'm surprised it's five in the morning. Soon I'll be able to see Kat, and I can't wait. I need to make sure she's safe. There's tension in the pit of my stomach that hasn't left since I got here.

"When will you take me to my daughter?"

"Rest a bit. She's still sleeping and has been all night. You haven't. Please rest and then you'll see her. Plus, I need to make some calls and figure out what's going on."

"No, I'll be fine. I want to see her. Now."

I throw the covers and get out of the bed. My legs are shaky at the thought he might not back down, but I will them to hold me up.

"I need to speak to several of my people. I've put it off too long as it is."

His voice sounds hard and unemotional, and I wonder if he's lied to me about her being here the whole time. Pressure builds in my chest, and I swallow hard.

"I'm not asking!" The quiver in my voice betrays my panic. What can I say that will force him to change his mind?

"Neither am I. I won't budge on this. I *need* to make sure you're okay. Your safety is of the utmost importance, and I can't protect you if I don't know exactly how many I'm up against. Knowledge is power."

A cold sweat trickles down my back, and fear grips me when his words from earlier ricochet in my head. I whip around, grabbing the gun that's still laying on the bed, and turn, I simultaneously bring my arm up, letting the cold steel rest under his jaw. My subconscious gives him credit for not flinching.

"You told me earlier that I'm your priority. *She's* my priority. Do you understand that?" Once again my heart rate has lowered, my breathing has become even. I've gone from hysteria to hostile in a second. I vaguely wonder why I'm perfectly okay with all this violence.

"I know. It's why she's safely here instead of at your home. I learn from my mistakes. Do you?" He leans in minutely, the barrel pressing harder. If he thinks I'll move because of this tactic, he's wrong. I press forward myself. It's got to be uncomfortable for him, but I don't care.

I stare into his eyes, searching for anything that will make me believe he's placating me. Long enough to make sure he knows I'm dead serious. "Obviously, I didn't. Because if something happens to her, I'll hold you personally responsible. If she's not here, and you're lying to me, I'll make you regret every word."

Pulling the gun away from him, I begin pacing. I didn't want to know anything else tonight, but now it's imperative I know everything, in case I have to make a run for it with Katrina. Fuck resting.

"Finish telling me what happened. I'm not sleeping." I raise the gun and wave it around, knowing damn well it's probably not the best threat. "And there's nothing you can say to change my mind. And in an hour or so, when she's awake, you'll take me to her."

He sighs dramatically and finally gives in. "The guys you killed deserved it. They were pieces of shit. They hurt you, intending far worse. They murdered your friend. And if it makes you feel better, they had a rap sheet. I checked. They weren't nice people."

I stop pacing to glare at him. "That doesn't mean I get to kill them. What did I do? I mean, how did they die?" The words peter out in a whisper. I don't want to know what I'm capable of. On the other hand, yes, I do. Knowledge is power. The hypocrisy of my actions isn't lost on me.

"You made them run into the street. A bus ran them over. Literally."

Concern shines in his eyes. The blood drains from my face. I can't be so cold-blooded. Can I? I'm a horrible person. My skin turns cold. Even my fingers feel like icicles. I mean, I just threatened him with a gun. Clearly, I'm capable of doing all sorts of things I had no idea I'd do, given the right circumstances. My stomach churns.

The Guardianship was right to keep tabs on me. I can't be trusted to be a nice, normal person. I tuck the gun into my waistband and grip both sides of my head. The ache of my conflicting feelings burns in my brain, giving me a massive headache.

Drew walks over and with the tip of his finger lifts my chin for the briefest second so I've no choice but to let go and look up. Warmth sizzles over my skin, briefly thawing the cold.

"What happened wasn't your fault. It was mine."

His admission jerks me back out of the cold feeling of guilt. What the hell is he talking about? "You didn't do anything. I did it. I caused them to run out in front of a bus. There's something seriously wrong with me." I waved a gun around just minutes ago.

Drew shakes his head violently. "No. If I'd been quicker, or if I hadn't lost my head and let rage rip through me, none of this would've happened. If anyone is to blame, it's me."

My mouth drops open, yet no words come out. How can he still believe he's at fault?

"I'm your Protector."

The deadly cold voice returns. He thumps his fist on his chest.

Thump. "I should've been there to protect you, and I wasn't."

Thump. "I should've never left the vicinity of the house, and I should've been there the whole time."

Thump. "I could've alerted the Guardianship that much quicker. I failed you."

Thump. "And because of *my* failure, everything that's happened has been my fault."

He walks out of the room. Stunned, I don't move for several seconds before racing after him. I halt at the door. Do I use this opportunity to look for Katrina? Do I search for Drew? My heart pounds rapidly. I don't know what to do. I don't know what's right. I don't know anything anymore. I shake my head, trying to clear the buzzing in it. Where's the sound coming from? I close my eyes, trying to keep calm and make it go away. I'm losing it. I really going to lose my shit.

"Katrina! Drew!" I yell, but there's nothing except the echo of my voice. To the left is the hallway dead-ending at a bookcase. So, right, it is. In bare feet, the marble floor should be cool, but it's surprisingly warm. Heated floors? Unreal.

The next door on the right opens to another hospital-type room. I shut it and keep going. The door on the left yields a storage room, massive and fully stocked with linens, medical supplies, bathroom supplies, and various other household supplies. Why would someone need a hundred cases of toilet paper? I shake my head and wander back out.

I keep moving down the hall. The next several rooms are guest rooms, bathrooms, showers, and even a full-sized kitchen. I've lost track of how impossibly big the building is. There are several hallways that branch off, but I remain on this path. I'm too afraid I'll get lost in the labyrinth.

Plus, I know I'm headed in the right direction. Towards Drew. I'd call it a hunch, but with a sinking feeling, I register my soul's ability to find its other half. It pulls me toward him. If I have any lingering doubts about what's real, this newfound discovery smothers it.

Opening the next door reveals a huge training room with a cavernous ceiling. There are various exercise machines, racks of weapons and targets. My eyes are drawn to a shirtless Drew viciously attacking a Mook Jong. The fact that I can identify it is no longer surprising.

I observe his form. To say it looks like a piece of art is an understatement. Every inch of skin appears to be sculpted from a piece of granite.

Does the man have any body fat?

It hasn't taken him long to break into a sweat. He's been gone minutes, but rivulets make their way down his back. He's obviously beating himself up. His voice jerks me back to the present.

"I'm sorry. I needed a moment myself." He finishes the last of the movement, bypassing the wooden dummy, and grabs a towel. He dries off and turns to me, pulling on a shirt. I vaguely register a tattoo on the left side of his chest near his ribcage, *exactly where mine is*, when I see the scar.

The oxygen is ripped from my throat, and I gasp loudly, dropping to my knees. How can this be? The faded angular scar dissecting his upper body from left hip to right shoulder no longer looks sinister. It looks positively angelic next to the last hellish image I have of it.

In my nightmare, it's torn open, his torso much like a Picasso painted with blood. My heart stutters in my chest. My soul weeps.

"Delaney!" Drew rushes to me and drops to his knees. "Are you okay? What's wrong? What happened? What hurts? Delaney! Answer me!" His hands are everywhere, on my shoulders, my arms, my hips, searching for something wrong. He finally leaves them on my upper arms, gripping almost too tightly.

The comfort of his touch, the familiar warmth, registers on my body and I don't care. I focus on his shirt and, reaching out, trace the scar underneath it. His muscles bunch and tense beneath my fingers. I barely notice as I follow the scar up. I feel the ridges of puckered skin. But I don't need it to be able to follow its path exactly. It's been seared into my brain. The blood and tissue exposed from a cut so deep it should have been fatal, now healed.

"I never thought it was real. That the image I carry in my head was ever real. This scar."

I drag my eyes from his shirt to his face. I don't know who did this to him nor do I know why. But I do know that it caused him an untold amount of pain, and to know he survived this gives me insight into his incredible strength.

"Fuck. You scared me half to death. I don't remember you ever being so dramatic." He rocks back onto his heels and examines my face. I'm sure he perceives a difference in the way I'm looking at him. Mistrust is slowly seeping away as the truth is nailed into my conscience with every irrefutable revelation. "Want to tell me about this image of yours?"

"Want to tell me what happened to *you*? And why I see you in this image?" I poke his scar with a finger. "Except this isn't a scar, Drew!"

Inexplicably, I'm pissed, and I punch him in his jaw. The force of it knocks him back momentarily and he sits back up, rubbing his face.

"Still favor that sneaky left hook."

"I'm going to punch you again, if you don't tell me what the *fuck* is going on! I mean it!" The air stutters in my throat every time I inhale. Who hurt him? Why do I care so much?

"I've said before I think some of your nightmares are memories. This confirms it doesn't it? Let's go." He holds out a hand.

I shake the feeling of déjà vu and clasp it, warmth flowing down into my arm. He pulls me up and quickly releases it. The loss of him makes me sad, and I do my best to ignore it.

"Are you a martyr?" He must be. Nobody just takes the blame for someone else.

"That's a strange question. No, I'm not."

"Then stop blaming yourself for everything that happened. I know I don't remember it, but from what you've told me, none of it's your fault. So, you're either a martyr or are just that egotistical." I peek under lowered lashes at his profile. The chiseled jaw and straight nose, the dark stubble on his cheek. He probably knew he was good-looking.

He sighs. "No. I'm not a martyr, and this isn't about my ego. I blame myself. I genuinely do. No matter what you say, if I'd been there, it wouldn't have happened the way it did. You wouldn't have had to deal with the consequences. You wouldn't have forgotten everything. You wouldn't have forgotten *me*."

I gasp loudly. "The consequences. That's right. I can't believe I forgot about them. You know what though. I deserved them, whatever they were." The small part of me full of guilt senses I need this. I need the punishment.

He stops dead in his tracks, fists tight, his jaw tightening. "You don't know what you're saying. You don't remember how bad it was. And none of that would've happened if I'd been faster, stronger, or, dammit, didn't lose myself in a rage thinking you were dead. I should have known I'd know if you were dead. I never stopped to think. Instead, you suffered, and I suffered, needlessly."

Something in my head clicks again and brings a sharp pain right down the middle. I want to grip my scalp again, as if I can prevent it from splitting. "Will you stop it! For one second, can you think of something other than yourself? These were people! Real people! And I killed them. Me. I caused it. I caused you pain. I was the one who couldn't control myself! I'm the one who should've died! I deserved that punishment! No one, power or no power, should go around killing people. I earned those consequences."

The stabbing disappears, and I know I must be right. I'm moving back to the hospital room, drained from all of the emotions roiling through me, when he grabs my arm and quickly spins me back around. He shoves his face into mine.

"You're not understanding the full extent of your power. You couldn't have chosen differently. It wasn't possible, because you did see the outcome. You had a vision while standing there, of the future, and we all died. Not just your friend, but me and you too. You chose to save us and to change it. That's what I meant when I said it wasn't your fault. And when I said the Guardianship should never have given you a black mark for it. I didn't understand it then and I don't understand it now. But don't you ever blame yourself. You're incredible. You're one of the smartest, kindest, and fairest people I've ever known. And I don't say that because we share a soul. I say that because it's the truth and I will not have you tarnish it."

I hadn't expected this outburst at all. I forgot the other portion of my power, the visions I see of the future. "How do you know this?"

"Because you told me later." He sighs. "Come on, you need to get back in bed."

We arrive at my room, and he opens the door. I plop myself onto the bed. Then I dig out the gun that's jabbing me in my back and put it on the tray cart next to my bed without a second thought.

"We thought this event would be classified as a normal course of action. Not as something personal," he continues. "The delay in consequences made the reality of them slam into you. We didn't know what Nature decided. It was unexpected. I've been researching why for years."

"Ugh, these titles of the Guardianship are killing me. When you said earlier that Nature demands it, I assumed...I don't know, the universe or something. A yin and yang type thing. I didn't know it was an actual person. One day, you need to sit down and draw up a list of all these classifications."

"One day, hopefully, you'll remember it yourself and we won't have to do that. The hallucinations started four days later. I'd been sleeping at your house, ready to help with anything that might come up. We had all just went to bed. Not that the situation was great to begin with. Believe me those four days of nightmares weren't a walk in the park either. An hour later, you started screaming."

His words cause something to curl in my gut, and for a moment, I think I'm going to get sick again.

"We were petrified. *I* was petrified. The first night they were bad, you kept trying to walk out of the house in the middle of the night. When you weren't sleepwalking, you were in bed screaming. I slept on the floor in your room. Laying on the floor in front of the door, in an effort to stop you."

Well shit. What good is my ability to create a future if someone else, like Nature, could override me and create another reality?

"You were scared to go to bed. You refused to tell me what the nightmares were about, but they were getting worse each day. When the hallucinations started, it wasn't anything I'd ever heard of before, nor anything I'd imagine it to be. And nothing I'd wish on even my enemies. You got two, three hours of sleep between the nightmares ending and the hallucinations beginning. I got even less. I was afraid if I fell asleep, I wouldn't be able to save you. You've no idea how powerless I felt."

Kind of like me right now. I can't get to my daughter.

"How long did this go on?"

"For a very long month. Four weeks of hell. I didn't think we would survive it."

"But I did."

"Yes, you did." Drew nods. "And now, you need sleep. Or your body won't heal."

I debate fighting because didn't I say I wasn't going to sleep before seeing Katrina? But honestly, at this point, I don't think my brain can take in any more. The faster I fall asleep, the faster I'll be able to see Kat.

He turns off the lights, and I tense, thinking of the dark,

but he's thoughtfully left the bathroom light on and the door open.

I try to sleep, but my brain won't stop processing everything I've learned. I'm worried about Katrina. Is she scared? Does she even know anything is wrong? With my eyes closed, I count sheep.

Chapter Ten

DREW

I turn on the TV monitor in the training room and click through to the cameras in the hospital room. The screen shows Delaney tossing and turning on the bed. I know she's dealing with the aftermath of everything I've told her.

Everything, except of course what happened to us. I overloaded her as it is. Whatever it was she'd created to protect herself is slowly falling apart, and the memories will start rushing forward. She'll need her strength, and sleep is the best thing for her. Her mind fracturing will be the end of this version of her, and I'll have to start all over again.

I'm torn between elation and hesitation. This is the furthest I've come with Delaney, without her shattering herself and the world. Without her creating chaos and murdering innocents. To think she's here and as close to being who she was makes me think this is it. That this Delaney is different.

My jaw clenches. Maybe this time I won't have to barter a piece of my soul. Maybe this time I won't be brought to my knees for days, wracked with the physical pain of losing her and the other half of my soul. Maybe this time we've won. But I've thought that before and been wrong.

Devastatingly so.

This time has to be different. The never-ending hope when it comes to her. I refuse to give up until I can no longer go on.

I'll never get enough of seeing her talk, laugh, smile. To see her alive. I'd never wish pain on her, and I'll get to the bottom of who's after her and threatened her child. But the last ten hours have been exhilarating. I've always been fond of battle, both the physical release as well as the mental challenge of outwitting your opponent. It's been too long since I've had the opportunity to do both. The best part of tonight, hands down, has been being with her.

It doesn't matter to me that our emotions are roiling. It doesn't matter to me that I fear for her. It doesn't matter to me that she fears for her child. It doesn't matter to me that I shattered her reality.

We can overcome all of that. She's strong. I'm strong. We've both been through worse. I'd do it again and again, knowing I can be close to her, knowing I can touch her. Knowing she feels the connection we have is worth every minute of pain I've ever experienced losing her.

She's still tossing and turning. Fighting sleep. Her mind needs to rest and to shore up for what's to come. I'll just go in and touch her briefly through the blankets. Soothe her enough to get to sleep. For her own good, of course.

I snort. Nope, nothing to do with how it'll make *me* feel at all.

Fuck.

I move out and head to my office to call Astrid. We had one regrettable night together. Business for me, pleasure for her. But she has a soft spot for me, and I've a spot for whatever intel she might have about the hit on Delaney.

I shove in the steak and potatoes that Charlie left sitting on a plate at my desk, quickly chewing and swallowing as I contemplate what to say. She's not completely sane and may want my body as payment. Not going to happen now that I have Delaney back.

"Hi, handsome. Tell me you're calling because you want me naked and can't wait to have me on top of you." Astrid's insinuating voice makes me wince. This isn't going to be easy.

"Not this time. I need your considerable resources to find out some information for me."

"Oh, babe. That's gonna cost you," she purrs.

"You know I can't get away right now. I'm on Guardianship business." Now that Delaney's back and hopefully permanently, (please Fates, let her be the right version) there won't ever be another night with Astrid. Or anyone else.

"Mm-hmm. What can I do for you?"

"I need to know who put out a hit on two people." I hear her rummaging around and then the click of a pen cap hitting teeth.

"Give me the names. I'm guessing this information isn't official Guardianship." Her voice is brisk, ever the businesswoman.

"Last name is Opmerker. Delaney and Katrina. And that would be a correct assumption. I've heard nothing above ground, and need you to listen under."

The pen taps against something wooden, a quick tattoo. "Why does that last name sound familiar?"

I don't answer the question, since I don't think she was asking me. "I didn't think you had a desk, Astrid."

"Oh, I don't. I'm finishing up a job."

"You could have called me back later."

"Not a chance, handsome. An assassin's work is never done, and I won't miss a call from you if I can help it." Her flirtatious tone is back. "I'll get back to you as soon as possible."

I once again hit the computer, searching the Guardianship files, quickly skimming through Delaney's. There's nothing new, and I know every piece of information by heart. I've had years to look over them. Over and over, trying to figure out what the Guardianship was doing. Why they had such a big file on her. None of the other Destinies had a similar file. In fact, they were all laughably small. Why Delaney? It was almost as if they had a bull's eye on her since the day she was born. But that is preposterous. The Guardianship isn't supposed to be the bad guy. We're the good guys. The ones that make sure humans don't destroy our way of being. Their hotheaded stupidity is not their fault. They simply weren't born with the gifts we have. Someone has to watch over them.

To think that something is turning sour within the Guardianship goes against everything we've been taught. But somehow, that's exactly what's happening. I'm losing faith, and the answer is under my nose. I know it. I just have to find it.

Chapter Eleven

DELANEY

I wake with a start, breaking free from the dreams that grip me. They came hard and fast, snippets here and there. Instead of giving me answers, I have more questions. If this is all true, and my brain is resigned to think so, I'm in way over my head.

Katrina! I'm going to see my darling Kat. Except now I don't think I'll be running away. If everything checks out, we'll be staying. I'm going to need to know how to keep us safe from the Guardianship.

I mentally throw all my thoughts about dreams of screams and bright fire to the side and jump out of bed.

My clothes from yesterday are folded on the chair in the corner. Someone has washed and dried them. There's no helping the cuts and tears, not to mention the faint haze of bloodstains. They're ruined. I pick up the first item in the next pile. It's a shirt. Brand new from the looks of it, and similar to the clothing I have on—just what I'd pick out. The shirt, made of soft cotton, is my favorite shade of blue.

Drew never did elaborate on why "my" clothes were here. Had he bought clothes for me? Did he know it would come to this? It doesn't matter at this point. I've nothing else to wear. The jeans are soft, as if from years of wear. Underwear, bra, and socks in my size. Loafers on the floor next to the chair. This is so creepy. I head to the bathroom and get dressed, and I'm nearly done when a knock sounds at the door.

"Come in." I tuck in the shirt.

"Good morning." Drew carries in a tray of food.

"Uh, good morning." It's been an hour or so. But if he can act like this is a normal situation, so can I.

I'm wearing clothes he bought, I'm sleeping in his house, he's bringing me breakfast. Oh yeah, and we're soul mates. Nothing awkward about this at all. Totally normal. Ugh.

"I'm glad you slept. Your body needs it. Eat, please. Then I need to check on your shoulder." He puts the tray down.

"I'm not hungry. And my shoulder's fine. I barely feel it," I lie. "I want to see my daughter."

"You eat, I'll inspect your shoulder, and we'll go." He stands, his arms behind his back, looking like he's got all the time in the world and not a care to go with it.

"Fine." I pick up a spoon. It seems to be some sort of chicken noodle soup. Soup for the invalid I guess, but I can't help my stomach rumbling as soon as I get a good whiff of it. It smells fantastic. "I am kind of hungry."

"Mm-hmm," Drew murmurs, wisely not saying anything. He sits in the opposite chair and focuses those shrewd green eyes on me.

"Are you going to sit there and watch me eat?" The man knows how to get under my skin.

"Yes, actually. For two reasons. One, I want to make sure you eat all of it, and two, don't end up vomiting. You got sick several times already. I want to verify it's not because of a concussion."

Begrudgingly, I lift the spoon full of the soup to my lips

and sip at it. It tastes homemade and reminds me of the soup Mom used to make when I was little.

"This is good." Just like the sandwich yesterday. "Did you make it?" I know I sound surprised, and I don't know why. At this point, it seems very little should surprise me.

"My chef made it."

"You have a chef." I open my mouth again, then close it. I resolve to sit and eat every last drop of this delicious broth and not ask why he has a chef. Or hospital rooms. Or the other rooms I've glimpsed. He has money, that much is blatant. He's awfully good at sidestepping questions.

My questions will have to wait till later. I don't want any more distractions or delays. I *need* to see Kat. As I finish the soup, Drew gives me another round of antibiotics.

"Isn't this overkill? Don't you think I've had enough yet?"

"Not even close. You have a couple more days of round-the-clock antibiotics. I didn't get you back now just to lose you to some infection. I need you to remove your shirt."

I choke on my own spit. "Excuse me?"

"Last I checked, I don't have x-ray vision, so take off your shirt."

I reluctantly do so, hugging it to my chest. My awkwardness is kinda ridiculous. Not only have I been in a bikini that shows less skin than this, but he bought this damn bra. He knows the color of it, the cup size. And yet, I can't help but be embarrassed.

Drew proceeds as if he's done this a thousand times, as clinical as any doctor. He carefully peels off the bandage taped to my shoulder.

"How do you know so many medical things?" I ask, hopefully easing the awkwardness.

"Part of my training includes first aid, CPR, the basics." He pulls out his cellphone, snaps a picture, and shows me the screen. The back of my shoulder sports six stitches *in perfectly healed skin*.

I've always been a fast healer, but this...this can't be normal.

"I need to remove these now." He takes out whatever instruments he has, but I don't bother to look.

"How? How did I heal this quickly?" I swear if he tells me magic I'm going to scream. The stabbing pain is back in my brain, and I carefully rub my forehead nonchalantly. I don't want to distract him from bringing me to Kat.

"We are really good at healing. And it's a bit of a bonus for us soul mates. Over the years, I've attended a bunch of classes. In my experience, having medical knowledge is a good thing that can keep you alive. And off anyone's radar."

I grit my teeth as the sound of snipping pushes through my head. Why is it so loud? Are my ears clogged? He gently dabs at my shoulder with something wet and slathers on an ointment. Each slight brush of his skin sends little waves of heat over my skin. I could close my eyes and relax right here with his touch. It pushes the pain away and my muscles loosen in my neck.

He rips open a new bandage and gently tapes it to my shoulder. I have to give him credit, I barely feel him. and the few wisps of heat dissipate as quickly as they appear. The care he gives both to my feelings and to my shoulder is incredibly kind.

"Is that what this place is? Off anyone's radar?"

"It is." He cleans the table with an antiseptic and throws it all in the trash, including the gloves he's wearing. I hadn't taken him for being a germaphobe or a neat freak but here we are.

"It's my home, my sanctuary. And yours as well."

My home? When will I be able to go back to my *own* home?

I jump up from my chair. "Can we go now? I've rested, I've eaten, you've checked me over. I need to see her. You don't understand what it's like being a mother. I need to know she's okay. I need to hold her and make sure she's safe. And I'm sure she needs me too. She must be so confused and upset!"

"You'd be surprised how much I can relate to that," he says dryly. He guides me out of the hospital room and back out into the hallway. We head toward the bookcase and make a sharp right to a set of stairs.

We walk down a flight of stairs and turn into yet another hallway. There's a chair by the door but it's empty. Adrenaline shoots through me, giving me a clammy, sick sensation. Didn't he say she was being guarded? Where's the guard?

"Mark isn't keeping watch now that Liza's with her. She's the one that's going to be overseeing Katrina while we figure out what's going on. Kind of a nanny if you're okay with that?"

I don't answer. First, I want to make sure Kat's actually fine. Then, I want to check out this Liza person.

"Momma!" Kat spots me the minute the door opens. She jumps up from where she's sitting on the floor playing a game with a slightly older woman.

She runs to my open arms, and I squeeze her so tightly she squeals. "Hi, baby. I missed you!"

"I just saw you last night before dinner, Momma." She giggles and pulls me by the hand. "Come see what I'm building with Ms. Liza."

Had it only been last night? A few measly hours before my world turned on its head? It feels like forever ago. I let her drag me over to a short plump lady. She's got steel-colored curls and glasses perched on an unlined face. She's younger than she looks from far away.

After oohing and ahing over the fort and city they had been building with blocks, I sit back on my heels and watch the interaction between the two. Kat really seems to like Liza, which is no small feat. She's always been extremely reserved in front of strangers, but the level of play and the amount of giggles erupting has me at ease. She clearly loves hanging out with her. Liza, on the other hand, seems just as smitten. You can't fake that kind of attitude toward children. Drew's remained by the door, standing stiffly, and I wonder what has him so irritated.

I shrug, returning my attention to Kat. "Do you want to stay here and have some more fun with Liza, darling?"

Kat's eyes light up and she nods vehemently. "Oh yes, please! Ms. Liza's said we can build a fort this afternoon with the pillows and chairs!"

The fact that Liza has already found a way to Kat's obsessions with building comfy spaces speaks volumes. Lots of adults don't talk to kids and get to know them. Kind of like Drew standing awkwardly—confidence completely gone for once.

"Okay, love. I'll stop by and see you later, then. I love you." I scoop her wriggling body back into my arms and blow raspberries into her neck. Her sweet smell wraps around me, and I keep my face burrowed into her until she hugs me hard. "I love you too. Is everything all right, Momma?"

"Yes, baby. Go have some fun." I put her down and walk out of the room and out into the hallway where Drew is now standing, propping up the wall. There's a strange look on his face that I can't identify. It's clear he doesn't like kids, but it doesn't matter. Kat's here and happy and he's done that for her. Provided her with a safe space and an entire room full of activities meant for a kid to have fun. People are hunting me, and therefore her, and I will do anything to protect her. Which means I'm going to be working with him to regain my memory. I'm going to do everything I need to do to make sure that my entire world, my Kat, is safe.

"You said there were other Destinies. Do you think we can contact them? Would they help?"

"Probably not. Destinies, in general, don't get along. I don't know if it's more than just a power struggle or what." He shrugs. "Regardless, we can't risk the Hunters finding you, and that much power concentrated in one area will draw them in as good as signs on a freeway. We're on our own. I have faith you'll remember everything you need to. You just need to be nudged."

"Tell me, what's a better nudge than your child being in danger? Because that's where we stand. I won't let them hurt her."

My lips compress into a thin line in an effort to control myself. The thought of them hurting her makes me damn near hysterical. And that won't help me. "I don't remember. And I don't know how to remember."

"I think I can help with that. We can start with muscle memory. You once had defensive and offensive training."

I perk up. Offense is good. If I end up having to go after them instead of waiting for them to come to me, I'll need offensive training.

He looks at me, intelligent eyes calculating. "No, you may not use it for your own gain."

The hell I can't.

"Of course not. I don't think I actually know how to fight."

"We'll see," he says thoughtfully. "Before that, though, food. We'll talk more while we eat." He throws up a hand, stalling my protest. "At least a snack in preparation of the calories you'll burn during physical training."

Then he grins. Why is he smiling? "You forget I know you. You'll accomplish nothing if five minutes into our exploratory training you collapse."

I think all this food is ridiculous, but whatever he thinks

I'll need to make this work is how I'll play along. For now. "Fine, but let's not dawdle."

"Yes, ma'am." He smiles widely. "You sound like a mom."

"I *am* a mom."

My lips lift in response to his. He's handsome when his face is stern, but oh, that smile. It must have made hearts melt. There's a cramp in my stomach, and it takes me a second to realize it's jealousy. What do I have to be jealous of? He may be my soul mate but that doesn't mean I have cause.

"Tell me, you must have some idea on what caused me to not remember any of this stuff from before? I've been mulling it over, and suppressing memories just because of some hallucinations and nightmares is a bit drastic, isn't it?"

We walk toward the bookcase, and Drew stops and presses a button on the wall. The bookcase slides forward silently and then to the side. My jaw nearly drops open as I look through the doorway and into a foyer ending at a front door. I step through and the whisper of the bookcase sliding shut behind me has me whirling around and gasping at the sight. If I didn't know better, I'd think I was staring at wall full of floor-to-ceiling bookshelves.

"Welcome to our home."

"This is...something else." What an understatement. We walk through the foyer, past a grand staircase. Everything is made of marble and screams elegance. We end in a dining room, more wall cabinets, and three large windows. There's a circular driveway out front and a long driveway. I can't even see the end of it. Are we out in the middle of nowhere? There seem to be trees as far as I can see. Unbelievable.

"Are you going to answer my question?"

Chapter Twelve

DREW

"Eat." I gesture toward the meal spread out before us. Charlie has outdone himself. More chicken noodle soup and a garden salad, salmon on a bed of wild rice with asparagus tips in a cream sauce. Not the snack she was envisioning, but judging by the amount she's eating, she was hungry. Doesn't she realize it?

My fingers tighten around the fork and knife in my hand. This is it. The last of the information I have to give her. I'm worried she's having headaches. She thinks she's being sneaky, but she has no idea that I'm extra careful with my observations of her. She rubs her forehead and the top of her head when she thinks I'm not looking. Was it really a slight concussion or a sign that I should be worried about?

I have no fucking clue.

"Remember when I said you hallucinated? They weren't your average run-of-the-mill nightmares or some drug-induced hallucinations. These were... horrible, twisted nightmares. You refused to tell me what they were about, but I saw *you* during them. Hallucinations so vivid, you lived them. If you want me to give you an example, I can show you the scar on my chest again."

"*I* did that to you?" Her face pales, but she seems fine otherwise, and I release my breath. I'm not really sure what holding it would do for me in the first place, but rationality seems to have fled last night.

"Yes. But only because you thought I was tied and bound to a chair, and you were cutting the ropes off to save me."

Like that makes it any better in her mind, but maybe it will help.

"Holy shit," she whispers. "I'm sorry. That doesn't even sound adequate."

"You don't have anything to be sorry for. You didn't know. That's hallucinations right? And it was for the best, I guess."

"I don't understand. It was for the best that I *sliced you open*?"

"I know you don't understand. Fuck, I don't understand it yet either. The bottom line is you changed the future. I don't know why you did. You left a cryptic message. Of course, I didn't get it for a long time. But you changed the future. Incident number four. And then you killed yourself." There. Now it's out in the open.

"What? How can I have killed myself? I'm still here, aren't I? You aren't making any sense. Every time I think that what you're saying is madness, the story you tell me gets stranger! I'd *never* kill myself."

Her pitch rises until she's nearly yelling, and I wonder if I should've withheld that last bit. Do I never learn?

"Yeah, you wouldn't kill anyone else either, would you?"

I know damn well she's thinking of going after the Guardianship. Which I have zero intention of letting her do. She shrugs as if it's no big deal, and I have to give her credit for trying to fool me. She thinks I don't recognize vengeance? She has no idea what that would do to her.

"Maybe I'd kill. Someone had to have told the Hunters to...hurt me? Those guys only follow orders, right? Who ordered it? Because somebody is responsible, and I'll find out who it is, and I will kill them! Piece by bloody piece."

She's gripping her fork in her fist and slamming it on the table with each word. Anger at those responsible, fear for her going out and getting herself hurt, and guilt that I still haven't been able to find out why they're after her fuel my frustration and I lose my patience.

"Will you get a hold of yourself? You have no idea what I've been through. What we've all been through!" Her mouth falls open in surprise, and I continue yelling at her. "You only worry about how you're feeling right now. Look at yourself! What you're doing. You have to control yourself."

"Of course, I am!" she shrieks. "I was attacked! And they might come after my child! You're damn right I'm thinking of what I'm feeling right now. And it's deadly. Plain and simple."

The fuck she thinks I'm going to do? Sit around and let them hurt her? Has she listened to nothing I've said? "You can't murder people for your own purposes. You're a Destiny!" I shove my hand through my hair and push my chair away from the table. "Did you forget there are penalties for these things?"

She shrugs again, and I want to shake her.

"What do I care about penalties? You keep telling me what I can and can't do, yet you've also told me I've killed people, and myself included, so there are obviously ways around such penalties. So, we'll find a way around it again. Because I'll protect my daughter if it's the last thing I do!"

If I can't make her see reason, I've already lost. She's got to get a hold of the emotions that can run rampant through her. That can mess with her mind so badly, she'll crack it into a million pieces. Right now, logic is my only weapon, and I don't know how to wield it successfully. Fear churns in me, making me nauseous.

"Fuck. It *will* be the last thing you do. The rule is there for a reason. Plagues that have killed millions, fires that have torn through towns. Dictators that have created mayhem and chaos. You think these things are all normal? You think these things aren't the direct result of people who have gone bad? Who have decided their actions are justified?"

"Wait," she drawls, studying her fork for a second and looking up, her mouth twisting into a sneer. "Let me guess. Those have all been Destinies."

Of all the times for her to be snarky. "No. No, of course, it wasn't all Destinies. You're only a small piece of the Guardianship. Yes, you are powerful, but there are other players here that are as powerful as you. My point is some of those have been by a power that's corrupted the sweetest souls. Some of that's been the result of corruption. Some of that's been the punishment of corruption."

Terror that they'll kill her floods me until I want to scream into a void. I can't live without her. I can't go through the permanent pain. I'm already on the edge of sanity. I *have* to make her understand.

"Yes. There's also punishment given that's been harsh and unimaginable. You're not just talking about affecting you. You could have an effect on innocent people. The people need you. A Destiny not being there to stop certain things, well, the world will continue on, won't it? But you won't be there to protect it. You need to care about things besides yourself!"

Desperation tinges my words, but I don't know if she'll hear it. She can't condemn me to eternal pain. She can't.

"I've been through this over and over again for years. I've felt guilt and betrayal and love and hate and fear and hope, and every feeling in between! Do you care? Get your head out of your ass and think about other people for fuck's sake!"

I'm losing my grip on my own reality. I get up and back away, breath coming short and hard. Breathing in through my nostrils, out my mouth, I struggle to control my panic—my emotions.

"I need you to focus on things other than your own revenge. You have no idea how badly I—and the world—need you to."

She leans her head against the back of the chair and takes several deep breaths of her own. She sighs loudly and relief shoves aside my panic.

"Did I get reincarnated? Is that what happened?"

Thank the Fates she's flipped back to seeing reason. "No. No, you don't get reincarnated. Let's go to the training room and burn off some of your anger. I think we're done here."

I push in my chair and stalk out of the room. Fuck, but that was close. She jumps up and hurries to catch up. We're both silent as we walk toward the sliding bookcase, until I continue the conversation as if neither of our outbursts had occurred. We can act normal. Can't we?

With a soft snick, the bookcase slides open. The lights turn on as we enter, and the wall shuts behind us. We pass the hospital room and several corridors.

"I meant to ask earlier. How many rooms are in here?"

"About thirty on this side."

"Thirty?" She frowns. "The house doesn't look that big from the outside."

"It's not. These rooms are all built into the mountain, that's where we are now."

Surrounded by concrete and impenetrable lead.

"I had this side of the house specifically built. The original part of the house is also built two feet into the mountain, and that's all most local people know. There are no public records of this."

"Doesn't the builder know?"

"He would if he were alive." I bite out the sentence and shut down my emotions. Kills scar you forever. Especially the innocent ones. But I'll do whatever it takes to protect Delaney. If only she knew how much I'm willing to give.

"Did you have him killed?" She glances over speculatively, with more than mild curiosity.

Not so fast, love. Thinking about killing and actually doing it are two different things.

"No, you don't leave that kind of stuff to others. I did it myself." And would do it a dozen times more if it kept her safe. It doesn't matter how much of my own humanity strips away with each innocent death.

She turns, surprise on her face. "After everything you just said back there, I didn't think you'd kill an innocent person."

"I don't...usually. And I *never* like it. Unfortunately, for the man who was building this house, no one can know about this place. Or it would no longer be safe for you."

And I'm not having that. I'll take the hit to my humanity —what's left of it.

"Here." I get to the door to one of the training rooms and flick on the lights. "This is one of my favorite places in the house. You were in here briefly earlier."

It's big, forty feet by eighty feet with high ceilings that soar fifty feet in the air. At the very top, the ceiling seems to shimmer.

"You probably didn't notice this." I point up

"Is that...water?" She gasps. "We're underwater here?

"Technically, yes. That's a multi-layer, bulletproof glass ceiling, and it has a doorway there"—I point to the corner of the room, near the ceiling—"where you can go through and into the hollow space that's between us and the bottom of what people think is a private pond on top of the mountain." I anticipate her next question. "Yes, I had the pond installed.

Yes, he's dead too." Unfortunately, only dead mouths don't speak.

"This is incredible. How is there an empty space there and how do you get up there?"

I point to the other side of the room. "It was designed that way. There's a spiral staircase there. See? A concealed door and a thin walkway goes from one door to the other. The other door there can only be accessed from the third floor of the house. The hollow space is between the glass ceiling here and the glass bottom of the pond."

If we ever needed to abandon it, we'd flood this out and hide what had been here.

"That's ingenious! I'm not sure what to make of the house. It's incredible, truly."

"Oh, it's full of surprises. The blueprints impressed me long before this was built." And had shocked me to the core. *What could we need such a safe house for?*

"You didn't design it?"

"No, actually. You did."

"Holy shit. Really?"

"Yes." I can't help but laugh at her expression. "That was precisely my reaction when I found out about it. That brings me back to what happened to you. Remember in the dining room, when I said you were, ah..."

"Cutting you open?" she supplies wryly. Her fingers twist together. I wish I could put a hand to hers, touch her, spare her some of the anxiety. But she probably wouldn't like that, so I shove my hands into my pocket instead.

"Yes. It didn't matter to them that the boys that killed your friend were evil. It didn't matter that you hurt me because of the hallucinations. None of it mattered to the Guardianship. They were going to come for you and exact their penalty."

And that penalty was death.

"I don't know to this day what you saw in the future. All I know was you killed people, you thought you killed me, on top of that, you had the threat of the Guardianship's penalty. Even though we were going to fight whatever it was. It was too much." No backing out now.

All or nothing.

"You killed yourself with a knife." The words are still capable of ripping agony from the depths of my body.

The horror of coming to, my own chest spread open like a burst, overripe tomato still makes me want to vomit.

I saw her, through the sheen of tears and searing pain. I couldn't even look at my own chest. I couldn't breathe. My eyes locked onto hers, the tears there. The regret, registering the knife in her hand. The garbled scream that had erupted from my own hoarse throat.

I hadn't heard her then. I saw her mouth move and say something as she fell to the ground. I was powerless to do anything.

I shake my head to clear the memories.

Now, her face is clear. Without the remorse and fear I'd seen on that bloodied visage long ago. Her face is more familiar than my own. I'd seen it when she was first born, red and wrinkly. Though of course I don't remember that memory.

I'd seen it flush with chubby cheeks. I'd seen it through childhood playing around, studying, training with bloody noses and puffy eyes.

I'd caressed it when it was shiny with the glow of adolescence and love. I'd seen it bloody and crazed, vengeful and full of hate in the years since. I've seen it in every variation it has to offer. I've loved every facet of it, no matter what expression it wears.

I'd endured months of pain, had countless dreams, and

relived that last moment, over and over again, before I was able to focus on what she'd said to me.

"*Trust me.*"

I did then, and I do now, with my very soul.

Chapter Thirteen

DELANEY

Drew's expecting me to shatter. And maybe I should. Perhaps I'm shell-shocked from everything that's been happening, but I can't think beyond...well, it didn't work because here I am. *Thank you, universe.*

"You said we can die. Am I immortal?" Would I want to live forever?

"No, you're not. Though remember we do age rather slowly."

"How slowly?"

"It depends on what we live through. None of us escape unscathed. You used to say we had nine lives. You know, like a cat? That no matter what, we always landed on our feet alive." Drew frowns. "We can be killed, though, in a variety of ways."

"If I killed myself, did it not work? I'm confused. I didn't kill myself or what?"

"No, you were definitely deceased. No heartbeat. But I eventually...pulled some strings, and you were brought back from the dead."

What the fuck.

"You're kidding me. I died, and you had me brought back

to life? Why?"

"Yes, that's the gist of it. Now let's see what you've got."

And he charges me, catching me completely off guard. I'm still trying to process my supposed past death.

I wheeze as my lungs grab onto whatever air they can manage to get. I hit the mat hard.

"What was that for? You couldn't give me a warning?" I manage to eke out, gasping.

"You're not going to get a warning when you get attacked. You have to be able to defend yourself from any position, even if it's flat on your back."

He puts his hand out to help me up. I grab onto his arm and half-heartedly try to pull him off-balance. Maddeningly calm, he hauls me up as if I'm not even resisting.

"But I want to talk about—" I stop forming words when he pulls me into his chest and pure lust shoots through me. His lips are so close, and I half hope he'll kiss me. I shouldn't want to. I've got ass kicking to commence, but for some reason, I find this entire scenario incredibly hot. Muscle memory my ass. The only thing my muscles seem to be remembering is that I'm attracted to him. He pushes me away, and it's like a shot of cold water poured over me. No gentleness here either. I see how it's going to be.

"Obviously, we'll work on how to be more aware of your surroundings than you currently are. At your prime, I wouldn't have been able to knock you down so easily."

I scoff, but there doesn't seem to be words that can eloquently be a jab.

I'll give you prime, jackass.

The conversation about my death will have to wait because I won't be caught unawares again, and I need to focus. He has the nerve to laugh and rushes at me again. But this time, I'm ready for him and I brace myself. He isn't taking me back down again if I can help it.

I gasp for air, dragging in another lungful or two as I again stare at the ceiling. Anticipating exactly what I'm going to do, he drops at the last minute and sweeps his leg into an arc, taking my legs out from behind, and my body slams down. Again.

Shit.

This is going to be harder than I thought. But I'll endure as many body slams as I need to remember my training. There will be no killing of bad people if I can't even keep myself upright, but no matter how many times I attempt to block his attacks, I end up in the same position—down.

"Need a hand up?"

Drew smirks, holding his hand out. Each time he's helped me rise, I've been rolled right up to his chest, his mouth taunting me. I'm starting to think he's trying to distract me on purpose. I stare up, breathing hard. This has to be the hundredth time I'm back on the floor. Each time, he's managed to easily get me there in a variety of ways, none of which are ever the same. Yet, I end up on the floor, without doing a single thing to stop him.

Redundancy is me.

"No." I try to growl, but I'm sure a mewling is what comes out of my mouth instead. I roll onto my side and sit, pushing myself up with both hands.

"Let's go again." I stand and keep him in my view as he circles me, considering.

"No. This isn't working the way I thought it would. Wait here. I've an idea."

He strolls toward a cabinet at the other end of the room. There's a line of sweat that shows down the back of his shirt, but otherwise, you can't even tell he's been working with me for the past two hours. I, on the other hand, look like I've been picked up and spit out of a washing machine. My shirt is sticking to me with sweat in far more places than is probably appropriate. But I can't help looking at his form, even from the ground.

My hair's still in its ponytail, as flat as ever, but it's lopsided, wisps flying every which direction. I shake it out and put it back up again, fixing it. My body's aching. I can't imagine what I'm going to be feeling tomorrow. Ugh, this is why I hate working out.

"Here. These might help." Drew hands me a pair of VR goggles. "Have you ever played virtual reality games?"

"Yes. But they make me sick to my stomach. I'm not a huge fan."

He puts them on my head and moves behind me, adjusting the straps.

"Standard VR goggles tend to do that. It usually happens when the brain's trying to tell them it's not real and their eyeballs are telling them something else. The conflict between organ and brain can get people feeling spacey, which in turns makes them dizzy, which makes them nauseous. You though, aren't going to use standard VR goggles. These are a special pair, enhanced. You'll feel every bit of anything that gets you. The reality of the attacks may trigger you to defend yourself, something I can't do when you know I won't hurt you."

I raise an eyebrow when he faces me.

"Regardless of what you may think, your body and brain know it. It's ingrained into your soul."

So the soul mate says.

But did I know that? Of course, his voice and touch make me feel safe, but do I think he's safe? I pause for a minute. I'll be damned, I do. Why? How? He puts a pair of earbuds into my ears and I focus on what he's saying.

"Okay. I'm going to turn them on and step back. The program won't start for fifteen seconds. Once it does, it's going to come fast and steady. This is one of my training programs, and there's no holding back. Are you ready for this?"

"Yes."

The goggles are light on my head, barely noticeable. Something I'm sure was designed to make the wearer less aware of the potential reality outside the realm of the eyes.

"If you need to get out of the program for whatever reason, double tap the earbuds," he says.

"Okay. Start it up."

There's a beeping inside my ear and the world around me goes pitch dark. I blink fast a few times, my body automatically checking to make sure I'm not blind.

"ARGH!"

I fall to my knees as something hits me from behind. How is this possible? Is he hitting me? I jump up and spin around. I get hit in the back of the knees, and I fall. I jump up again. Dammit.

"Don't let the program get the best of you. It really is all in your head. You aren't actually getting hit, but for fuck's sake, stop falling to the damn ground." His voice is definitely far enough away that it can't be him.

I grit my teeth and squint, looking around. It's still dark, but I'm starting to see the dark isn't as black as I thought it was. I can just make out shadows that are a shade darker. Those must be my attackers. A searing pain hits me in the jaw as I take a punch to the face, and I again fall to my knees, gasping in pain. It hurts, badly. I get up again. I refuse to back down.

I'll remember this. For Katrina's sake.

I try to control my breathing. The shadows are converging, dancing in and out of my limited sight.

How the hell does he do this program?

And why can't he fight normal people instead of shadows? In the light instead of the dark. Damn Drew anyway. I swing out with my own fists, hoping at some point to connect with something.

"Don't go on the offensive, Delaney." His voice soothes my pain as I hear him somewhere next to me over the earbuds. I sigh, momentarily pain free.

"You're supposed to be defending not attacking," he continues.

"Yeah, well, I can't see anything." I hate that I sound whiny.

He chuckles low. "That's the point of this program. Defending yourself against what you can't see."

Air rushes out of my lungs as I'm back on the floor. On my back. Again. Even the shadows attacking me know how to knock me down flat.

"Concentrate. Get up and feel the attacks coming."

"How the fuck am I supposed to feel the attacks coming?"

"You're going to have to open yourself up to your senses. Everyone has a different way of doing it, and you can't be taught that. It just is. And it should be second nature to you. You've already learned this. It's like riding a bike."

"ARGH!"

I yell as I get punched again. This time, my lip splits and blood pools on my tongue.

Fuck you and your bike, Drew.

"Stop distracting me."

Again and again, I'm punched. The side of my head feels like it's exploding. Another punch and my nose is spurting blood. I can't see it, but I feel it dripping down my face.

"You're not even trying! Is this how you're going to avenge your daughter?"

Drew's sarcasm makes my head snap up, and I'm furious. But a punch to my stomach doubles me over, taking my fury and breath right out of me. I clutch myself hard, grinding my teeth. I refuse to back out until I learn how to defend myself.

Over and over, the shadows dance in and mark their hits. I'm thrown to the ground. I'm picked up and tossed some more.

"Delaney. Put a stop to this," he snarls.

He's angry I'm not defending myself. And so am I. I keep thinking that one of these times I'm going to do something that'll put a stop to it. Each time he speaks, the pain recedes, if only for that brief moment. I hold it like a lifeline. Finally, he realizes what I'm doing and refuses to talk. Silence rings, spotted with the slap of skin on skin.

The last punch to my kidneys makes me see white. Quite a feat, since I can't even see out of my swollen eyes. I topple over and double tap the earbuds. The world explodes around me as Drew gently removes the goggles.

The sensation of pain, the aches and sheer agony of it disappears. The blood and the peculiar metallic taste of it evaporates off my tongue. I'm panting as my brain adjusts to the reality that is.

There were no shadows. I was never hurt. What the fuck kind of VR goggles were they?

"Here, lie back down and take some deep breaths. I'll get you some water." He stands up from where he's kneeling by me and walks over to the fridge next to the cabinet. He pulls out a bottle of water and returns, shaking his head.

"I honestly thought you'd remember this way." He frowns. "At this point, I'm not sure what triggers your memory."

"I think training is a viable option, if not our only option now, right?"

"For now. I'll keep thinking and check out some things."

"Then we keep trying. But not anymore today. I've had enough. I didn't think I'd have my ass handed to me so many times."

Drew laughs. "Oh, you didn't get your ass handed to you. You just took a couple of hits, nothing to worry about."

"Oh? Just some hits? So in your world it's okay to get sucker punched multiple times until you're bleeding and ready to pass out? It's okay though because it's just some hits?"

This is bullshit.

"It isn't real," he points out. "No blood, no passing out. You're fine. Just wait until you actually get sucker punched multiple times until you're bleeding and ready to pass out. Wait until your life's blood is bleeding out. Your chest ripped open. Your soul tossed to shit. Then you'll know what real pain feels like."

Drew scoffs and stands up, offering me his hand once more. Suddenly, the fear and panic from the assassination attempt, his condescending attitude, the tears I've shed and the constant veil of possibly leaving my sanity behind blend together and an inexplicable anger rushes through me.

Fuck this.

"But my brain thought it was real. I thought it was real. Do you have no sense of compassion? I don't remember any of my past life that you're talking about. I don't know what you've been through, what I've been through. You act like you care about me but dismiss my pain. You sit there on your high horse and scoff. You laugh as if it doesn't matter. It matters to *me*, asshole." I get up and stalk out of the training room.

I hesitate in the hallway. We've discussed me having a bedroom in the main part of the house, but he hasn't gotten around to showing me where it is. I head to the hospital room first, but when I flip on the lights, I see it's in pristine condition, patiently waiting for its next patient. I guess I'm on my own. I head back to the bookcase and push the button. It does nothing, and I realize I don't know how to get out.

Damn it. I blow out air. I refuse to ask him.

Chapter Fourteen

DREW

I sit down on the mat, my arms linked around my knees. There're sweat spots all over the place. I drop my head onto my hands. She's right. My humanity has slowly been stripped from me over the years. It's easy to harden yourself against things, knowing it's all going to disappear. Fuck.

All those times I've failed, maybe it's been my fault instead of hers. I wince. Maybe I'm the variable. I don't know what to do anymore. I don't know how much more I can go through. I don't know how much more I'm able to shoulder and push through. I clench my jaw.

I don't know how much is left of my soul.

That's my pain, my reality. I love her, yet time and time again, it hasn't been enough. "Trust me," she'd mouthed. And I did. I trust her with my soul. But will it be enough?

I walk over to the wall nearest me and push a button on the TV. Changing the channel, I pop up the monitors. There are cameras everywhere. She has nowhere to go, and I know she'll need some alone time. I doubt she wants to see me now, and I don't know what to say to her anyway.

I search the screen for her until I see her standing in front of the bookcase. I forgot she doesn't know how to open it.

I pull out the remote, pressing a button, and the bookcase opens. Startled, she looks around, but with a shrug, she walks through—with the slightest limp.

Even though she hasn't really sustained any hits during the VR program, she's gotten pushed by me. I haven't thought of how it might hurt someone who isn't used to it anymore. Another point against me. So many things I fail to think about. I'm back at square one. But first, Delaney needs a bedroom and something to eat again. She doesn't remember how much our bodies need to refuel.

I tick down my mental list. She's going to need a pain reliever. She'll be sore tomorrow, and we'll put in more hours in defense.

Shit. At some point, I'll need to test her in the offensive arts. I don't want to. This is the closest I've been to her in a long time. Being able to see her daily, to speak to her, to touch her is a balm to my soul.

Of course, I want more. I always do when it comes to her, but I'll take what I can get. It won't be possible to have what I want, what we need. She barely knows me; she certainly isn't going to fall in love overnight.

I head to the kitchen. My chef's thrilled to be cooking for Delaney. I may have let slip that she's a food snob. I find Charlie's excitement amusing. If only everything was so easy.

"I'm going to need you to create some kind of schedule for food."

"What kind of schedule?" Charlie stops chopping and turns around, wiping his hands on the towel looped at his hip. A retired Navy SEAL Commander, he has a quiet strength belied by his apron. Anyone who doesn't look past it would be blindsided by the wrong end of a Krav Maga combination, and it wouldn't go well for them.

"I'll need to have food prepared each day with an assortment of snacking opportunities in between regular meals. Keep it light, but high protein. We're going to be physical most of the day, and I don't want Delaney vomiting."

"Physical?" His eyebrow lifts, and his brown eyes twinkle.

"It's not what you think."

Unfortunately.

"We'll be in the training room mostly and hopefully get in some runs in the early mornings."

"As early as you usually run?" The Healer in him is probably already thinking of the foods to be prepared for our optimal health.

I run the energy expenditure calculations quickly in my head. "No, I think she's going to need more rest, but we'll still be pretty early. Make sure it'll also sustain her. She's going to need her strength. And stop smirking. It's beneath you." I grab an apple and a granola bar off the counter and head out.

"Of course."

There's a hint of laughter in his voice, and I grin and head to my office. My next phone call is to Mark. He's more than a housekeeper, but he repeatedly reminds me that that's his title. Mark and Charlie are the closest things to friends I have.

Mark, too, is part of the Guardianship, and both are of the few who know some of what I've been doing. Not everything, of course. No one knows everything except for me. And Delaney's closed-off brain. Besides being a confidante, Mark also manages the house and grounds staff along with a good chunk of the security. These things combined make up most of his day. The rest of the time is spent training with me. That'll have to be put on hold for now.

"Hey. Did you have the bedroom next to mine cleaned and prepared?" I dip my head to hold the cell to my shoulder and pull up the Guardianship's remote website and log in.

Dammit, the website is down for maintenance for the next two hours.

"I did. Are you sure that'll be wise? Maybe we should put her in the one on the first floor. We still don't know what she's capable of, and we should keep an eye on her."

Our personal bedrooms and the bedroom next to mine don't have cameras set up in them for us to monitor. What she does in her bedroom isn't any of his business. I lean back in the chair. Holding my phone again, I pinch the bridge of my nose. It's not his fault he's questioning everything. It's mine. This is what I get for retraining him from following every order the Guardianship hands down.

"I don't recall asking you your opinion on this matter. I need to be next to her."

I'd like to be with her, but that's just not going to be possible.

If I'm close to her, I can work on our connection. Temptation isn't coercion.

Mark's voice goes up an octave in excitement. "You think there will be an attack on the house? No way they're getting through the grounds."

"They will. I'm counting on it. And we have to be prepared. No one makes it out alive, do you understand?

"We'll be ready. They won't get through to the house." Mark clicks off the line.

I sigh. He's not naive, just lacking experience. Not having as much training as I've had doesn't help, even with me remedying that.

That's one of the things I can't stand about the Guardianship. Keeping everything to each group. Always fucking keeping secrets.

I crack my knuckles. I want someone to make it through the house. Whoever is capable of doing that also knows damn well who's in here, and that information will make them very interesting. I've plans for whoever that person ends up being. They're going to give me answers.

Too bad it won't be enough to save them.

I get up from my desk and head toward the stairs to shower off the last several hours of panic and sheer determination.

Chapter Fifteen

DELANEY

Slipping into the hot water of the bathtub soothes my muscles and the bubbles soothe my mood. Wisps of steam curl up with the smell of jasmine. I shouldn't be surprised that my favorite scent fills the bottle of oil in the vanity. That isn't the only thing in there. Bottles of my favorite shampoo and conditioner, body wash, and lotions are all lined up in a row underneath the sink. When my skin wrinkles and the water turns tepid, I step out and wrap myself in a towel far more luxurious than the ones at home.

I walk into the big closet to pick out some clothes. Everything in it is exactly my size and suited to my tastes.

Creepy.

I prepare myself for seeing Drew and the awkward conversation sure to occur. I don't want anything from him except his help. And I'm certainly not going to apologize. I guess I'll just see how this plays out.

I open the door to find him leaning against the wall, arms crossed. He must have just gotten out of the shower himself. His dark hair is wet, a droplet hanging from a piece that flops over his forehead. I've a brief urge to wipe it away, so I stick my hands in my jeans.

"I'm sorry I pushed you hard."

Well, well.

I hadn't expected an apology.

"You're right. I should've been more compassionate. I promise to be more so in the future."

Wow.

A man just told a woman she was right. Maybe he isn't so bad after all. He gestures toward the stairs.

"Charlie has promised to whip up an amazing meal for you. And I'm thinking a glass of wine won't be remiss?"

"I'd dearly love a glass. Why for me though? Doesn't he make amazing meals all the time?"

He laughs. "That would be a no. He says he can't make masterpieces for just one person."

"I like him already."

True to Drew's word, there's French onion soup, the broth so flavorful and light, the cheese crispy and perfect, followed by a delicate arugula salad with a lemon vinaigrette, and grilled chicken pesto paninis. Each course has its own wine. I enjoy a glass with each. I notice Drew's favoring an amber drink.

I pop the last bit of the panini into my mouth. Charlie's going to spoil me. "Not a fan of wine?"

"I need something stronger every once in a while. Numbs the pain, you know."

I lean forward, curious. "What's your story? Why are you in pain?"

"Let's skip that portion of the evening, shall we?"

He downs a healthy swallow. Touchy subject?

"Why don't you tell me how you brought me back to life instead?"

He wipes his mouth on a napkin and throws it down. "That's all kind of tied together."

My eyes narrow. Why isn't he answering my questions?

"I called a friend of mine who has an ear to the underground world. She'll let me know if she finds out who put out a hit on you and your daughter."

I lean back weakly in my chair; finally some progress somewhere. "Thank you. Thank you from the bottom of my heart."

"You're welcome."

He pauses for several seconds, and I continue to stare him down, my eyes boring into his green ones. I attempt to will him to talk. He said I could just will things to happen, but clearly I'm not capable. He sighs loudly.

"It doesn't work on me. But I'll tell you anyway." I gasp, but he continues talking. *Did* I actually will him and he's doing it or is he just humoring me? "It was some time before I was able to think more coherently. As you know, you had cut me open pretty well. But on top of that, you died. The other half of my soul was dead, and it was…gut-wrenching."

He takes a long swallow from his glass, draining it. He pours himself another glass, the amber liquid swirling. He stares into the contents for a moment. I don't push him.

"The last thing I'd seen was you falling to the ground. The Guardianship came and took your body. There's a lot we do as a formality. They have to make sure you're actually dead, of course," he says bitterly, toasting the air with his glass.

My own, considerably not-dead body is rigid. I'm waiting for the bombshell. At the rate he's consuming alcohol, it must be a doozy.

"But there was a ton of paperwork, especially since there was such a cloud surrounding your death. You were in violation of rules, you were going to be reprimanded, only the Guardianship knows in which way. I'm sure all had to be dealt with. Then a new Destiny is born and must be found and documented, of course."

Who took my place? Where are they now?

I sip my water, eying him as he pours himself yet another glass. I raise my eyebrows, but who am I to judge?

"In the meantime, I had therapy to go through."

I tilt my head. "For what I'd done to you?" My shoulders hunch with a faint sense of remorse.

"Well, the loss of your soul isn't exactly a walk in the park."

My brain grasps the reason for the drinking. I'm guessing reliving his experiences now isn't any more pleasant. "You figured instead of dealing with it you were going to bring me back to life?"

"No idea if that can even happen."

I slam my hand on the table, startling Drew out of his faraway gaze.

"Well then what happened? I thought you said I died. And you told me we don't get reincarnated *and* I'm not immortal. You said you brought me back to life. How the hell am I here?" For fuck's sake, what else could there be?

"I'm getting to that."

He drags a hand through his hair again. Is it anger, frustration, fear that makes him do that? He picks up his glass and plays with it, rolling back and forth.

"It took some time. I lived in a numb, grief-stricken, and... painful state for a long time. I barely tolerated it all. There was nothing I was interested in. I ate because I had to, when I could. I relived those moments over and over again. Waiting to die. Was there anything else I could do?" he whispers quietly, as if talking to himself.

Shouldering the blame and the guilt too, I know. Waiting to die?

I reach across the table and put my hand on his arm. He

looks up from his glass, surprised. This is the first time I'm willingly touching him, in an offer to comfort. The warmth spreads throughout my body, soothing my muscles far better than the bath had. There's a minute or two of silence. Drew clears his throat and moves his arm away. The sensation of warmth receding abruptly leaves me bereft. He doesn't want me touching him.

He continues his narration. "It took me far longer than I care to admit to realize you had said something as you fell to the ground, dying.

I'm curious if it was a typical declaration of love. A farewell? An apology?

"You said, 'trust me.'"

I frown. Why would I have said that?

"Yeah, that was my reaction as well. Why would you tell me to trust you as you kill yourself? It didn't make any sense. I searched for a clue from you. Anything that would explain this away. I knew you wouldn't have committed suicide, if anything, because you knew it would hurt me. I'm sorry, you don't want to hear it, but you loved me once. Very much. Besides, we have always been told the pain that we feel when our soul mate dies."

He drains his glass again. And pours another. "Then I found a piece of paper."

I perk up. "Did I write a letter?"

"No. It was an address halfway around the world. It also had one word on it."

Betwixt

My brows furrow. "Doesn't that mean *in between*?"
"It's actually just *between*."
He swirls the liquor in the glass slowly, perhaps lost in his

memories. "You loved that word when we were kids, and we'd use it for anything we wanted to have between just the two of us and no one else was supposed to know. I went to the address and told no one. I took great pains to make sure there was no trail. Hard to do when everyone is worried about you. When you feel your body ripped in half."

I wince at the reminder that I'd done just that, literally.

"But I managed to do it."

He sighs heavily and swallows the remainder of the alcohol. He looks up. "Only to find it was a safety deposit box. With another address and betwixt written on it.

"And so it went. On and on. I went to safety deposit boxes in banks in various countries. I went to churches, graveyards, libraries, and a million places in between. I damn near killed myself. I beggared and stole, and it took me two years to get an answer."

"I was dead for two years?"

Every time I think he's told me a fantastical impossibility, it quickly becomes a mere possibility and is supplanted with something even more incredible.

"And all this time you were without my soul?" My voice tightens.

"Yes."

I get up and walk around the table to him. I take the empty glass from him, pour a measure, and toss it back like a shot myself. He raises his brows.

"By the amount of alcohol you've just drunk, I can imagine what you went through."

I pour again, and this time I hand it to him. He looks at it and throws it back, pouring it smoothly down his throat. His Adam's apple bobs, and I'm surprised that someone who has drank so much can still speak coherently.

"No, you can't."

He shrugs and fiddles with his napkin, folding it over and over, until it's a small square.

"You went through the effort and trouble to make sure no one could follow a trail. There were clues, there were addresses, there were things only we would know."

I place my hand on his arm again, only slightly reveling in the warmth coursing through my muscle groups.

"I don't know why I did it."

He leans forward. "There was no choice for me. I trust you. With everything I have. With my very soul. I always will." His eyes are glassy, his face slightly flushed.

Not so unaffected then.

The warmth curls around my body, the wine and whiskey curls around my stomach, and my soul begs me to lean forward as if hypnotized. His gaze drops to my lips for a small second before his hand shoots out and he grasps the back of my neck, pulling me forward. Our mouths collide, my lips part, and the warmth of his tongue invades.

His desperation is evident in the frantic movements of our tongues, yet the sensation I always feel with him intensifies dramatically, and I can't breathe. It continues to skitter along my skin, building into a crescendo as the warmth in my body explodes in a shower of fireworks, leaving me burning.

I pull back with a gasp. If that hadn't been the best kiss I've ever experienced, I don't know what could possibly top it. My brain immediately plops in a vision of us having sex, and my nipples tingle in response and I'm immediately wet. My fingers trace my lips and I contemplate shoving everything off the table and showing him that I'd be down for some sexual activities.

"I'm sorry. I shouldn't drink when you're here with me."

Oh. Maybe he doesn't feel the same way? His words may as well have dumped a bucket of cold water on my head. My face flushes. There's nothing worse than throwing yourself at someone who doesn't want you. His cellphone buzzes loudly on the table and he picks it up, glancing at the screen.

"It's Astrid."

A girlfriend? I never asked if he was single. Dammit, I'm an idiot. No wonder he pulled away.

Wait. "Is she the one with information about the hit?"

Suddenly, my knees are weak. I sit down in the chair, hard. The spice of alcohol lingers in my mouth, and the heaviness of guilt settles on my shoulders. I should've been thinking about Kat, about protecting her, and getting my memories back. Not romping about on the dining room table. Nodding in response to my assumption, Drew answers the phone, his voice slurry.

"Yeah."

I barely make out a feminine voice, low and throaty. She sounds sexy, and I frown.

"What?"

He sits up straight, and I grip my hands together. There's no way, judging by his reaction, by the anger in his voice, that what he's hearing is good news. My heart starts pounding and sweat slicks my palms.

"I had no idea. Thank you."

His lopsided smile as his gaze cuts to me gives it away. If she isn't his girlfriend now, she certainly was at some point. Guilt rushes over his features quickly before disappearing, and there's a hollow feeling in my belly.

"Maybe one day soon," he continues into the phone, and hangs up.

And just like that, the urge to straddle his lap, to devour his mouth and bend him to my will overcomes me and I'm horrified. How can I want to force someone to be mine from a few seductive noises from another? It's not as if I have a claim on him. And it's not as if I don't have other things to worry about. Maybe the Guardianship was right about me. There's something not right within me.

"What did she say?"

I'm afraid to hear the answer. Afraid not to hear it.

"Your *fucking* husband," Drew snarls, his hands fisted till the knuckles turn white.

I inhale hard, dizzy with the sudden influx of oxygen. I must not have heard him correctly. "What? What about Tyson?"

Drew walks over to another cabinet, opening it to yet another screen. There are an obnoxious amount of cabinets and screens in every room in this house.

"Look at this."

He turns the TV screen on and gets out a portable keyboard. As I walk over, what must be the Guardianship insignia floats onto the screen. With a few taps and a couple seconds of typing, Tyson's face pops onto the screen.

My breath hitches again.

What the fuck just happened?

Chapter Sixteen

DREW

"Why's Tyson's face on the Guardianship site?" Delaney asks, but I'm already thinking ahead, analyzing the possibilities. Or trying to.

I shake my fuzzy head.

Well damn.

I knew that bastard would be a buzzkill.

"Hold on." I search the cabinet for a little blue vial. "I need to sober up."

I shake out a pill then, glancing at the nearly empty bottle of whiskey on the table, shake out two more and down them with a glass of water.

Delaney's cheeks are flushed from wine and our kiss. Her dark eyes, wide and worried, dominate her face, and I can't blame her. I'm worried too. Fucking petrified. How the hell did Tyson fly below my radar? How far does this go?

"Astrid explained why the name sounded familiar to her earlier. Opmerker. It means observer in Dutch. Astrid's brother works for the Guardianship overseas and one of his assignments was a rogue Watcher."

"A Watcher," she says slowly, her brows furrowed in confusion.

There's no easy way to tell her this. I take the plunge and hope to hell I can contain her if she falls apart.

"Tyson was a Watcher. Part of the Guardianship."

"A Watcher? The Guardianship?" Her face drains of color. "What does that mean? How? He never said anything. I've never even heard of any of this until you."

She's not connecting the dots. Dammit. I hate being the bad guy when it comes to her. "And he wouldn't if he'd been undercover, would he?"

Her head snaps up, her eyes searching mine for any sign of a lie.

"He'd been watching you since high school. Which means, the Guardianship knows who you are. This version of you. *They always have.*"

"This doesn't make sense. And he's been gone for years."

Shit.

Why would they just be watching her and not do anything about her? How long have they known that she wasn't permanently dead? Did they know about my involvement?

"I don't understand."

I shove my hand through my hair again, wanting to rip it out in frustration and instead grip the back of my neck, squeezing hard, hoping to force insight into my brain. Think.

"I don't know what it means that Tyson was part of the Guardianship." I groan, dropping my head to my chest in an attempt at...something. Some kind of meditation that will make me focus. I raise my head quickly, almost feeling lightheaded.

Fuck.

But then my gaze finds Delaney, and she's gone deathly pale. She cannot faint right now. I need more information from her. "Put your head between your knees." I push her head down gently, and my fingers can't help but rub the strands of her hair. "Slow your breathing. Remember? Breathe in one, two, three. Breathe out one, two, three."

"Drew."

She grips my arm hard, and the constant protectiveness rises to a higher level. She needs me and is reaching out. Damned if I'll fail in that. Her face inches from mine, eyes burning with fear and tears, etches onto my soul. Another memory ingrained into me. I hope I never need to pull it up. I refuse to falter.

"Delaney," I whisper, fearing that this might be the last time I touch her if I can't get her calm. I frame her face with my hands, my thumbs caressing her cheeks, fingers entrenched in her hair, protecting her delicate scalp. Heat waves pound against me, her emotions reaching out just as much as she did. Her hands grip tighter onto my forearms, and the muscle flexes almost of its own accord. They're steel beneath her fingers. Steel that will crush anything out to harm her. I won't let them hurt her. I won't let her hurt herself or anyone else.

"Nothing will happen to you. Nor to your daughter. She's yours and therefore mine. I promise you, Della, that I'll protect you with every breath and movement of my body."

I press my forehead to hers, noses touching, lips close. It wouldn't take much to lean in and brush them with my own, but for once I'm not thinking with that head.

If I fail her it's only because I'm dead—and she would wish for death also. And I won't allow that. Her body trembles, and it does nothing to ease the urgency within me. I can't make her believe me with words. Only actions.

I pull away, and her hands fall to her sides. I want to rush back in, touch her. Let her touch me for comfort. But soothing our souls will not save them.

"In the meantime, let's talk about Tyson."

"What about him?"

I grind my teeth together and my fingers tighten into fists. I focus on relaxing them. I don't want to know, but I need to know the details of this life, of this version of her. Fuck me, but I want to bring the man back to life only to beat him to death.

"Let's start at the beginning. How did you two meet?"

"It was my first couple of days of high school. I was nervous, never sure of where my classes were. One day, a senior student ran into me when we both turned the corner at the same time. He knocked me back."

I'd like to knock back some of his teeth. Classic, 'oh I ran into you.' Fuck that asshole.

"Of course, I dropped the books I was carrying. I had a bunch of sheets from my last class that I hadn't put in my binder. They went everywhere. The senior laughed and told me I needed to figure out school. Tyson was right there, and he took pity on me, I guess."

He wasn't the senior. Fine. But he's still an asshole.

"He helped me pick everything up and walked me to my next class. He was a senior too. We talked every day in the halls and pretty much were dating within a month or so. I've only ever dated him."

She'd never dated me. We didn't have to. We knew we had each other from birth. But she would never have looked at another because we were made for each other. What if she never looks at me like that again? Raw emotion boils through me and into my throat until I think I'm choking on my own air. I don't think I ever knew what fear was until this moment. Fuck the world. Fuck everything else. What if she never loves me again? I lock my knees to keep them from dropping me to the ground and pleading with her to forget him.

She looks back up from her clasped hands, and rage replaces panic. I want to kill anyone who's involved and causing this sadness in her eyes. Even if it was that asshole.

"I don't understand any of this."

"You two dated all through your high school?" I know the words are coming out in a growl and I can't help it. I despise the fact that he had opportunities to be with her. That she *chose* to be with him. She never had to choose me.

"Yes."

"What did he do after graduation?"

I can't just keep watching her become a wreck over the man I never knew but hate with every fiber of my being. I head back to the keyboard to see what files I can access.

"He became a lineman with the electric company, then moved up to a managerial position. We got pregnant, and then he had an accident at work... He died. But he loved me. I know he did. None of this makes any sense."

She may as well have taken a bat to me. Kicked me while I was down. I clench my jaw and uncurl my shoulders. Well, I'm still fucking standing here, aren't I?

"Look, you may be mad and jealous or whatever, but I had a good life with Ty. I loved him. There must be some mistake here."

And she just keeps twisting the knife.

Tyson Opmerker's dossier is unrestricted. Shit. I flip through screen after screen. Fuck. How am I supposed to tell her the man she thinks loved her so much was actually a Guardian hired to make her think so? In the last twelve hours or so, I've flipped her world upside down. Now I'm going to tell her it didn't even exist. What if this is what pushes her over? At the same time, I can't hide it from her. Fuck.

"There's no mistake. He'd been in the Guardianship since he was twelve. He rose in rank quickly, and he's one of the youngest Watchers awarded an undercover assignment. You. There are reports." I turn the screen. Rage flows through me at the anguish on her face as she slowly walks closer. I wish I could protect her from the hurt.

'Target entered class.' 'Target is taking SATs.' 'Taking target to Prom.' Receipts for the limo, corsage, tux, and dinner are attached.' The whispered words sound like they're wrenched from her mouth, and I want to wrap her in my arms and kiss away her pain. But our healing doesn't work that way.

A red PAID stamp mark bleeds onto the screen. The reports never deviate from keywords such as target, plan, diversion, reimbursement, goal, and assets. From what I see, he never calls her by her name in a single report.

"'Recommended Plan: Marriage and Children.' I was nothing to him." I count each tear that leaks out of her eyes with a sick compulsion. That's how many people I will kill to avenge the pain that's ripping her to shreds.

The screen flips again, and her gasp vibrates through my chest. *That motherfucker.* The rage I felt a moment ago seems flimsy compared to now. I gather her in my arms, pulling her against my chest, heart to heart. She simply leans her head against me and collapses. I'm not sure if I'm more pissed at the underhanded schemes the Guardianship authorized or the bastard who went along with it. But swapping out birth control with placebos and orchestrating fake weddings was something I never imagined would be condoned. The body count is rising. And when they see me coming, they better fucking hope I have a shred of humanity left in me to be merciful.

"I need...my daughter for a bit."

I let her go. Not only does she need a moment to wrap her head around the betrayal she just read about, but I need to figure out if there's anything in the files about what Tyson's mission was. I can't hold her and protect her at the same time.

I'm pissed at myself. How had I missed this in all the research I've done? What the fuck is going on?

The Guardianship and Tyson had poured time and effort into this. What was the end goal? Obviously, Delaney, but they had her for years. And did nothing. For what purpose? And who's watching her now? My hand trembles, and I stare at the tremors, turning it from side to side.

I thought I knew fear, pain. I never thought much beyond the next time-turn. But everything I've known just flew out the damn window and I'm flying blind.

I sift through files and with each one, the sheer complexity of the mission becomes apparent. The Guardianship made an effort to have Delaney in their grasp, but never made a move against her. Why? They aren't known for their leniency. The question repeats over and over in my head and fear burns in my throat.

Damn the Guardianship and their fucking secrets.

Chapter Seventeen

DELANEY

Katrina sits in my lap and reads me a story. Besides helping her when she stumbles over the bigger words, it's easy to think about other things when a five-year-old is just learning to read and stubbornly independent with it. It leaves room for my mind to wander. Why would Tyson do that? Why would he make me love him and act like he loved me too? What kind of person can live a lie every day for years?

What have I done to deserve this?

I killed people. This was my punishment.

Karma. What have I done?

I don't know what I hoped to find in Kat's room, but there's nothing that will make this make sense. Kat's face is as familiar as my own. I've stared down at it in wonder, searching for Ty in the baby face when she was born. Besides her darker skin color, she's almost an even split between us. His nose, my eyes. His hair, my lips. She's perfect.

Looking at her now solidifies that I will do anything for her. That I'll go to whatever lengths to save her from the

Guardianship. To save myself from them. Those bastards know nothing of a mother's feral fear for herself and her child.

But I won't have much time for hand holding Kat, for being home or even being here and spending time with her, and I'm pissed they've put me in this predicament. Pissed they're making miss time with her. But if I'm going to win this, I need to remember. And I'm going to remember. I need to do all the things, whatever they may be.

I force myself to my feet, kiss her curls, and head back up to my new room to shower. Water has always been a comfort for me, and I don't have much better to do here. Plus, I need to remove the stink of betrayal before it brings me to my knees.

The water pounds on my back. I turn the handle higher, and still it's not hot enough to wash away the lies. I don't know where the water ends and my tears begin.

The water cools, and I turn the tap as far as it goes, until the shower simply goes from hot to warm to tepid to cold.

I'm shivering when I step out, wrap myself in a towel, and stare at the reflection in the mirror. I'm supposed to just be Delaney, a normal mom. Then I'm supposed to be a Destiny, controlling the fate of millions. I can't even control my own life. Or see it for what a lie it had been.

I stare at the woman in the mirror with soaked hair and a towel, her eyes wide and shimmering with tears, shoulders hunched. And rage builds in me. The woman is weak. A plaything in an intricate game of chess.

Oh, hell no.

I'm a Destiny, dammit. And I'm done playing by the rules and being moved like a pawn.

Fuck them all.

I'm going to learn *everything*, and they'll regret their actions. The woman staring back at me straightens with eyes glittering with rage.

There's a knock on the bathroom door, and Drew asks if I'm okay.

I'll be fine, just fine.

I'm no longer Delaney. I. AM. DESTINY.

I open the door, not caring I'm only in a towel. Probably not something he hasn't seen before anyway. And honestly, I don't give a shit.

"Nope. No, I'm not. But I'm sure you've seen me naked before, so it's not anything to be embarrassed about, right? Let me get dressed, you can come in."

"I'm sorry Tyson wasn't who you think he was." At the muffled words, I lean against the closet wall briefly before remembering that I don't give a fuck.

"I guess you're pretty happy though, right?" I stroll out pulling on a T-shirt. "You're legitimately free to hate the guy without worrying it will bother me."

Just like I hate him for what he's done to me.

"I'm not going to lie. I'm overjoyed you hate him right now...but I'm here for you. I never want you to hurt, and you are hurting right now. You loved him, and that won't change, I'm sure."

I'm not hurt. I'm angry. Can't he tell the difference? The ache begins at the base of my neck, and I rub at it. I step forward somehow, wondering if I can be soothed by his embrace, but he steps back. What? Now he doesn't want to be around me? Fine. I glower, letting the emotion roll through me, giving me some kind of anchor—even if it's the wrong kind.

"Found some compassion in that stone-cold heart of yours, Drew?"

"I'm not going to let you rope me in. You're in pain, and I'm sorry for it. But I'm not going to be a whipping post for you. We have a training room for that. You want to work out some shit, go there."

Wow. What a way to comfort me. Didn't he say he was my soul mate and how that was so different from my definition? I snort and turn away from him. "Figures you could care less."

He grabs my elbow and whips me around, heat drenching my arm before spreading through my body. His words start quietly before escalating to a near yell.

"You think you're the only one that's been hurt here? You think everyone else lives peachy lives, dancing around? Well, let me tell you something. You have no *fucking clue*. Your pain is a walk in the park compared to what some of us have endured. *Some* of us have been endlessly dancing to the tune *you've* been whistling for years.

"You're my soul mate. I hurt when you hurt, even if I don't understand it or want to understand it. I'd die myself, *I'd even kill you,* to protect you and to protect the world.

"And maybe I have hardened my heart. Because I only have so much of it left. You can't fault me for trying to protect it. And I'll do whatever I have to, over and over again. But damned if I'm going to sit here and let you parade around half naked and tell me I don't care."

My anger disappears as quickly as it appeared. My own drastic moods are going to get me killed. I flop into a chair and try to control my breathing.

"I'm sorry. I really am. I don't understand what's so special about me or why this is happening." Apologies never come easy, more so when you were blatantly an asshole. I forge ahead.

"I know it doesn't excuse my behavior. And you're right. It's easier for me to have someone to blame, and you're convenient. It's wrong and I'm sorry. Please forgive me?"

His brow furrows and his lips compress. He looks shaken, but his forehead smooths out.

"It's fine. I know it's a lot for you to handle." He jams his hands into his pockets. "That's what I've been trying to figure out since you left me downstairs. There's something I'm missing here. Yes, you're a Destiny. Yes, you were supposed to be punished. And dead. But none of this makes sense. I'm extremely concerned with the fact they knew about you for years and yet they've done nothing.

"This is a problem I haven't anticipated. I don't know how much they know about me and you, about what I've done. I don't know what they've planned for you, and that has me worried. I'll figure it out. You need to get up to speed though. It would be really helpful if we could figure out how to trigger your memories."

"What is it you've done, Drew? We keep circling around, and I still don't have that answer." I pick at a strand of thread on the upholstered arm. Anything to keep from leaping up and rubbing my hand down his.

"And I promise we'll talk about it." He holds out his arm, and I get what my body's been craving. Skin-to-skin contact.

"I want you to rest. Just a couple of hours." Drews voice softens, pleading. Does he experience the exact same things I do when we touch?

He pulls out his cellphone, and I notice the screen looks like the hallway outside of Kat's room.

"You've got cameras? Where?"

"Everywhere, except my room and your room. And bathrooms, of course. They're all hidden."

There's a twitch in the middle of my back and I roll my shoulders.

"Stop freaking yourself out. First of all, they've been here the entire time."

"Yes, but I didn't know it. It's creepy."

"Is it? I guess it can be. It's to keep everyone in it safe. I'm so used to it, it doesn't bother me. Every room has a cabinet with a screen in it. You have full access to everything. It runs on a thumbprint and retina scanner, as well as your voice imprint. See? You can always check on your daughter."

He pulls up the camera in Kat's room. She's eating and seemingly enjoying every bite. "Ah, food. The way to her heart. She's my mini me, there."

Drew jerks, startled at my statement, a frown creasing his forehead.

"You're thinking something. What?"

He shakes his head. "I'm not sure exactly, but something you said made me think of something. There's some stuff I need to look over."

He stalks away quickly, tapping into his phone again. What did I say? And damn it for not triggering my own memory. You know what? He can't brush me off anymore. I need to do everything I can to get those damn things back.

"You could tell me what happened instead of walking away and doing things on your own. Finish telling me. About me and you."

He stops, and I wonder why he's hesitating. It can't possibly be worse than killing myself.

"Right." He sits back down, still tapping on the phone.

"I told you I was traveling all over the world trying to find you with all the clues you had left. Why did you set all this in motion?" He shrugs. "I don't know, and it doesn't matter. Like I said, I trust you implicitly. Naturally, I followed you through this wild goose chase of yours. It never once occurred to me to stop. When I got to the last box, I found a note that didn't have another clue on it. You can imagine how happy that made me," he says with a slight drawl.

"You never thought to stop? To think I was crazy, or you were crazy?"

After knowing what Tyson had done, I don't want to comprehend that kind of complete loyalty. It makes his betrayal rise from massive to colossal.

"Never. In the box was an address, a name, and money. And a passport. This was a first for me. I opened the passport and found my face staring back. Except I had a different name and address. I went there, thinking I was going to be calling on someone at high tea from the driveway length. Imagine my surprise when I found that it was in the heart of a mountain. This mountain. Of course, the house wasn't as built up as it is now. I found out it was owned by the name on my new passport. I broke in and looked around. It was empty. It took me days to spot the loose floorboard. I followed the cryptic directions you left for me, searching for some cave. I found it and went inside by tunnel."

He lays his phone on his thigh and closes his eyes, his chest rising deeply. Linking his hands behind his neck, he brings his elbows together in front of his face. The silence stretches out and he pauses for so long, I worry that he doesn't want to tell me. After everything? I dare not wonder how bad it could be.

"What was there?" So much secrecy. Why?

Finally, Drew gets up, punching numbers into his cell, and my bedroom door locks. My head swivels as the bathroom lights click on by themselves and the exhaust fan turns on. The radio clock by my bed turns on and a country singer croons out a ballad. The closet door closes. The fan above me whirls to life. Metal plates slide out from the wall and cover all four seams of the closet and bedroom doors.

The cell screen turns green and dings. Have I entered some kind of James Bond film?

"What just happened? And more importantly, can I breathe in here?" I fan my face, suddenly claustrophobic.

Drew moves closer and lowers his voice. The hairs on my body seem to wave toward him.

"Yes, the bathroom exhaust has an oxygen feed in it. We're perfectly fine. The room has been scanned and is on lockdown. This is the part only you and I can ever know, and it needs to stay that way, at all costs.

"I found a stone at the end of my journey. You can't imagine the shock I felt at finding a rock." The words are quiet and devoid of emotion.

"What kind of stone?" I whisper back. What a letdown. With all the theatrics, I thought for sure he was going with treasure.

"A peculiar one. It took me some time to figure out what it was and what it meant. What you obviously wanted me to do. It was a bit difficult, seeing as the stone isn't supposed to be real."

"What do you—" But his hand stops me from speaking. His eyes burn into mine. Emotions I don't recognize flicker behind the green.

"And for a time, I wasn't sure that it wasn't my soul speaking to me instead of my head. I wanted you back so badly, I questioned if I conjured the whole thing. If I really was mentally unstable and back in my bed at home."

The intensity in his gaze never wavers. This is it.

This is how I'm here now.

Chapter Eighteen

DREW

I thought I had finally gone insane. The hope, the pain, the time that I'd been away from her had converged into that single thought. But the need for it to be real had burned the hottest.

"But I'd turn the stone over and over in my hand, pushing past the pain, thinking there's no way I pulled this out of thin air."

I'd floundered for too many days between the highest points of hope and the deepest depths of despair, not knowing which one was right. Not knowing whether I'd cracked after all and I was going to die in a mountain—by myself—my own soul shriveled up.

"One day, I figured what the hell. I honestly thought I'd gone crazy and should kill myself. I didn't for one moment think I was completely lucid and that it was real."

"What was it? What did you do?" Her eyes are huge in her face and her arms are wrapped around herself, but her whispered words sound excited, and I recall that feeling when I had held the smooth rock in my hand, my fingers tracing it round and round until I decided to do something about it and test the theory.

"I summoned the Time-Turner."

"What the hell is that?"

"Not what, who. There are legends of them. I had no idea they still existed. Last I heard, their race was killed out centuries ago. When he appeared, I couldn't believe my eyes. He looked ancient and young. All those of the Magical race did." I shake my head, still remembering the first time I'd seen him. How petrified I was that he was going to kill me. That it had all been for nothing.

"Do. Ageless in an extreme, peculiar way. All of his features are a washed-out version of a man. Pale-blond hair, pale-blue eyes, pale skin. He only asked me if I was willing to pay the price with my body and soul. It was like he knew what I wanted, what I was doing. And he did. All I had to do was agree to it."

"You just *agreed*? What happened? What was the price?"

"Of course, I did." I snort. Does she think I'd have given up so easily? All that time, my only thought was to trust her as she'd asked. "I didn't go all this way to not agree. Time simply changes back to some unspecified point they pick. One minute, I'm with the Time-Turner in the present, the next I'm not. I never know where or when it's going to be. It's always different points of your life—never the same."

I clench my jaw. But it's always the same pain, pain, and more pain, until I can get a hold of myself. Breathe through the worst of it, and as time went on, kick and scream my frustration that I can't just sense her and find her so easily.

"It's a life I don't know or understand because the point I'm sent back to doesn't have me in it. Which changes everything. Your life ends up on a different path each time. It's up to me to find you and figure out—"

She sinks into a nearby chair, and I rush over to her. Is she okay? Did I miscalculate? Should I have waited?

"You're saying this as if you've done this more than once. And you have to figure out what?" She grips the arms of the chair, her gaze boring into my face. I have no choice but to answer her. I can't deny her anything.

"I don't know. I'm going blind here. I just know it's never what it's supposed to be."

"How do you know that? And *how many times*?"

She interrupts me, but I finish the sentence. "Because it always ends with you destroying the world."

Her gulp seems loud to my ears. "I destroy the world? Like, infinitely? And you fix it. You just keep turning back time?" Her voice wavers softly.

"Yes."

"Why would I destroy the world?"

My heart nearly stops as I recall all the times I've had to essentially end that version of her by turning time again. "Because your mind fractures and...and you didn't know what you were doing. You're too good to do that on purpose and you'd never—if you had complete control of your mental faculties. So, I summon the Time-Turner each time that happens."

Her jaw drops open, as she stares off into space. Then she shakes her head and focuses back on me. "But what's the end goal? What's the plan? I mean, besides keeping me from destroying the world. Which I'll tell you right now, I have no plans to do. Ever."

Adrenaline shoots through me. That would mean she's in control, and I'd give anything for that.

Anything. I've given that and more.

"I'm glad to hear it. And I don't know. Each time, I'm hoping either I do something that changes it, or you remember what you did and that it becomes clear. Or whatever it is that needs to change. Except it never does." The adrenaline leaves me just as quickly as it shot through me. It's always the same. It's always wrong.

"Obviously, what you're doing is wrong."

I grimace at her echo of my thoughts. *Thanks, love.*

"Nice to meet you, Captain Obvious. It's increasingly difficult as I'm fast running out of options and scenarios. Sometimes, you're in that particular existence for a long time, sometimes for a short time. Sometimes, it takes a year to find you. Others, you're right there, nearby." Weariness anchors around me.

"How does this work? And why can't you find me all of the time—with our connection?

"That's unfortunately part of the price. My connection doesn't work until I find you again. I haven't stopped aging. I mean, we age much slower anyway, but I'm still aging, whereas everyone else goes back to the age they are at that point in time."

"How does the Time-Turner pick the time?"

"I don't know. We don't exactly have a conversation. I yield the stone with the intent to call him out, but before I do, he pops up out of thin air. It's always the same. He asks me if I accept the consequences with body and soul. I say yes, and he turns back time."

"What you've described—is that all of the consequences?"

"No. I remember everything, every time, while no one else does." I run my hand through my hair and down my neck. I grit my teeth hard, hoping she won't ask anything else. I've told her enough. No need to make her worry.

"What else? Don't hold back."

Damn. "Legend has it that my life span will be shortened because of it. And that I'll lose a little of my humanity and sanity with each time."

She jumps out of the chair. "How could you agree to such a thing?"

How can she even ask that? For me, there was no other choice. "Because you asked me to trust you and I do."

"How many times have you summoned the Time-Turner?"

Does she need to know?

"Drew?" Her eyes are full of worry.

"Thirteen times."

The words seem to hang in the air as if they're able to be seen. A shiver rolls through me. Thirteen times I've gone back into the past. Thirteen times I've killed innocent people—over and over—attempting to recreate the things she specified. Attempting to find the version of her that doesn't kill everyone. Twelve times now that I've failed. I'm really fucking hoping this isn't the thirteenth round of failure.

She plops back down and huffs out a breath. "Why would you do that? I don't know what to say. Do I thank you? Do I tell you you're crazy to have agreed to it? I don't even know how to thank you. And I'm *so* sorry I've put you through all of this." The words rush out of her mouth, confusion and panic lacing through the words.

"Della." I lean forward, hoping that I'm still capable of pouring emotions into my words, of letting her know that I speak only the truth. "You're my soul mate. I love you with every fiber of my being. I exist because you exist. I can't live without you. I know, I've tried, and it was literally hell. There's absolutely nothing I wouldn't do for you. It's as basic as that."

Maybe I'm already not capable of the compassion anymore, of the true meaning of right and wrong that I used to have. Maybe my humanity's permanently stripped from me and this...this shell of a man willing to do anything it takes is all that's left. And maybe she won't want me anymore when all is said and done. But I don't know how to be anything other than what I am. The Protector to my Soul Mate. She's silent, just staring at me, wordless, but there's nothing else I can say. I just don't have the right words.

I punch in the numbers to deactivate safe mode and the metal sliders slide back into the wall. The radio shuts off, the fan stops spinning. The bathroom goes quiet. Doors unlock with an imperceptible click. The silence is almost eerie, and still she just sits there.

I walk to the door and glance over my shoulder. She's still looking lost, now with tears in her eyes, and it does nothing but break me that I put them there. I may love her but I'm not good enough for her. Not anymore. All I can do is my best and hope it will be enough...for anything left.

"Get some rest. We have a lot to do in a short period of time and you're going to need it."

Chapter Nineteen
DELANEY

That's it? I sit on my bed for over an hour, mulling over the things that I've learned in the last several days. My brain won't shut off long enough for me to sleep. Incredible doesn't even begin to describe the fantastical elements. I'm stunned Drew trusts me, loves me so much that he'll in all probability kill himself over me.

Let's not discount saving the world from you.

There's no way I can remember what I'm doing here. If the real me is even the real me in this world. Is that how it goes? Everything I've learned so far has been in pieces thanks to my own inability to conquer my emotions. I haven't pushed Drew as much as I should because I'm afraid of myself. Because I can feel myself cracking. Is that even possible? Maybe not. But I sure as shit know that I'm not acting like my usual self, and from what he's told me, I can only surmise that I'm close to that edge.

But I need to figure out how this all happened. It's obvious to me that all the versions of me have failed because I have failed. And damned if that doesn't sound like the weirdest thing out of all of this.

At fourteen, I killed myself and sent Drew, with clues, on this wild goose chase all over the world for reasons unknown to me. For two years. Clearly, I'm the worst soul mate ever. Who fucking does that to someone they profess to love? Me, obviously. I grimace when a sharp pain pokes me in the skull and my chest tightens with pressure. That should be my cue to stop, but I can't. Kat's safety depends on me figuring this all out.

When my mind has shattered in Drew's previous attempts to reach sane me, he summons the Time-Turner who just throws him back in time, willy-nilly. So my age has reset to wherever that is, but Drew's doesn't. Which would make me still twenty-four, but him twenty-six, even though we were born the same day. I shake my head as if I can suddenly make a more rational sense of the information with the movement.

I jump out of bed. That's it! We probably just need to summon the Time-Turner together, and then maybe we'll have a different outcome!

Throwing the door open, I race out of my room.

"Drew!" I bang on his bedroom door. There's no answer. He can't be sleeping already. I crack open the door. I didn't know that his rooms were soundproofed until I'm blown away by sound and sight. I enter and shut the door, leaning my back against it.

He's sitting in the chair facing a window with rounded shoulders. A glass of alcohol in hand and a nearly empty bottle of amber liquid on the table. He's drinking the finer stuff with a higher alcohol content. Music blasts from the walls.

He senses me, and opening his eyes, gets up and turns the music down low.

"What are you doing?" I gesture toward the bottle. Dammit, we can't summon a Time-Turner while he's drinking so heavily. Can we?

"Catching some relief."

"Were you always a drunk?" I don't know why it bothers me, but it does. Is it my subconscious? Is it a memory? Or am I just losing my shit already?

"Well, I can't exactly feel some of the pain recede in the normal way. Seeing as how you aren't of a mind to cooperate."

"The normal way?" I tilt my head. What's he talking about?

"Yes, by prolonged physical contact with you."

Oh.

"You feel some of the same way I do at your touch," I breathe out.

Of course, he does. Why didn't it occur to me that he felt the same way?

"What you feel? No, you have no real idea. You only experience small wisps of what we feel when we touch because you're holding back."

Small wisps? What does that even mean?

He swirls the alcohol in his glass. "I'm not sure how many times or in how many different ways I can explain this to you in order for you to get it. The soul mate bond is true. It's real, no matter how you feel about being a part of it. And it's powerful. You only know of the human soul mate definition. The man and woman who choose to fall in love and want to be together. That's your only experience. It's just not like that."

"Falling in love is debatable and subjective, apparently."

Has he forgotten what we just learned about my relationship with Ty?

"Be that as it may, you think you were in love with him and that he was your soul mate. That's not what we've got. I want to die when you're not near me. My soul craves your soul. When you're close, I feel alive. When you touch me, I *am* alive. Our touch is a power in its own right. It gives us clarity and strength. It strengthens our natural abilities."

He turns the chair around and straddles it, studying me. I move farther into the room, drawn in by his compelling energy. I feel alive when he touches me too.

"The true bond that includes"—he clears his throat—"extended amorous touches, like kissing and lovemaking, can also create a powerful strength in both of us. One so powerful we can literally heal each other through that touch."

My breathing stops. "Heal each other? Kissing? Lovemaking?" I pluck at the words that dangle in the air as if I can touch them. Yes, please.

"Yes. Through regular sexual contact, we build an even stronger bond. So, when we have physical wounds, we can heal each other through a touch that isn't sexual. Which is always a plus on a battlefield. Can't exactly be making out then, can we?"

He laughs bitterly, but my heart picks up its tempo.

Battlefields? Making out?

I slowly look his body up and down. I can't imagine—well, maybe I can—having sex with Drew.

My palms grow damp, and now I'm quietly breathing faster. Oh, yes. I definitely can envision it. My soul dances in anticipation and my body yearns for him. My hormones say hello, what are you waiting for? My brain says no, absolutely not. It doesn't matter how my body responds. I back up slowly.

"I can't just have sex with you. I don't even know you." But honestly, one-night stands were meant for this kind of thing. But we weren't going to walk away at the end of the night. And he's in love with me. I hope he hears the desperation in my voice. I'm not sure what kind of desperation it is though.

"I'm not saying you have to." He blows out a breath. "Don't get me wrong, I want to, desperately. The peace that would come with it alone." He shudders, briefly closing his eyes. When they open, the green holds me in place. "The need to touch you intimately."

He gets up and slowly stalks toward me. My heart races faster and my mouth goes dry.

"You don't know what it's like, so you don't miss it." There's a feverish sheen in his eyes. His breathing's faster. Or is that just mine? I know what sex is like, and I damn well miss it.

Panting, I hold his gaze with a tenacity I can't break. I back into the door again, hard. Slamming the breath out of me. I drag air in, sharply, but all I smell is him. Woodsy and spicy. Sexy.

"I can't say that I don't miss it, that I don't want it, and you. Because I do. But I understand. Fuck me, I understand how you feel and what you're going through right now. The downfall of knowing you so well and being attuned to your emotions," he says, a lopsided smile appearing.

He reaches out, and I think he's going to touch me.

Yes, please.

Warmth pools between my legs in anticipation and I exhale hard when he doesn't. Instead, he reaches around me and turns the knob, and I scoot sideways out the door.

"Yes, I understand you, even when you don't understand yourself, and I won't push you."

He looks at the doorframe as if considering it, sliding his hand up the wood, and finally gripping the frame. I follow the movement, fascinated by the way his knuckles turn white.

"Even though a good bout of hard, sweaty sex, slammed up against this door would be best for the both of us."

I drag my eyes away and lock onto his face. Telling myself not to imagine sex with him is pointless when he paints such a vivid picture.

"Which means I can and will tell you to fuck off when you're judging me on the small ways I do get some solace."

And he slams the door in my face.

Chapter Twenty

DREW

I shut the door without any remorse. How dare she sit there on her high horse and judge me? She's a solid seventy-five percent of the cause. I'm not even drunk yet. I've only had half a glass, and though I'd originally thought of smothering the tatters of my soul with an alcoholic haze, my brain has already prevailed.

They'll come for her, and I need to be stone-cold sober and ready.

This is the one time I think it's a shame I still have a shred of apparent decency. It wouldn't take much to seduce her, and we would both be better for it. Far better for it.

I wasn't lying when I told her our strength is incredible when we're together, sexually. We were too young to experience the actual act when I'd lost her the first time. I had enough of an inkling from kissing and such that it would be a powerful thing when we did.

I experienced it with the first alternate version of Delaney. Saying that it had been beyond even the scope of my imagination was an understatement. I'd understood then the awe people used when they spoke of soul mates.

It's a tangible, living bond. It's the bond all soul mates forge.

But it also requires her brain to be on board, as well as her soul. One without the other is futile.

I make the rounds while making a quick call. "Mark, what's the status out there?"

"All quiet here, boss."

"It won't be for long. They'll arrive tonight."

"How do you know?"

"It's what I'd do. They'll try to catch us unaware." Too bad for them, I've a whole lot more to lose and as such won't be caught asleep.

"Like we discussed, I'm taking this shift, so go sleep some."

I settle in to keep guard over my domain. I walk the house, the large monitors on in every room for ease of keeping tabs. I keep one eye on Katrina and one on Delaney. And my mind roams, questioning why she had set this in motion. What had she seen? What was the end game? As usual, it's fruitless.

I stalk the halls and check my personal arsenal. Each time I pass the weapons room, I add another one to what I'm carrying. Something tells me I'll need it, and I always listen to my gut.

On a pass through, I pick up a pair of Glock nine millimeters for Delaney. She'll need to defend herself when the assault breaks loose as it surely will. They'll be fighting hard for her. I stop in front of the door and knock quietly. When she doesn't answer, I crack it open.

She's asleep on the bed, fully dressed, facing me. One hand under her cheek, the other arm cradling her head. Dark smudges stain the delicate skin under her eyes.

It'll take some time for reality to catch up to her current version. I know how hard it can be. At least, she has me to lean on if she needs it.

I'm cautiously optimistic she's the one. That the world won't fall around my ears. That my soul won't have to feel the pain of tearing away from her again. I brush a strand of dark hair from her face gently, hoping it doesn't wake her, and lay the Glocks on the nightstand, checking to make sure they're fully loaded. I put four extra magazines next to them.

Shortly after I switch with Mark, the first sensor trips and shoots an electric jolt through my body. I jump up from the bed where I'd laid down fully dressed and armed.

I'm no longer tired. I train for these things every day of my life. I'm Delaney's Protector. I live for this shit. The intruders have no idea what they're in for.

I join Mark in the security room, dubbed the war room. There are no windows, and walls of screens are everywhere. "Did you give Charlie a heads-up?"

The first group of men infiltrates the grounds. One at a time, slithering in like the serpents they are.

"Yeah, boss. He's on a cot out in the hallway in front of the kid's room. Wouldn't it be better for him to be in front of Delaney's door?"

"No, I left her with a pair of Glocks. I'll watch over her as I'm sure you will too." A low growl slips out of my mouth.

"Boss. Dude. You gotta chill. You know I know she's my first priority." He shakes his head with a grin. "I've no problem watching her." He winks.

Mark's the only one who has ever had the temerity to joke with me. "You know the only reason you're alive after comments like these is because I trust you to value your life." I casually inspect the Beretta in my hand.

"I'm not afraid of you." Mark laughs.

"And that would be the last mistake you'd make." I jam the gun in my back holster. "Here we go."

Showtime.

The first round of ten men goes down fast. One by one,

they all step on randomly placed units in the ground. With enough pressure, the unit engages faster than the booted foot can be removed. The pressure-sensitive trigger drives a metal spike with enough force to puncture most rubber-soled boots that assassins like to wear. As the spike penetrates skin, it simultaneously courses enough voltage through the body to electrocute them on the spot.

The first wave is over in seconds.

The second round of armed men takes slightly less time to kill, their downfall in thinking the first group had hit the only defenses. Stupid. They're unprepared for the fortress that's my home. The third wave is warier, smarter, and makes it to the second round of defenses.

The trees on the property are a great cover for the base of automatic rifles. Like mini stationary sentries. They target a certain weight and height, in order to preserve the abundant wild game. Mark and I watch the screen as the entire third wave falls with bullets in their heads. The fourth round falls just as quickly. By my count, they've lost about fifty men and still haven't gotten within a thousand yards of the house.

How frustrating for them, how satisfying for me. I rarely get to see this many men attempt to breach the defenses. They'll keep coming, as I predicted. I gleefully anticipate the couple that should make it to the actual building. I doubt more than one or two will gain entrance. I crack my knuckles and stretch my fingers in preparation. At the possibility of finally getting some answers. At being able to hit someone for daring to threaten my soul mate. I can't wait to break down the one who's smart enough, or stupid enough, that manages to get in.

The last group of thirty men seem to be the smartest of the bunch. Bringing in so many men ensures the probability that some will storm into the courtyard. Mark and I are outside waiting. The group of twenty or so remaining men halt abruptly, facing us. They look at each other.

"Just the two of you here?" says a mercenary who looks like he can dead lift two hundred pounds. The group of heavily armed, burly men starts laughing, probably thinking they'll get their mission completed easily.

I don't bother to tell them that the defenses they were getting themselves killed on was a cake walk compared to what Mark and I are capable of.

I raise my voice. "Whoever wants to give me information, please let me know. We can step inside, have a beer. And I'll be merciful in killing you. If you don't give me information now, the last man standing will do so in far less welcoming circumstances."

I wait. No one responds.

"Pity. Then let's proceed. Mark, no one leaves here alive."

And I pull out my gun and shoot two of them in the head and neck before the group can even react.

I throw myself sideways, shooting two more on the way to the ground. I shoot one in the shoulder as he's running away.

Their vests prevent back and chest kill shots. To protect their heads, mercenaries tend to run with their heads hanging low, like a bull, making the head a smaller target.

The force of my bullet hitting his shoulder spins him around enough for me to put a well-placed bullet through his ear.

Mark's busy with four men who are trying to wrestle him to the ground. Little do they know that he was a reigning underground boxing champion before I pulled him from the standard Guardianship detail to work with me. The things people do for fun.

His grin should tip them off but instead spurs them on.

I spin just as one of the mercenaries manages to come close enough to kick my gun out of my hand, sending it skittering.

I reach into my shirt and whip out a set of throwing knives, one in each hand. I throw them, each one landing in the throat of two separate men. As the blades embed themselves, I grab the man who kicked out my gun and slam him to the ground, rolling with him to break my momentum.

The knife from my boot is in my hand and ramming through his heart before we even stop. His vest is made to stop bullets and normal knives. My knives are made of rhodium, a peculiar metal that's so rare and expensive that most defense companies won't pour money into it for protection purposes.

My adrenaline surges. With a yell, I run straight into another group of four men, arms spread wide in a fall from grace, T-boning them all. These idiots don't even know when to run.

My hands crush one throat, and I bring up my knees to snap the neck of another while he's still lying there trying to catch his breath. It'll be his last.

I jump up and kick out one foot. It lands on his neck, and with a quick pivot, he's no longer trying to get a good grip on me. I reach out, yanking on the collar of the one trying to get away and throw him backward into Mark, who shoots him point blank.

The two of us move back-to-back as ten more creep out of the bushes surrounding us. The haze of gunfire sits in the air.

"You loaded?" Mark asks.

"Yep, still have my spare on my back. You?"

"I've only fired the one shot. Still fully loaded in the other. And one at my back you can have."

"Showoff."

"Carousel?"

I briefly consider which one will unwillingly give me information. "Yep, to the right. And I want the one at my three o'clock."

"Gotcha."

"On two. One, two." I'm yanking my Beretta out of its holster, and Mark draws a Sig Sauer from his. We spin in a coordinated circle we've practiced so many times we could do it with our eyes closed, drunk, and still be the victors.

It's over in three seconds. Smoke lingers on the air and the thrill of adrenaline courses through my veins. I stare down the lone man facing both our barrels.

"Guess you've won the lottery." I walk over and hold the gun to his forehead. "You and I have some talking to do."

"I don't know anything, and even if I did, I wouldn't tell you," the surviving mercenary says. "You think I'm afraid of you? You've only gotten lucky so far this evening. You're nobody."

"You're right. I'm a ghost you can't hold onto and can't kill. Let's go." I cuff him with zip ties from my pocket and frog march him toward the garage.

"We aren't going inside the house?" the man asks.

"You think I'm going to welcome you into my home? I offered a beer once, and you declined. This is no longer a social visit."

Inside the garage, there's a room outfitted for these kinds of purposes. Anything needing killing can be done in the violently sterile room. Tile covers the floor, walls, and ceiling. The floor slopes into a drain in the middle of the room. One side has a metal sink and counter with a hose attachment. The wall adjoining it holds a variety of tools, knives being a predominant feature. Mainly, the room is used for dressing hunting game. Many a time, Mark and I have stood side-by-side cleaning out an elk or deer we bagged. But the room will suit this purpose too.

I flip the light switch on, illuminating the room in all its white glory, and the man I'm dragging in realizes he miscalculated.

"Yes, you very well should whimper. We're going to have a

nice chat." I grab the metal chair propped up against the wall and set it next to the drain, tossing the man in its general direction.

"How long this chat is going to last is up to you." I walk over to the wall of knives and consider my options. This dude looks like someone who understands the game of torture. A large knife will only make him breathe a sigh of relief.

Whoever said bigger is better was just stoking their own ego. I take down one of the smaller knives with wickedly sharp teeth. The merc's eyes widen. Too late, he understands that I may be experienced. Skills in the assassination trade are prized and touted. And not for the faint of heart.

He raises his chin, and I groan inwardly.

Fucking fabulous.

Someone who thinks he's a badass and can't be broken. Everyone can be broken if you find the right button. I've never been a fan of torture. It takes as much out of the torturer as it does the one getting tortured. But there's nothing I won't do to protect Delaney.

This merc will find out quickly his will is nothing compared to mine.

Chapter Twenty-One

DELANEY

I wake up drenched in sweat. My dreams consist of pale people wielding magic and of people so dark they're part of the night sky. I don't know any of them. Gunfire breaks the silence.

Katrina!

I run to the TV and change the channels. The screens pop up, and I home in on her room. My knees almost buckle with relief. She's sleeping. I turn the volume up high enough to hear breathing, deep and even.

She's safe.

I turn back to the other channels and gasp. Drew and another man are standing back-to-back in the middle of a dozen or so men. Drew's unarmed, and the other guy has one gun. It seems laughably inadequate compared to the men surrounding them.

I search the room, panicked, looking for a weapon. I spot a pair of handguns and pick them up. They're comfortable and familiar in my hands. I tuck one in the small of my back and run out and down the stairs.

At the front door, the cacophony of bullet after bullet

being discharged from multiple guns, impossibly fast, echoes on the airwaves.

NO! Drew!

Heedless of any possible danger, I open the door and stop. Two men are unceremoniously dragging bodies toward a garage. Drew's nowhere to be seen. I've no idea how they managed to be victorious so fast, but it's obvious they won.

"Where's Drew?"

"He's in the garage, but...Delaney!"

I *need* to make sure he's safe. In the building, there's a door with a light showing under it. This must be another room in the mountain. That can't be good.

There are muffled yells and screams, groans and slaps. Oh, shit! I run the last few steps and throw the door open, gun in hand.

Drew's in one piece, and I breathe a sigh of relief. My stomach drops at the sight of the man tied to a chair in the middle of the room, bloodied head hanging to the side, and slumped sideways.

"What are you doing?"

I can't imagine living in a world where torturing someone is commonplace. I know exactly what this room is used for. My stomach churns with the need to get sick.

"Let him go."

I lift my gun arm. I don't know if I can fire it and trust myself not to hit either man, but neither one needs to know that.

He growls low. "Put that down and get out. Right now."

"No. Let him go." The man in the chair looks up with a barely audible gasp and straightens.

"She's here too," he whispers roughly through split lips.

"Fuck."

Drew swiftly closes in on the man and snaps his neck. My

arm starts shaking wildly and my breathing stops before I drag air in again.

"You killed him. You—you broke his neck."

I don't understand why he did that. Drew's eyes look dead, murderous even, and I step back, pointing the gun at him.

"Why? Why did you kill him?" The dreaded spots float in my vision.

"Because he knows who you are, and he was surprised you were here. Fuck!"

He runs his hands through his hair, pulling on it, thinking. He's silent for less than a few seconds.

"Katrina. They were here for her, not you. But now they'll know. You need to get inside. Now."

Drew steps forward, and I step back. At the thought she's in danger, panic sweeps through me and combines with the nausea of what he's been doing.

"Don't touch me. You killed him for no reason. You... tortured him."

I'm in shock, I think. From everything I've learned in the last couple of days, this puts me over the edge.

"Delaney."

He walks up and grabs the gun as if it's incapable of harming him, twisting my arm behind my back in the process. It's all been a sham. I've never been able to defend myself from him, even with the guns he gave me. What a fool I've been.

"Stop and think for a minute. Of course, I'm a killer. I'm your Protector. You think that comes with negotiations? Diplomacy?"

I struggle, a futile attempt to get free from his iron grasp. They probably have blood on them right now, and the acid burns higher in my throat.

"For fuck's sake, they didn't know you were here. Are you

listening? They came for Katrina. Now knowing you're here, too, they'll redouble their efforts. There's no way these guys aren't bugged. Get into the house where it's safe."

He shakes me slightly then lets me go. He sighs in exasperation when I don't move.

"I was asking him questions he didn't want to answer. Not my fault." He shrugs. "If he'd have answered them, I would've been more merciful."

At his words, I back away. "Don't touch me. I'm coming in because I need to be with Kat, but don't touch me. And stay away from me."

I back all the way out of the room and move toward the house. Fear lances through me, and I worry that I'm not quite rational right now. I've never seen anyone tortured before, and the need to run pulls through my muscles.

"Stop!" He runs in front of me faster than I know is possible and looks out the garage door.

Dread fills my stomach and a cold sweat slides down my back. Are they here for her? How am I going to make it to the house to protect her? I was stupid to have left. "What? What is it?"

I stand behind him, resisting the urge to huddle against his back. What is wrong with me? How can I be disgusted and horrified by what he's capable of and what he was just doing, yet want the very safety he offers by such actions? I step aside.

"I don't need your brand of protection."

And I step through the doorway.

Drew pushes me out of the way. There's a slight breeze from the bullets spitting from his gun as he shoots while shoving me to the ground and throwing himself on me.

"Oof."

Made of solid muscle, he lands on me hard, covering my body with his own. My soul reacts swiftly. I'm nearly dizzy with the contact of his body down the length of mine. Heat floods through me.

He yanks the gun I miraculously still hold out of my hand and rolls over. Crouching, he fires the guns from both hands until one is empty, tossing it to the side.

I can't do anything but watch as he jumps up and charges the last guy, still firing. I'm morbidly fascinated and on some level horrified at the attraction weaving through me. My emotions have zero stability, clearly.

I watch him run through bullets whizzing in the air as he charges another shooter and tackles him. When he whips out a knife—What is he? A walking arsenal?—and slashes it across a neck in one smooth motion, I can't help but be impressed by the fluidity.

He immediately slumps over like a deflated balloon. It takes my brain a moment longer to understand that this is all wrong. I get up, racing toward him.

"Drew!" I scream, but there's no response.

Another man runs out of the woods, heading for us. Without hesitation, I yank the second gun out of my pants at my back and fire, hitting the man in the middle of his throat. For a moment, I stare at the body that falls to the ground, unmoving, and at the handgun in my hand.

The realization that Drew's still on the ground crashes back, and I run to him, flipping him over and off the dead body he's on and check for a pulse. It's there but faint.

"You have to get up!"

I shake him but he isn't moving. There's blood everywhere, and I don't know how much of it is his. Voices echo out of the woods, and there's no way that can be a good sign.

"Dammit, wake up."

I grab his legs, pulling him across the driveway. Getting him close to the door of the house is the easy part, but I can't pull him up the stairs without hurting him. The voices are getting louder, and I turn and plant myself in front of him and point my gun at the woods.

The seconds seem like hours as I wait to see who's the next to be killed. Two familiar men break through the woods, holding each other up, and I breathe a sigh of relief as my arm drops, suddenly limp.

"Help me."

The men who were clearing out bodies earlier both stand there, staring.

"Have you lost your minds! Get over here and help me! I don't know what's wrong with him! He needs you."

They hobble faster toward us. They must have injuries of their own. As soon as they get to me, I run up and open the door. One of them grabs Drew under his arms and the other picks up his legs. With a grunt, both rise and carry him up the steps.

"Lock that door," says the man with his back to me.

I shut the door and spin around. "Where are the locks? I don't know how to lock the doors!" Panic twists my stomach and forces my voice out in a screech.

"That button right there next to the light switch. Hold it in for ten seconds. The entire ten seconds."

I press and hold, counting to myself as the guys carry Drew toward the bookcase. He's out cold.

At five seconds, there's a whir and deadbolts slide into the door from the doorframe. I can't count the number of simultaneous snicks. At seven seconds, a metal sheet of some kind lowers over the windows, obscuring the rising sun and plunging the room into darkness. At ten seconds, an automated voice sounds out of speakers I can't see.

"Full lockdown complete."

The lights automatically turn on in the hallway, and I run after them. At the bookcase, I curse the seconds used for the scanners to scan me. It slides open and I run down and peek into the hospital room. I need to go see Kat, but I need to make sure Drew's okay too. I inch backward.

"We'll work on him. Go check on your daughter."

I nod and barrel down the stairs and through the hallway toward her room. Gathering lungfuls of air, I calm myself and quietly open the door to peek in.

I tiptoe in and carefully smooth Katrina's curls from her forehead. Liza's sleeping on the cot on the far side of the room, and she snores once and rolls over, snuggling into her pillow.

Careful to close the door quietly behind me, I race back to the hospital room.

"How is he?"

"He was shot, twice. I'm Charlie and Mark's getting some things I'll need to fix him up. But he should be fine."

"What? Where? He never faltered. He was fighting, and I never saw him get hit. I never saw a reaction."

"Looks like just the shoulder and chest. He'd have kept going as long as you were in danger."

Guilt weighs heavily on my shoulders and I wince. If only I'd stayed behind him. If only I wasn't so disgusted by the violence he exhibited. Violence I didn't turn my nose up for when it was used for my protection. Violence I used myself and would again to protect Drew and Katrina.

What a hypocrite.

If only I could turn back time like Drew did. A hint of a memory nudges my brain. This is the second time I've felt a memory stirring, and I close my eyes, hoping to bring it to the surface.

Nothing.

"It's okay," Charlie says. "It's not your fault."

I open my eyes and sigh. "Yes, it is."

Drew's still in his clothes, but one of the men ripped open his shirt. There's a large clear, plastic-type bandage on his chest. A hole and darkness. I don't want to know how bad it is. The guilt eats at me.

"How bad is it?" I ask anyway.

"Just missed his lung, I think." He turns around and gets gauze from a tray near the bed. He soaks it in some kind of liquid and turns back.

"What's the plastic stuff on it?"

"It's a chest seal. It's used to prevent air from getting into his lung and collapsing it in case it did puncture a lung."

I place my hand on Charlie's, needing him to ease my throat closing up. "Please tell me again he's going to be okay."

He sighs and shakes his head. "I don't know. It depends how long he fought with a bullet hole in his chest. How deep it is." He points to Drew's shoulder. "This one here grazed him. It's a mere flesh wound." He pats the hole with the soaked gauze. I've never seen such a large, muscled man be so gentle in his movements.

This one looks worse. Blood crusted around it, and the skin an angry red. What scares me the most is the chest wound though, with its dark, cavernous hole. I think I'm going to vomit. I focus on what Charlie's saying instead.

"The next couple of hours will be critical. We're hoping they don't attack again while we're short an army."

"What army?" I don't remember other people.

"Drew. He's like a one-man army. The man is a beast."

I believe it after what I saw today. I'm sure when there's time to analyze it, I'll be in awe if not proud of my Protector. But now fear tastes bitter in my throat, and guilt chokes it. I can't breathe right.

Mark returns carrying some clothes. "Hey, you okay? You didn't get hurt, did you?"

"No. Thanks to Drew. And to the both of you for protecting me and Katrina. I owe you our lives." I don't know what the body count is, but the three of them are a formidable, deadly team.

"Of course. We'd do anything to help him, and yourself. You should go shower, sleep while you can. We're going to clean him up as best as we can and get him stable. Charlie here will hopefully feed us before we starve to death."

I put my hand out to shake first Mark's hand, then Charlie's.

"Thank you, guys. Really."

As soon as I get out of the quick shower, I pull up the monitor. Katrina hasn't moved in her bed. I'm grateful she's sleeping. It makes spending my time with Drew easier.

Someone dropped off a tray of food at my door, but I can't eat. Guilt sits like a lump of stones in the pit of my stomach. I snag some pieces of bacon because I know I need it, but it tastes like cardboard. My stomach is in knots, and a ball of dread curls in my gut. Something's wrong. I know that, somehow, I'm sensing Drew. Urgency quickens my feet as I run to the hospital room.

I jerk the door open, breathing a sigh of relief at the soft beep of monitors, and I walk in quietly. Drew's eerily still. I don't remember our previous memories together, but I've been around him long enough to know this is bad. His natural nature seems to be always alert. He isn't necessarily always moving, but he's always analyzing everything. The environment, what I'm doing, what others in our vicinity are doing. Nothing gets by him. But now, that alertness isn't here. A shell of a body is lying on the bed, gurgling.

My heart stutters before bucking into place. Dread invades my senses and pours into my body. He shouldn't be making that noise, should he? I don't know where any of the cameras are.

"Mark? Charlie! Can you hear me? Something is wrong with Drew!"

Mark barrels through the door. "What happened?"

"I don't know. I just came in, and he's lying here so still. But I heard a gurgling sound. That can't be good can it?" We both hold our breath. Silence. Then the soft sound again.

"Shit." Mark pulls out his cell. "Get in here. We've got a problem."

"What's wrong? What's happening?" I grab his sleeve, interrupting him from getting supplies from the closet.

"I think his lung is collapsing." He shoves by me while I stand there, numb. Charlie runs in and the two of them begin working on Drew, but I can't see what they're doing.

My body is cold. So cold.

The numbness creeps up from my toes. Crawling along my skin like a black fog. Like an inky squid, the tendrils of it lick and curl through my body. When it reaches my soul, the numbness turns to hot molten lava.

My entire body is a volcanic eruption of knives. I vaguely hear myself screaming. My body simply drops to the floor, boneless with each nerve ending dialed to hypersensitive.

I can't stop my body from convulsing on the floor.

I can't close my mouth to stop the screaming.

I can't shut off my mind to stop the endless howling in my ears.

My soul is grieving in a way I can never mentally comprehend. But my soul can only understand one thing.

The death of the other half of itself.

Drew is dead.

Chapter Twenty-Two

DELANEY

Curling into a ball, my body protects itself as well as it can. But how can you shield yourself when the pain ripping through you is internal?

I wrap my arms tightly around myself and push my knees into my chin, trying to squeeze out the mounting pressure. But it isn't enough.

I rock rhythmically, rolling from side to side, desperate to soothe myself. But it isn't enough.

Tears leak from my eyes, the overflow of pain seeking an escape. But it isn't enough.

My mouth opens, the voice box trying to do its part to release the terror. But it isn't enough.

Mark yells from Drew's bedside, but I can't understand what he's saying. A hand's on my shoulders, uselessly offering comfort. "Hold on, hold on. It'll be over soon."

"Dammit, hurry up and save Drew's ass!"

I don't feel anything but excruciating pain. I can't think, I can't move. From far away, Mark's voice calls out, "Fuck, move faster! Stop fucking counting! We can't lose them both. Not on my watch."

The slap of the paddles—the whine—barely penetrates my ears. I can't hear over my own screaming. And then suddenly, it's gone. The torture wrenches from me viciously and I lie in a heap of wiped-out emotion.

A soft whirring and beeping penetrate my ears. Strong antiseptic scent fills my nostrils. I don't want to open my eyes. Or move any part of me. My body aches in places I didn't know existed.

There's an army of ice skaters training for the Olympics in my throat. My eardrums hum in time to the beeping. The good thing about the giant bruise—my body—pulsating with every heartbeat, is that I'm no longer in the depths of hell.

I open my eyes and a groan escapes my lips. The grit in my eyes can't control the tear that leaks out.

"Here. Take some of this, it'll help." Charlie holds out a small bowl with a spoon. "Honey. It'll coat your throat. Get a spoonful and sit it on your tongue. Let it liquify a bit and slide down your throat."

I slowly lean up on my elbows, my shoulders protesting the pressure, and follow his instructions. After a couple spoonfuls, I risk speaking.

"Drew?" I whisper hoarsely, wincing at the fire that burns my vocal cords.

"He's stable. But he's going to need surgery."

My abdominal muscles scream at the torture of moving to a complete sitting position so that I can get a better look. My muscles shake with tension. Drew's laying on the bed, deathly still, but there isn't any more gurgling. A machine inhales and exhales for him,

"Life support?"

I shudder hard, unable to control it skittering up my spine. I can't live through his death again. I don't know how he did it for years. My hands shake at the possibility of reliving hell. My soul curls in on itself in fear.

"Yeah, because of the hole in his chest. Once the surgery is completed, as long as everything goes well, he won't need it." Charlie bends close, peering into my eyes. "How are you feeling? Besides your throat?"

"I hurt—everywhere. Did Drew act this way too? Is that how you knew it would hurt?"

"You were screaming." He heads to one of the cabinets and peruses the bottles and vials there. "I can give you painkillers through a needle. That way you don't have to swallow a pill."

"Yes, please."

Choosing one of the small vials, he removes a syringe and opens the packet, prepares the dosage. He puts on gloves, grabs a packet of sanitizing wipes, and slides my sleeve up my arm. He wipes it clean and uncaps the needle to inject the clear liquid into my vein.

Dizziness washes over me as the painkiller flows through my veins and hits the neurons in my brain. Some of the pain shuts down, and I'm floating on a pretty cloud.

"Charlie," I say too slowly, "you may have given me too much." I brace my arms on either side of me on the edge of the couch.

"Give it a few minutes. The dose is higher than you need, but that's because your body will metabolize the drug ridiculously fast. If I were to give you a normal-sized dose, it wouldn't do you a lick of good." He throws the needle into a syringe collector and removes his gloves. I blearily watch him —there are two of him now—put on another pair of gloves.

I scrutinize the Charlie on the left, hoping it's the real one. "I didn't know that."

"No? You never needed extra Novocain at the dentist or more of an epidural when you delivered your child?"

Oh.

"I assumed they just didn't work on me."

He moves around the room, gathering equipment and supplies on a large tray on a metal cart. The movement makes me nauseous, so I close my eyes, hoping to regain a measure of equilibrium. If only the room would stop spinning. But it's useless and only makes my head swim faster, so I reopen them.

"Yep, you need more stuff like that. It's also why you eat massive amounts of food compared to normal people."

Huh. I have so much to learn. *Normal people?* "Charlie, are you part of the Guardianship, too?"

He nods as he injects Drew with another syringe. "I used to be in another unit. Drew helped me out a long time ago. I was a Healer with them." He disposes of the syringe and changes gloves again. Drew must get his germ protocols from Charlie.

"And now you're a chef."

He nods again. "Food has a way of putting things in perspective. I chop at it, slicing and dicing, but I don't cause pain. I can boil it, mash it, shape it, and it doesn't scream in terror. And correctly prepared, it can naturally heal you. It brings me peace and joy like nothing else."

I rearrange my facial features so I don't betray my concern. *What had Charlie done in his lifetime?*

"I, for one, appreciate your cooking. Everything I've eaten has been divine."

He beams a smile so wide it dazzles me. "I'm humbled you enjoy it. How do you feel now?"

I sit up straighter. I'm no longer dizzy, and though my body aches and my throat is raw, I don't feel half as bad as I did five minutes ago.

"Much better. I don't feel like I've taken flight anymore either."

He chuckles. "Good. Why don't you go check up on Katrina. Then, if you don't mind coming back and sitting with Drew, I'm going to head out and prep some food for us to eat. We'll need sustenance before anything else happens. I'm planning on conducting the surgery this afternoon, as long as he remains stable."

"No, of course I don't mind." I glance at Drew's still body. "I'll be back. Thank you for everything. For saving him, for saving me."

Impulsively, I wrap my arms around him. He stiffens and awkwardly pats me on the back. I pull back, smiling, delighted to see a pink flush on his cheeks. He's so sweet.

"You're welcome," he says gruffly.

I walk slowly to Kat's room and back after making sure she and Liza have breakfast and more importantly, plans for the day. It seems I'm going to be focusing a lot more on Drew. Nothing drives home the point that we're soul mates any clearer than his death. I understand now what he meant by saying that people who have lost their soul mates go insane.

I couldn't handle five minutes of his death. I don't know how he survived two years of mine.

My body tightens and my heart drops at the possibility of being without him. He's right, our version of soul mates is nothing like what I had with Tyson.

It's pitiful in comparison to my need for Drew. I hate to say it. Normal people have no idea what the concept of soul mates means, and I'm not sure they aren't better off without firsthand knowledge.

Even Kat. I'll do anything for her. Do anything to protect her. I'd kill, violently. I'd sell my soul to the devil if I needed to. And yet, that's nothing compared to what I'd do for Drew.

It's my own self-preservation after all, and I need to live for her.

Back in the hospital room, Charlie hands me a cell phone. "This is yours. It's got Drew's, Mark's, and my phone number programmed into it. I'm sure I don't have to tell you that you shouldn't contact anyone—not one person you know."

The sleek, silver phone is thicker than the prized slimness of new phones, but thinner than most cell phones encased in heavy-duty protective cases. Except this one doesn't have a case. I flip it over. I'm sure the tech in this thing will put every known cell maker to shame, if it follows the technological capabilities of the house.

"Drew programmed it. It'll only open to you and him. It's got all the biometrics. You place any finger on it and it has to scan your face, too. It's pretty user friendly, with the dark web installed and more firewalls and security than Fort Knox. You can google or whatever to your heart's content and no one will trace you. And it's bulletproof, literally."

He taps the side of the phone. "Here, you slide out these earpieces. Use them like headphones. When you're done, you squeeze them to thin them out and shove them back in their slot. It doesn't look like they'll fit, but they do. I'll be back in shortly with something to eat."

I tug on the earpieces that popped when Charlie tapped on the phone. They're incredibly light, and though they look like they're made from carbon fiber, they feel like silk. When I pinch one, it condenses like a foam earplug. I insert it into my ear canal and wait while it expands to fill it. I slip the other one in. They're so light, I can't tell they're in there. Experimentally, I hold up the phone in front of my face, my thumb pressing on the screen. The phone blinks and lights up, showing a deceptively average background.

"Good afternoon, Delaney," a smooth, male voice speaks into my ear. Curiously, Drew's recorded voice doesn't give me any of the bodily sensations his actual voice does.

I pull the earpieces out, pinch them, and push them into the slot they came out of and slide the phone into my back pocket.

Drew's covered with a sheet, the edge tucked in under his armpits. His tanned arms lay by his side. So still. So quiet.

His hands lay open, palm down, and his hair is in disarray over his forehead. His face looks peaceful, the skin smooth. No frown lines or furrowed brows—something I haven't ever witnessed.

The tube coming out of his throat looks ominous, and I can't stand the hiss of air softly flowing through. His vulnerability makes me want to punch someone. He's too strong to be in this hospital bed.

"Dammit, Drew. I don't know what to do. I need you to wake up. I need you. Do you hear me?" He doesn't move. My hands curl into fists. "I'm sorry. Is that what you want to hear? I'm sorry. I should have trusted you. I should have listened to you. I shouldn't have been scared of you. Of all of this. I'm sorry. I need you to wake up and tell me it's okay. Please."

Nothing. My balled fist hits the side of the bed. The clear bandage with its black hole builds a mountain of fear. He wouldn't be here if I hadn't been so stubborn.

The guilt weighs on me, and my fists clench harder so I don't reach out and shake him awake. I need him. The small slice of ink peeking out from the sheet on his chest beckons me. I pull the sheet back.

Like my tattoo, it's a quote of some kind. The words, inked in the same spot as mine on the ribcage, causes an involuntary shiver. "And time goes by so slowly. And time can do so much." The words nudge my brain, branded into my memories. Why can't I unlock them? Gently tracing the words, my fingers delicately hover over the skin.

Mark suddenly backs into the room, pulling a cart loaded with food. Did he see me staring at Drew's ribcage, my nose inches from touching him? The flush heats my cheeks.

"Charlie'll be right in." He brings the cart to the table and pulls out a metal folding chair from a nearby closet.

"What's he trying to do, feed an army?" I ask, nervously laughing. Could I be any more obvious?

"Nah. The three of us are going to eat in here. Plus, you eat enough for two grown men."

"I should be offended, but it's the truth." I shrug. I make no excuses; I love food.

"It's cool. It doesn't put me off my feed none." He sets out plates and forks. "You want orange juice or apple?" He lifts a decanter of each.

"Juice? What's wrong with water?"

"You can have that, too. But we need juice. Charlie says so. And since he's in charge of the food I get to put into my mouth, I don't argue."

"Apple then, please."

He pours it into a glass. His large hands are scuffed and bruised, the knuckles scraped. Where Drew is lean, steel muscle tantalizingly hidden, Mark reminds me of a bull, with a wide chest and a short neck. His generous muscles bunch, even with small movements, like pouring juice. I'm slightly fascinated by the ripples.

"Are you with the Guardianship, too?" I'm assuming, at this point everyone here is. Or has been. I'm not sure that's a good thing, considering they seem to be the enemy.

"Yeah. I'm what folks call a Housekeeper. It ain't just running a house you know. And it ain't just for women." He puffs his chest up, the muscles obscene in their visibility. Ah. The muscular build, the body whipped into a frenzy so that it exudes stereotypical masculinity and virility. Stereotypes suck and bullying affects everyone. I hate people for what they do to each other.

"Of course not. I imagine you have a million things here to keep this fortress running smoothly."

He nods. "I do. I run the house, the grounds and the staff. But Housekeeping is more than that. It means keeping your house clean, literally and figuratively. I'm in charge of security, making sure no rat gets in that shouldn't be here."

It takes me a second to realize he doesn't mean actual rats. "Are you still in then?"

"Nah, I got out long ago. Joined in with Drew and Charlie. I used up my usefulness there."

"Your usefulness? At the Guardianship? What do you mean?"

"I helped Drew when I shouldn't have."

"With what?"

"Getting to you."

Yet another person I've hurt with my existence. "I'm so sorry, I didn't know. Thank you."

"Well, how could you? Drew helped me many times over, saved me a few times, and his mission is true. That's more important than any high and mighty Guardianship rules."

"What's his mission?" Finally, someone who can tell me things that may not be fantastical.

"You are. And saving the world. It has its perks." He winks.

So much for hopes and dreams. Saving the world from what? Me? Or something else?

Charlie walks in, all business. "While we're eating, we need to come up with a plan and schedule for sleeping. Until he's up and running, we've got a lot to cover."

"What are you thinking?"

"Well, Mark's going to need to finish retrieving the bodies on the grounds and resetting our defenses. We still have live traps, enough for now, but if we get attacked like we did earlier, we won't be as well defended."

"I can help with that." I shudder. I can't imagine moving dead bodies, but I don't want them outside rotting either.

Mark chimes in. "Nah. You can't go outside. They have us pinged via satellite by now. There's no way we can hide you from that. Matter of fact, we're sure they already know you're here. Seeing as how quick they got another round of men in from the time you came outside of the house, till you came out of the garage. That wasn't coincidental-like."

Charlie nods in agreement, a mouth full of a salami sandwich. He motions toward my plate, and I pick up mine.

"Ok, what do you want me to do then?" I take a bite. I always forget how hungry I am until I eat.

I don't know a whole lot about protecting a house and the people in it. Prior to shooting that man earlier, I didn't think I was capable of killing someone. I'm conflicted by the relief that I can avenge Kat properly, and chagrin I can do so handily. I swallow hard and sip my water.

"Stay here and keep an eye on Drew. I'll take the first shift sleeping." Charlie pops the last of the sandwich in. He pours himself some of the apple juice and downs it, grimacing slightly. "When Mark is inside, he'll watch the monitors for an attack. I'll keep an eye on Drew and you can sleep. Then, you'll stay with Drew, and Mark will sleep, and I'll prep for anything incoming. And we rotate. Once all of us have had some sleep, I'm going to get him into surgery. I won't risk him, running on no sleep and full of worry."

The plan seems complicated. Isn't there something else I can do to help? Unfortunately, with my elusive memories and forgotten training, I'm more of a hindrance than a help. I sigh. It seems I'm not good for much in this lifestyle either. I eat some more.

"Will they attack again?" I study them. Are they capable of defending this house, and Kat, without Drew?

Mark's face stills and my stomach drops. "Drew said they would, and he's never wrong. I don't know how much time we have. Call us if you need anything at all and one of us will be here. We better get moving."

Dismissive, he continues eating his sandwich with one hand, and clears off the table with the other. I'm like a female trophy being shuttled off. Useless.

Charlie pats my hand sympathetically. "I know it doesn't feel like you're doing much. But you are. We couldn't do it without you. We need three of us."

I brighten my expression because I don't need them worrying about me on top of everything else. I force a smile to my face. "Of course." I shove as much sweetness as I can into my voice.

Mark stares at me with wide eyes and shakes his head. Charlie, too, briefly looks startled, and then contemplative as his brows furrow. The blond arches relax and he chuckles softly, understanding in his eyes, but he says nothing.

They both clean up, waving my offer of help away, and I officially take the first shift with Drew.

Chapter Twenty-Three

DELANEY

He hasn't moved an inch. I wipe the table, picking at imaginary crumbs. I straighten up the couch. Nothing from him. I fix the sheets on his bed, fiddling with them. Not one sound, not one movement. Pulling up the chair, I plop myself in it. I'm helpless and can't assist the men putting their lives on the line protecting me and mine and have even caused them to be down a man. A one-man army they called him.

It's crushing. The weight of knowing he's in this bed because of me. I get up and pace. There's got to be something I can do. I can't sit here for hours. I'll go crazy with self-flagellation. Maybe I can distract myself by seeing what the guys are up to. I open the cabinet and switch channels on the TV until I see Mark. He's walking back and forth, hauling dead bodies. What will he do with them? I watch him throw a body into what appears to be an incinerator.

Bile sears the back of my throat. I want to vomit, but I force myself to watch.

Mark strips each body of every item, all of which are weapons. The life of an assassin boiled down to simple metal.

Each body brought back, stripped and tossed in to burn, adds to my pile of shame. I lose count on how many bodies Mark brings back.

All of them dead because of me. Or because of Kat, if Drew's to be believed. I'm grateful she has no idea what's going on, what's happening, in the name of her protection.

Can I rewind the footage?

Morbidly, I watch the events unfold while I was sleeping. My body shakes with terror at the sheer number of assassins. What do I or Katrina mean to the Guardianship that it's literally wasting people to bring us in? What have we done?

I watch while they are surrounded by armed men. Mark's formidable in his own right, but my eyes are drawn to Drew repeatedly. He moves with precision and speed, his target hit every time he aims. No hesitation, no remorse. If anything, he looks excited at the prospect of the fight. I jerk, and my heart hammers while I stop and rewind the footage again for a few seconds.

A man steps out of the woods and then falls to the ground from a bullet. It's only a second, but he looks so much like Ty that a tremor runs through me. Now I'm seeing ghosts. I shake my head at observing myself running out of the house in a panic. Running straight for the garage and Mark yelling for me to stop. If only I could pause the monitor and tell the girl on screen to get over herself before she ruins it all.

There's footage for the garage room too, but I don't want to see Drew doling out violence. I may be less judgmental now, but that doesn't mean I'm an advocate of it.

I watch as I step out of the garage. I see exactly when Drew gets shot. Both bullets hit when he steps directly in front of me—while he shoves me out of the way. He takes down close to fifteen men *after* being shot himself.

I close my eyes. I'm such an idiot. The guilt doubles. The

man saved me. I mean, even if it's self-preservation for him to do so, I kind of value my life.

I slump into the chair by the bed again. His arm lies there, unmoving. Because of me. Like Mark, he has scratches and bruises on the knuckles. Even the fine, dark hairs on them are still. It's unnatural. I glance around, as if I'm doing something I shouldn't. What difference does it really make?

I swallow hard and tentatively reach out. As my skin brushes his, the warmth slithers into me and I snatch my hand back. Why am I still afraid? Nobody is here to pass judgment. And even if they did, who cares?

Drew said because I was scared, I couldn't feel the connection with him the way I would if I wasn't. I turn his hand over, putting my palm in his, and straighten my posture. I can do this, make myself feel more. They're cold, not the warmth I usually associate with him. But then heat creeps back in. But how am I supposed to open myself completely? I do the only thing Drew has told me to do.

I empty my mind. And imagine everything black.

I picture the white light, a pinprick of it, until it nears and surrounds me. I breathe slowly and deeply, letting myself drift in the warmth. I focus on his hand, warm now from our contact, the skin rough, the hands strong, on the heat that travels along our limbs, like steam curling from a hot shower.

It slides sinuously through me, relaxing each muscle. I don't feel pain. My heart steadies and slows. Once the warmth seeps through every molecule, it settles in my core, content. I blissfully sigh. With my eyes closed, I picture Drew in my mind.

The lean body, the scruffy face. Instead of his scent, I inhale the antiseptic sterility of the hospital room. My heart rate stutters and increases. I let my shoulders slump and lean back against the chair. This is pointless.

I don't know what else to do. There's no increase in the

sensations I normally feel from him. Maybe he's wrong. I'm not experiencing any more than the subtle softness and warmth. I open my eyes. He hasn't moved either. I slide my hand out of his palm and gently turn it back over. I gasp as my eyes assimilate what they're seeing. The scratches are gone. There's still some faint bruising, but the scratches are completely healed.

Even my throat feels remarkably better. Drew said we're able to heal each other with amorous acts. I swallow hard, shaking my head at the sudden thought.

Even if I would, I couldn't have sex with an unconscious man. My finger taps against my lips. What could I do to heal him? Could I actually do it? Could I fix a hole in his chest? An image forms in my head, the two of us together in bed. My cheeks heat up.

It has to be worth a shot. A way to be able to get him back on his feet. Get him conscious. So he can tell me what he meant about Katrina. Before I change my mind, I call Mark on my cell.

"Hey, can you spare a minute? No, no, Drew's fine. I'm sorry, I didn't mean to worry you. I have an idea. Can you grab Charlie, too? I hate to wake him, but I might need him. It's important. Hurry."

I pace the room, waiting. I can't talk myself out of it. I have a plan, and it has to work. If it doesn't, I'm going to die of embarrassment. I hope he doesn't wake up while I'm attempting to heal him.

Mark enters, wiping his hands. I school my face against any disgust. I know he's doing what needs to be done and that it's all for Katrina and me. I imagine he doesn't want to be burning bodies any more than I would.

"What's up?"

I expect him to be irritated, but by the expression on his

face, he's relieved to be inside. "I want to wait for Charlie to get here, but can you answer a question for me?"

"Sure. Shoot."

"What do you know about soul mates?"

My fingers twist in my hand as Charlie limps in. He's hurt, too. Sleeping is probably his only solace. I hope my idea isn't a wild goose chase and I'm not robbing him of precious rest. I grip my fingers harder.

"Soul mates?" Mark scowls. Ah. There's the irritation I expected. His finger jabs the air. "Lady, you better have a damn good reason other than wanting girl chat, because that's not what I'm here for, and I'd hate to think that's what I woke Charlie up for." He crosses his arms, the muscles unyielding bands of steel, flexing.

Heat steals into my cheeks again. That's not what I meant. Charlie lifts a hand, halting Mark's judgment, and studies me. "We don't know much, having never experienced it ourselves. We know theories, nothing more. The Guardianship isn't keen on willingly sharing information. Why?"

"Drew said soul mates can heal each other. He mentioned... sex." My face must look like a tomato. I've never been particularly prudish, but both men are staring. I hurriedly continue.

"Obviously, I can't do that. Not—not that I'd be willing to if he wasn't." I vaguely point in his direction. "I mean, he can't. I can't..." This sounds stupid.

Charlie takes pity on me. "I guess that means it's not a myth. I've never seen it though, since I'm not—ahem—into watching others..." Charlie trails off, a rosy hue on his cheeks. The awkward silence grows.

Mark steps forward. "So. What is it that you think you can do? Cause I'm of a mind to assist." He winks.

I can't help my burst of laughter. Charlie's face reddens more as he purses his lips, looking like he's going to bust open, trying desperately to hold in his laugh. There's a slight wheezing noise, and finally, he lets out a loud guffaw, too. Mark joins us, howling with laughter.

It's a good minute before we get ourselves under control. Every time we look at each other we start up again. Finally, we all manage to catch our breath, with only the occasional snicker.

"I know it doesn't change anything, but damn it felt good to laugh. I needed that." I wipe tears from the corners of my eyes.

"Laughter is good for the soul," responds Charlie, still wheezing slightly.

"But back to the business at hand. What is it that you're asking? Really," Mark says, a small smile still twisting his lips.

"I don't know. I know touch is important. I held his hand earlier." I refuse to look at either of them. I walk over to Drew and hold it up. "Look, the scratches are healed."

They both walk over.

"I'll be damned." Charlie rubs his chin. "I wonder how long or how much you'd have to hold him for his body to heal."

"I don't know, but I could take the next shift. I know I'm supposed to sleep, but I could lie with him. In the bed I mean." I want to smack myself. Where else would I lie with him?

Mark and Charlie glance at each other.

"It's worth a shot," says Mark. "And I don't see him complaining if he were to wake up." He winks again.

"Can you turn off the monitors in here? I'd feel better with some privacy, and well..." My cheeks burn. "I'm planning on lying with the least amount of clothes as possible. I think it'll be better with skin-to-skin contact. And no comments from you." I point to Mark.

He holds up his hands. "Nope, not saying a thing." But he can't seem to help the wink that slips out again.

I grin. I like Mark.

"What is it, exactly, that you need me for?" Charlie asks. "And no way am I watching." His voice sounds like it's choking him, and I bite the inside of my cheek to stop the grin.

"I'm hoping to heal him enough that he'll be able to regain consciousness."

"And you'll need me to help him medically when he does." Charlie exhales a sigh of relief.

Trying desperately not to acknowledge yet another wink from Mark, a giggle threatens to escape my lips. I clear my throat instead. "Yes, but since you won't be…observing…" I clear my throat again. "Can you hang out nearby so I can yell for you and jump out of your way? Covered," I quickly say at the horror in his widened eyes.

"Yes, I can do that. I'll give you five seconds extra, just in case." Charlie's cheeks are turning from pink to red.

"Okay." I bite the inside of my lip as hard as I can. Charlie looks at Mark, then me. "Oh go ahead, I know you're laughing at me."

Mark and I lose it completely for the second time, holding our sides and valiantly trying to contain our laughter. Charlie shakes his head at our immaturity.

"Let me know when you're done laughing like loons. I'll be outside." All this does is set us off once again.

Once we regain our composure, Mark says, "Honestly. Good luck. I hope for Drew's sake it works." He sighs heavily and brushes his pants. "I've got to get back to it." But there's a bounce to his step that wasn't there when he came in. Laughter really is good for the soul.

Charlie pops his head in. "Mark said to give him a minute and he'll turn off the monitors. Turn on the channel on the

TV. Once the screen goes to black, you'll know it's off. Good luck. And thank you for thinking of this. It never occurred to me."

I smile shyly. "I hope it works."

"I'm sure it will." He leaves the room, closing the door tightly behind him.

I get a towel from the bathroom so I can sufficiently cover myself if—no, *when*, Drew regains consciousness and I need to jump out of the bed. The monitor turns black. I wipe my damp palms on my pants and pull back the covers. He's in some sort of drawstring pajama pants. I tug on the string. What a gross violation of privacy. I was so upset at the idea of him doing it to me when he first brought me here. And now I'm doing the same damn thing.

Of course, what I'm doing is even worse. I'll be lying next to him in bed half naked myself. What would have been my reaction if our situations were reversed? I close my eyes, ready to stop. This is a matter of life and death. Mine and his. I open my eyes and continue.

And somehow, I don't think he'll mind.

I tug off his pants, gently, grateful he has boxer shorts on. I'm not sure what I would've done had he been commando. I quickly strip off everything except my bra and underwear and, laying the towel near me, I fluff the blanket and spread it out over Drew. I move his arm out and sit on the bed. There's barely any extra room.

Draping myself over his body in such a way that I can have as much skin-to-skin contact as I can, I situate myself and lay still, tense. I don't want to hurt him or bump the tubes and wires everywhere. I settle myself half over his chest, mindful of the gaping wound inches from my face. One leg is plastered along the length of his and the other draped over him. It's going to be an awkward couple of hours. Amazingly, warmth slides through and over my body, and with the scent of male sweat and gunpowder in my nostrils, I slip in and out of consciousness.

I jerk awake to monitors beeping and Drew struggling in bed. His eyes are wild and panicked. He's attempting to breathe, but the oxygen being pumped directly into his lungs is causing him to strangle on his own autonomous attempt. I jump off and grab the towel, yelling for Charlie.

I get out of the way as soon as Charlie barrels in, standing there helpless, then gather up my clothes and rush to the bathroom to get dressed.

I'm not ready to go out there and face Drew. Turning to the mirror, my jaw drops. There's a slight flush to my cheeks. My eyes are shiny, my skin dewy. I peer closer. My hair looks thicker.

I flex my shoulders, tentatively stretching. No pain. It's as if I've had the best restorative sleep of my life. The contact with Drew didn't just heal him, it healed me, too. My throat no longer feels like the pyres of hell. I slowly brush my teeth and my hair, pulling it into a ponytail. I can't stop staring at my reflection. Unbelievable. I can barely get the elastic around twice. My hair has more than doubled in volume. I fidget with my shirt, pulling at the hem. Charlie hasn't yelled for me. I hope everything is okay.

There's nothing else I can do in here. It's time to face Drew and the obvious elephant in the room. Us. In bed, practically naked, together.

Why me?

I creep out of the bathroom like a squirrel getting ready to run across the road. Except I'm pretty sure I'm going to get run over...by a giant embarrassment car. Heat already spreads over my cheeks.

Charlie's standing next to the bed, talking to Drew, who's still lying down. His color looks good, and the hiss of the life support machine is missing. No tube coming out of his throat.

He looks like his old self. They both turn toward me. Drew's face is inscrutable. I can't tell what he's thinking. Charlie walks over and speaks quietly.

"It worked well. I think you could do more and heal him completely, so I don't have to suture him externally. Get him on his feet faster, but the hole looks to be gone internally. I hope it's mostly gone, anyway. No way of telling right now." His animated voice betrays his medical interest and amazement.

I nod, not taking my eyes off Drew. He hasn't looked away either. Charlie clears his throat.

"I'm, ah, going to update Mark. And I'll make something to eat for us, some soup for you, Drew." He mutters as he walks out the door, and I've no idea what he's saying. I walk over to the chair and sit in it. Drew hasn't said anything yet. I clear my own throat.

"How are you feeling?"

"I feel...fine. Are you okay?"

"I'm fine. Why wouldn't I be? I wasn't the one that got shot!"

"Charlie told me I died. And how you reacted. Are you sure you're okay?" He reaches out some, but lets his hand drop back down. He seems genuinely concerned for me, and I'm astounded by this man's protectiveness. There are no bounds to what he'll do for me, despite everything I've done and how I've treated him.

"I'm fine, really. I, too, healed while I was healing you." I pause. How do I tell him that the knowledge of our souls has changed my life? That his importance has grown drastically? How afraid I was? How afraid I *am now*?

"I didn't know if it would work. Or what I could do to help you. I'm so sorry. I never..."

He pulls my hand in his and the now familiar warmth curls in. Like a long-lost friend, it warms me. "I know everything you've been through the last couple of days is a lot to take in. Believe me when I tell you, you're reacting far better to everything than I can hope for," he says fervently. "I can't thank you enough for what you did. I know that couldn't have been easy for you."

"It was...awkward. I've never even slept with anyone besides Tyson. Literally sleeping, I mean." I glance down. Somehow, our fingers have intertwined.

He laughs quietly. "Well, I'm grateful you chose to do it."

"You stepped in front of a bullet for me." How dare he risk his life? Doesn't he know I can't live without him?

"Two bullets." He grins. "And I'd do it again if I needed to."

"I know." My fingers tighten in his. Our hands feel right together. I still can't believe nor comprehend this level of commitment. Even my own husband hadn't—no. I can't think of that.

I jump up. "I'm going to see if Charlie needs a hand bringing the food in. And I need to check in on Kat." I tug my hand from Drew's grasp and he slowly lets go. "I'll be back soon."

Just as I open the door, Charlie walks in with a tray. He barely looks at me, and I suspect he's awkwardly thinking of Drew and I in bed together.

"Hey, just bringing in some sustenance. Oh, Delaney. Katrina's taking a nap. I thought I'd save you the trip there. Liza's keeping an eye on her and said she won't leave for anything."

"That's perfect. Thank you." I sigh. He's thoughtful, but I wish he hadn't been so right now.

He leaves the tray on the table. "I'm going to go tell Mark to catch a nap. He's got to need it by now." The traitor's leaving me.

"Oh. Thanks." I wasn't planning on hanging out with

Drew, but Charlie has efficiently and effectively removed anything I might've used as an excuse to leave. Sweet man isn't helping me. At all.

"I guess it's you and me."

"Yep, just us."

I pick up a bowl of soup and a spoon and hand it to him. He takes it, studying my face, a small line in between his brows. He looks concerned, but what does he want from me?

The awkwardness stretches the silence.

Finally, he gives an exaggerated sigh and slowly sips at the broth. I sit at the table to eat the thick sandwich Charlie made for me, glancing in his direction beneath half-lowered lids. What am I supposed to say? I liked lying next to you?

The silence yawns uncomfortably. I know he's waiting for me to break it, letting me take the lead. I wish he wouldn't. But at least I can ask him my most pressing question. The whole reason I helped heal him.

"Why do you think they're after Katrina?"

Drew lowers the spoon on its way to his mouth. "Because they never said anything about you. When you walked in on my interview with the mercenary in the garage, he said, 'She's here, too.' Which means two things. One, that somewhere, there's a price on your head, and two, he didn't know you were here. Ergo, they were coming for Katrina."

My heart begins galloping in my chest. A price on my head? They were coming here strictly for Kat? No. No, no, no.

"Maybe they were coming to attack you? You're in the Guardianship. You've got—" I pause, as Drew shakes his head and puts his finger to his lips. "Stuff here."

I switch stone to stuff, remembering at the last second not to say anything about it.

"The cameras are off in here, by the way, for privacy. For me. For earlier." So much for not bringing it up.

"The cameras might be off, but there's staff here. I don't trust anyone one hundred percent, except for you."

"Really? Not even Mark and Charlie?" How sad he lives his life without anyone to trust.

"No one except for you. You, I trust with my life."

I've learned that the hard way. On the one hand, it's incredibly distressing. That kind of responsibility sits heavily on both of us. On the other, it's freeing. To know there's someone you can always rely on with your best interest at heart. To know, no matter what, he'll always have my back.

"And no," he continues. "They weren't coming here for me. They aren't that stupid."

"Right. Well then do you know why they'd be after her?"

"Not that I know of. I was looking through the files before and didn't find anything. Of course, that doesn't mean it's not in there. I'll keep digging. Maternal bias notwithstanding, is there anything special about her? Guardianship wise, I mean. Anything they'd be interested in her for?"

The blood drains out of my face, and horrified, I stare at him.

"You think that's it? That they might have an interest in her? To see if she's like me? No. No, she's never exhibited anything, and surely even with me not remembering anything about the Guardianship, I'd notice."

My fingers tremble and my knees feel like jelly. She can't have any sort of special powers. Can she?

Drew stops eating. "I'm going to go through the records again. I'll get on that as soon as I'm done. And I'll keep thinking. Hopefully, I'll come up with something." He coughs wetly.

"Are you sure you're all right? That doesn't sound good."

"Yeah, I'm sure they'll be some surgery to finish fixing me up." He wheezes slightly. "It's nothing for you to be concerned with."

He avoids looking at me and methodically eats his soup. I narrow my eyes. He's not feeling better, but certainly trying to act like it.

"I could outright ask Katrina, but I'm not sure what I'd be asking."

"No, at her age, unless she had some kind of physical ability like healing, you'd know by now."

"Like Charlie?" What does a Healer actually do?

"Yeah."

"How long do you think they want me to hang out with you?" I ask bluntly. Too bluntly. Drew's face grows somber.

"I don't know. Why don't you lay on the couch and get some rest? Before you do, can you hand me the remotes in the screen cabinet and the portable keyboard?"

"Sure."

He somehow transfers the screen from the TV to the monitor next to his bed, replacing the vital signs that had been showing on it. I shake my head. The tech will never cease to amaze me. I lay on the sofa, trying to get comfortable. There's no way I'll be able to sleep with him in here. My body is way too attuned to his.

He taps away on the keyboard, and at some point, it lulls me to sleep.

I dream of chaos and murder, of a world gone dark. Everything has lost all meaning except for one thing. Katrina. She stands like a beacon of hope. Like some divine angel, pale and beautiful. Lit from within till she's a pale version of herself. She's so bright, I shield my eyes from her.

When I wake up in a cold sweat, panting, in the darkened room, Drew's sound asleep, softly snoring. The keyboard is still on his lap and the monitor by his bedside dark.

What the hell did I just see? Am I paranoid? Scared?

Please. Let it be anything but a vision.

Chapter Twenty-Four

DELANEY

I'm torn with the need to check on Katrina, but I don't want to leave Drew. I'm not sure what he'd done earlier, but I hope I can still see on the TV screen the monitors for the other rooms. I open the cabinet and turn the screen on. Thankfully, the soft glow shows the regular screens. I click through until I find her room. Both Kat and Liza sit on the couch engrossed in a movie.

I breathe a sigh of relief. No glowing child. No world filled with destruction. I turn off the monitor and turn around. Drew sits up.

"Shit!" My hand presses on my chest. "You scared me half to death. I thought you were sleeping." I inhale and exhale, trying to slow my racing heart.

"I'm sorry. I didn't mean to scare you. I'm a light sleeper."

"I didn't mean to wake you. I wanted to check on Kat." I frown. He needs to rest.

"No problem. Really."

"Did you find anything in the files?"

"No. Nothing in the entire file from Tyson and no file made for her either. She's barely a blip on the radar. What bothers me is that I can't figure out the end game for you either. I don't know why they kept you under surveillance for so long."

"Don't look at me. I've no idea."

I head to the table and pour some juice for myself. "Want some?" I ask, turning around. My mouth goes dry. Drew's out of bed and putting on the pants I'd removed earlier. The muscles in his arms bunch and move under the skin and his hamstrings tighten as he bends down. I can't ignore the fluttering in my belly at the memory of his skin against mine.

"Yeah, if you don't mind, whatever it is you've got there."

I whip my head back around to give him the privacy he deserves. He shouldn't be ogled like some candy dish. At least, not when he's recovering from a gunshot wound. I clear my throat.

"Are you dressed yet?"

"It's taking me a minute. I'm woozy, probably from laying inert for so long. But I've got to pee, and I'm sure you'd rather me do that in privacy."

"Do you need help getting dressed?"

Please don't need help. Please don't need help. I'm not sure I can kneel in front of him and put his pants on without the thoughts running through my head showing clearly on my face.

"I think I've got it now."

Grateful, I turn around and watch as he gradually shuffles his way to the bathroom. Mm. That ass though. What is wrong with me? The man's clearly not feeling well!

Be normal, nothing to see here. Normal woman pouring juice. And when the bathroom door opens, I don't look. I'd rather him be in the bed covering his lean, flat stomach with a sheet. I *don't* need to be staring at it, practically drooling.

"Delaney."

"Yeah?" My voice sounds breathless. Dammit.

"Can you help me? I don't think I can make it back into the bed without passing out on the floor."

I run to his side, terrified by the miniscule hole in his chest openly bleeding. I place my arm around his waist and put his arm around my shoulder. I won't think about the usual warmth that courses through me or the silky feel of his skin beneath my hand or the steel band of muscle wrapped around my upper body. No. I'm going to think about helping a weak, bleeding man. My knees are shaky again. We're both panting by the time we get to the bed, and I gently help him in. He's solid muscle, and the way it bunches under my hands has my heart rate up too fast. Maybe he won't notice.

"I'm going to call Charlie to look at that."

"No." Drew grabs my hand, and more heat shoots through me.

"Why not? You need medical attention, and I can't help you." And I can't keep staying here.

"Because he needs to rest. When they attack again, he'll need to be able to protect you. I'm not going to be of much use. And I can deal with the pain."

When, not if. A trembling starts within me and has nothing to do with his nearly perfect body. Fear for Katrina replaces the horniness, just like that.

"When do you think they'll attack?" I glance around the room, as if I can spot them coming.

"If it were me, it would be now, already. So we plan for any moment now."

"Are the guys capable of staving them off?" I'm sure they'll do a good job, but I also know how much they'll be missing with Drew down. Will I need to step in?

"They're capable. By now, they'll have reset most of the defensive devices. They should be able to handle the same amount we had last time."

They had a one-man army with them then. I know

because I watched the playbacks. They were all capable, but Drew had more at stake. And that made him far more dangerous.

I can't risk Katrina, not for should and should nots. I quickly make my decision.

"I'd like to kiss you. See if you can heal more. Will that be enough?" My breathing speeds up. What if he needs more than a kiss?

A strange mixture of desire and need crosses his face. "You don't have to do that. You and your daughter will be protected. This house is secure and fully stocked. We could wait them out for weeks if need be."

The thought of being stuck in the mountain for days on end sends a shudder through me.

"I know. But I'd feel better if you were on the mend. I need you running at one hundred percent too."

Is this want he needs or what I want?

"If you're sure, I'm not going to turn it down." Drew grins. My heart flip-flops, my soul dances, and my palms sweat. I walk over and stand at the side of the bed. My fingers twist together. Should I kiss him, or will he take the lead?

Drew's expression turns serious. "It would be more enjoyable if you didn't look like you're headed to an executioner."

"I'm sorry. Kissing you is...unfamiliar." And exciting. The last thing I want to do is throw myself at him like someone who's been without sex for a good long while. Which I am, but he doesn't need to know that.

"But it's not." He grabs both of my hands. "We've kissed before. Even before I lost you the first time. You're overthinking it. It's just a kiss. Relax."

Just a kiss? Suddenly, panic rolls through me. I wasn't enough for Tyson to want to marry for real. I haven't had many dates since he died. What if I'm not a good kisser? What if Drew is disappointed? I've just gone from desperate with need to just plain desperate.

"Can we get this over with?"

Drew sits up higher in the bed and scoots over, as much as possible, making room for me to sit. He pats a spot on the bed. I stare at it before sitting. Nervous, my fingers twist and turn.

He reaches out and softly strokes the length of my hair. "Close your eyes."

My eyelids flutter, but it's hard to keep them shut. I want to peek out and see what he's doing. He continues to play with my hair for several seconds. I wait, but nothing happens. My back hurts from holding myself stiffly. My body droops gently.

Slowly, softly, he caresses my cheek. The warmth of his touch invades my body, and I turn my face into heat. Cupping the side of my head, his fingers near the base of my skull, and he gently tugs me forward. I lean closer.

A whisper of breath flits across my skin. The stubble of his cheek grazes mine. The sensations leave, only to be replaced by barely-there, airy kisses. I'm not sure he's even touching his lips to my skin. My body pulls in, drawn by need.

He inhales, gently sniffing my skin. The scent of sweat, blood, and Drew wisps into my nostrils. Slightly spicy, hot. He invades my personal space in such a slow and sinuous manner, my body accepts without conscious thought. I lick my lips in anticipation, my teeth catching slightly on the skin. The warmth curls in my stomach and my underwear dampens. I'm like a teenager at her first make-out session.

Light kisses trail down my neck and back up to my jaw. His lips graze mine with the barest space in between us. I shiver, my nipples hardening. I tilt forward again. Any farther and I'll be crawling onto him. He kisses the other side of my cheek, neck, and jaw. Repeating each movement, silently asking for permission.

Yes, dammit, yes.

Accepting him, I turn, meeting his lips with mine. Fire lights up in me capable of warming the earth. Liquid heat melts any resistance I may have had, and I lift my arms, gripping the back of his head. I drive my fingers through his hair, pulling him to me. More. I want more.

Our breaths mingle and our tongues dance in an ancient rhythm. Hot and wet, the familiar ritual leaves no room for shock. My heart pounds in time to his. I curl my fingers harder into his hair, the silkiness of it contrasted by his rough facial stubble. Seconds turn into minutes and the inferno rages in me. Soft kisses change to a hard mashing of lips, tongues darting out, licking. I can't focus on any one thing.

Kisses turning back to softness, breathy promises of pleasure. Desire barrels through my veins. Sweat glides on my skin from the heat. I lean closer, pressing against him as much as I'm able, desperation in the movement. Why did I think we couldn't have sex? Pure, hot sex. Yes please. I groan, my hands sliding down his neck and gripping his shoulders. Pulling him closer. At *his* groan, I remember his injuries and pull my lips away. Did I hurt him?

Panting, I stare at his shoulder. His perfect shoulder. The flames recede from my body. The world crystalizes into focus. His skin is unmarred.

The hole is completely healed. My eyes travel, taking him in. Drew's eyes are heavy-lidded with satisfaction evident on his face, desire evident in his lap. I jump up.

My fingers to my lips, I back away. Drew looks sexy as hell. Hair rumpled, lips swollen and completely healed, even the shadows under his eyes are gone. I'm sure I look the same, healthy and dewy and oh, so satisfied. That cat that got into the cream. And dove into it, headfirst.

"I don't even know what just happened. I didn't mean to let it get so…" I trail off because how do I put words to such an experience? I can't believe it.

Drew jumps out of bed, and I back into the cabinet.

"Why are you afraid of me?"

Voice low, the timbre of it rough from desire, echoes through me. He leans in, and I lean back. "I'm not afraid of you." I don't consider leaning on the cabinet a form of assistance.

"Then why do you keep backing away until you have nowhere to go?"

"Because. Because...I don't know why. Because I'm afraid you'll kiss me again."

"And if I do?" He frames my head, trapping me against the unyielding cabinet.

"I don't want you to kiss me again."

Yes, I do.

But I shouldn't. Should I? I'm supposed to be thinking of Katrina. Yes, her safety. I should be remembering all the things. Not *doing* all the things.

"You don't? Maybe *you* want to kiss *me*. It sure seemed like you liked it."

"I was only doing it to help you heal. And since you're healed, we won't need to repeat this."

Why not?

Because I had a husband who didn't actually marry me and didn't love me. And maybe that means something is wrong with me. Maybe I'm the problem. My stomach clenches. Why am I thinking about Tyson? His death five years ago was hard, but this new betrayal of his hits even harder. I step forward minutely, in the only space left, and stand my ground. My body wants to lean into him.

"Well then, thank you for your services."

He pads out, barefooted. I slide into a boneless heap on the floor. That's not how this should've gone.

DREW

I leave the room with a bounce in my step. She can't hide her attraction for me. And we're all still here. So far, she's held up against all the information I've bombarded her with and the death of me. This has to count for something. It has to.

And I feel great. She feels great. In my arms. Right where she should be.

This Delaney is the one, I know it. Finally, I'll have answers on what the hell happened. Why she put us all on this path. It's been a long time coming.

"Holy shit, man! You look great. All that from lying next to a pretty woman? Man, I need to get me one." Mark strides down the hallway and claps me on the back. "It's great to see you up and around. Charlie held out on me—he said you still weren't a hundred percent."

He looks tired. I know the guys have been worried about me. They know my priority is Delaney, and the responsibility of that must've lay heavy on them when I was down for the count.

"It's good to be a hundred percent. No, he didn't hold out on you. I got up too soon and tore the hole in my chest. It was bleeding enough that Delaney felt she should do more."

"Oh, like that is it?"

"Now, you know I'm not going to give you the particulars. You need to get yourself someone."

"Nah, I'll live vicariously through you. You couldn't pay me for that shit. You should've seen her. She wouldn't stop screaming. So loud I thought my eardrums were gonna burst. I'm going to be hearing that in my sleep." He shakes his head. "Nope. Definitely not for me."

I frown. I have more than an idea, of course. I'm jaded. It's getting to be too common for me to feel that anguish—and learn to ignore it till it's shades of what it was. But I remember those first days when Delaney killed herself. I remember the agony of my soul ripping me to pieces, pissed the other half was gone.

"We all grieve differently."

The sickening pit of my stomach contracts at the thought she had to live through it. This is one battle I couldn't face for her, and it's clawing its way through me.

"Hey, man, it was quick. Charlie moved real fast, getting your ticker up and running again. I tried to soothe her as much as possible. Yeah, yeah, I was sitting on the floor patting her back. Not that it did a damn thing."

"It's the thought that counts. Thanks for that. He's still sleeping?"

"Yeah, I'm getting ready to run some eggs into an omelet for Liza.

"Do you mind making some for Delaney and myself, too?"

"No problem, was going to do it anyway."

"Thanks. I'll be in my room. I have to shower and get some of this hospital bed off me. I've got work on the computer. Delaney will more than likely be with her daughter. Once you're done there, go catch some sleep. I'll keep watch till Charlie gets up."

"Sounds good. Hey. I'm glad you didn't die, man." And that's as close as he'd get to letting me know he'd miss me. I nod and head up to my room. I desperately need a shower.

A cold one.

DELANEY

My pounding heart slows. When it's at a more normal rhythm, I slowly gather myself and head to Kat's room. Mark's just coming out.

"Perfect timing. I dropped some grub for Liza and

Katrina. There's some extra in there for you. Drew said you'd probably be in there. It ain't nothing special though. Charlie's sleeping. But I do make a mean omelet."

"Thanks. I appreciate it." My stomach rumbles in anticipation. The downside to a fast metabolism. I keep walking.

"Hey, Delaney?" Mark's eyebrows wing up, but his mouth is drawn into a frown, and I wonder what he's trying so hard to say.

"Thanks for healing Drew. That's decent of you. I feel better knowing he's up and running by our side."

How difficult it must be to always try for a stereotypical macho look, scared to seem emotional or less than. Sympathy spreads through me, and I tip my head in acknowledgment. "I couldn't sit by and do nothing. I'm glad it worked."

Liza nods to Kat and points at her plate, and she stops talking long enough to shovel some eggs into her mouth before she continues whatever conversation they are having. My throat thickens, but I refuse to allow any tears to fall. It's not the time to deal with the emotions of what's happening. The rage that Kat has to stay trapped in a room until I can figure out a safe way out of here and out of the Guardianship's radar bleeds through me. I need to focus and redouble my efforts on regaining my memories. I need to train.

Liza looks up and smiles and I mouth, "Thank you," and silently back out. It makes it easier to know she's with Kat. You can always tell when someone genuinely likes children, and I'm grateful Drew has her on staff. I haven't been attentive to Kat at all. And I won't. I *have* to figure out why they're coming after her. I don't have time for cuddles, as harsh as that is. With Liza here with her, I don't have to feel as guilty for doing my job as a mom. Protecting her at all costs.

My shower leaves me with too much silence and my mind wanders to Drew. Kissing him was an eye-opener. Nothing I've felt with Tyson compares to what I feel with him. More than the attraction, it's...a familiarity. And I know that sounds out of this world, but so has everything that's happened.

I flop onto the bed. I'm no longer tired after our kissing match. It seems I'm re-energized. Can I help Drew find out what the agenda is from the Guardianship? No. I know next to nothing about the entire group. Energy buzzes inside of me until I can't stand it. I head to the training room to run a virtual reality program and practice some more. I despise being a drain on this team.

I'm not there long when Drew joins me.

"Looking for something to burn off that energy?" A smile dances on his lips.

I know a double entendre when I see one, but I refuse to acknowledge it. "I was hoping to do some training. See if anything jars my memory."

He clasps his hands behind his back, seeming to consider options.

"Let's see if there's anything you remember offensively."

My eyebrows wing up and adrenaline races through me.

Oh, yes.

I'm going to kick some Guardianship ass, and it would be spectacularly helpful for me to remember how to do that.

He stands facing me. "Throw a punch."

"Like, at your face?" I frown, but he nods. "Just remember, you asked for it."

I ball my fist and throw it forward. He moves his head sideways and my punch misses his face by several inches.

"You've got to move faster than that. Don't hesitate. If your first one misses, your other fist should be backing it up from the other side. Whoever you're hitting isn't going to stand there and wait for you to try again. They're going to block you and attack. Again."

I punch a second time, but this time I follow through with

the other fist. Both miss him as he ducks one way and then the other.

"This is ridiculous. I don't remember, and you're adept at deflecting. What's this going to remind me of?" Anger and frustration sizzles in my veins.

He sighs. "You're right. It's not. If you'd like, I can show you some maneuvers on the mat and let you practice them. Muscle memory will assist you. I've got work to do anyway."

He demonstrates several movements and leaves. I'm hopeful but cautiously so. Nothing so far has worked. I spend an hour working up a sweat in the training room. It doesn't help. I don't remember any of this and blunder through. I pound my fist onto the floor mat. This is hopeless. And now I need another shower. Plus, my hands are shaking from overworking them. I should just give up. Looks like I wasn't good enough to be a wife and apparently not good enough to be a Guardian.

I run into Charlie on my way up the stairs. "Getting a workout in? What, is Drew rubbing off on you? Or is he putting you to work? Either way, you tell him you need your rest, too." His shrewd gaze drifts to my hands. "When's the last time you ate?"

"I don't know...the sandwich you sent to the hospital room?"

"You didn't eat the omelet Mark made?"

"No. I wasn't hungry, and I was too worried about...things."

"Lady, you have to eat. Don't want to end up in the hospital bed, too, do you?"

"Yes, sir." I salute. "As soon as I'm done with my shower, I'll come to the dining room."

My head swivels too fast and my hand reaches out to grip the banister of the stairway as the room spins. I don't say anything and neither does Charlie. Maybe he didn't notice.

Back in the shower, hot water pounds my back and steam billows around me. With eyes closed, I rest my head on the wall.

Suddenly, my vision darkens, and I grip the bar hard and slide down the wall. I'm lucky I don't drop like a bag of stone and crack my head. I weakly slump on the floor of the tub. My vision darkens more until I barely see. I open my mouth, but no sound emerges, and my eyes flutter shut.

Chapter Twenty-Five

DREW

My cell vibrates and my stomach clenches when Charlie's name pops on the screen.

"What's wrong?"

"I passed Delaney on the stairs. You might want to check on her. I'm going to bring her up some juice and fruit. She was pale and shaky. She told me she hasn't eaten since she had a sandwich earlier. I'm sorry. I should've made sure she ate before I went to bed."

"Don't apologize. Meet me in her room. I'm on my way now." I hang up, shoving my cell into the pocket as I dart up the stairs. Different Guardians have different health issues. Both of us have high metabolisms and need fuel constantly.

If we don't get it, we end up in something like hypoglycemic shock, somewhat like diabetics. I hope she doesn't pass out somewhere.

Or die.

I push my legs faster, taking the stairs two at a time. I skid into her room to the sound of the shower running. Damn, like it isn't hard enough to be in her presence as it is.

Karma is laughing, I know it.

The steam billowing out of the bathroom spurs me on faster. The obvious heat of the shower won't help her state at all. I grab the towel hanging up and rip open the shower curtain. She's sitting on the floor of the tub, leaning against the shower wall, her legs splayed. I turn off the water and cover her with the towel, refusing to look anywhere in particular on her naked body.

"Delaney."

Taking her face in my hands, I rub her cheeks with my thumbs. So soft. Her eyes squint open. "Hey, that's good. Open your eyes. Stay with me here. I'm getting you a juice to drink. Okay?"

Her eyes flutter and her head lolls to the other side. Panic sinks its claws into me. Dammit. I'm not going to lose her to low blood sugar of all things. My hands move to her wet shoulders, and I shake her. The heat slides between us, and for the first time, I curse it, knowing it will only bring her body temperature up.

"Pay attention! You want me to haul your naked ass out of there? Or you coming out yourself?"

Her eyes flutter again, and she tries to straighten her head. That's good. "That's fine. You don't mind then. I'll just sit right here and get my fill of looking at you. Nothing I like better than to carry a naked woman into bed."

That's it, tell her I'm an asshole.

She opens her eyes wider. Through the narrow slits, her pupils are constricted into tiny specks. She forces her head up straighter. Charlie hands me a bottle of juice with a straw in it, his face averted.

"I'll just stay out in the hallway." He backpedals as fast as he can.

"Here, take a couple of sips." I guide the straw to her lips, and she pulls and swallows. "More." She drinks again and moves her head away.

"No, no. You need to drink at least half of this, just to allow you to stand up."

With a groan, she turns her head and opens her mouth. I insert the straw again. Some of the liquid disappears from the bottle. I wait a few seconds. The worry clawing through my chest finally evaporates along with the return of her color.

"Can you stand up on your own? I'll keep the towel up."

"I can get up and you better not look."

Her voice is faint, but at least I hear it. My heart slows out of its hectic racing. She's going to be fine. Rage seeps in. How dare she not take care of herself? I clench my jaw tightly to stop myself from spewing out words and then release it.

"A few more sips."

She weakly reaches for the bottle, and I hand it to her, making sure she brings it to her mouth. My eyes wander to where the towel slips at her breast. Why is it I can never stop wanting her, no matter how dire the situation is? On the one hand, I hope it never stops, on the other I know she'd kill me if she only knew. Soul mate or no soul mate.

Delaney stands up shakily, one hand at the towel, another at the bar. I reach across the rim of the tub and grab the towel ends, holding them securely in one hand and assisting her with the other.

Slowly, we walk out to the bedroom, and I sit her at the table. I retrieve another towel from the bathroom and dry her hair. If I don't focus on taking care of her, I'm going to yell at her. And that will get us nowhere. I swallow some of my anger.

"Charlie brought this fruit. I need you to eat all of it and finish that juice. You should feel better shortly. Then I'm going to make you sit and eat. You have to make sure you eat more often."

"I know. I didn't feel like it with everything going on. I'm emotionally drained."

My hands fist in the towel. "That's not an excuse. You need to eat every couple of hours. You can't afford to skip any meals."

"Yes. I get it. I said I already know. I'll make sure I eat more."

She doesn't *get it* and I'm tired of pulling my punches. I'm tired of being nice. And I'm tired of being backed into a corner, tiptoeing around every version of Delaney and still coming up short.

If I'm going to lose my soul, fine. I'm done with it. Fuck it all. Someone else can take over trying to spare the world of being brought to its knees.

"No, you don't." I slap the towel onto the table. "You don't remember this life. You don't remember who you are and what you are. You don't understand the gravity of you being here. No. You don't get any of it. Let me apprise you.

"When you killed yourself and set me on this path, you did so for a reason. You don't know the reason, I don't know the reason. But you keep trying to end the world, and I know damn well that wasn't why. I keep turning back time to prevent that. But there's a price. Besides what I've told you before, I also lose a piece of my soul. *A piece of my soul.* Do you understand what that means?" I yell, picking the towel back up and throwing it across the room.

She stares without comprehension. Of course, she does. I'm disgusted with myself. Why do I keep thinking if I just tell her, everything will be fine? Am I trying to push her to the brink of madness? The anger drains as quickly as it built.

I flop onto her bed, my shoulders sagging. What does it matter anymore? "It means I'm losing a piece of my soul each time I turn back time. I don't know how big these pieces are. My soul isn't infinite. At some point, I'll barter the last piece. And when it's gone, I'll be dead. And in time, you'll end the world without it having any protection *or* you'll be in horrific pain until you succumb. That could be days, it could be years. Depends how strong you are."

Finally, horror shines in her eyes. At the least, she understands what that means for her.

I'm such a dick.

"Yeah. You should be scared. On multiple levels. Regardless, we have to figure it out and soon. I know I'm getting close. I've lost a good portion of my humanity, my compassion. I can feel it. We're running out of time. And I can't fucking afford to lose a piece of my soul because you died from hypoglycemia.

"You. Have. To. Eat. You have to pay attention to your body. I'm not willing to let you die for some dumb shit. We've got bigger things to worry about."

DELANEY

I can't leave Kat without a mom, and I can't live without Drew. "I'm sorry. I know it's not just me at stake. You, the world, Kat. I'll do better. Set a timer or something. I never knew I was hypoglycemic. I always eat, because I love food."

"We have a fast metabolism. And we aren't hypoglycemic like people with diabetes, we just literally burn through our fuel and our bodies need it. If Charlie hadn't seen you and noticed your hands shaking, he would've never alerted me. You would've been dead in the tub before anyone found you. It's important."

I understand what he's saying, and I already feel better than I did earlier today. Clearly, the sugar makes a huge difference. Guilt piles on top of what was already there. That's all I need.

"Let me get dressed and I'll eat. Then we can discuss how we can open up the jar of memories in my head. I'm tired of waiting for it to unscrew itself."

Plus, I don't want to die. I like being alive. And I like being with him.

"I'll be downstairs waiting. Don't take long, that fruit won't last in your system."

He leaves, and I hurriedly get dressed. I can't believe I almost died because I did something so stupid as not eat. I can't risk leaving Kat alone. Even without the Guardianship after her. She needs me. Drew needs me.

Charlie went full out, preparing a massive meal. Huge cheeseburgers with all the fixings; lettuce, tomato, raw onions, pickles, avocado, and topped with crispy bacon. Sweet potato fries and coleslaw rival any five-star restaurant on the side.

I can't shove the food fast enough into my mouth. There's nothing delicate about the amount of food I eat. Drew eats the same obscene amount. I've never noticed it. Tyson used to make fun of me for how much I ate and how I worshipped food.

"Why is it that Tyson didn't eat like us? I thought you said Guardians metabolize food quickly?"

"We do. Not everyone in the Guardianship is equal. He probably doesn't have the metabolism we do. Different abilities have different needs, talents. We're all different and it's all secretive. The Guardianship has long kept everything silent. Like Turners. No one knows much about them. I think that's something that needs to change. I've been keeping journals of what I've learned from Guardians like Charlie, Mark, and others I've encountered. The one good thing out of my time here is that I've been able to see far more than otherwise."

"That's good though, right? I mean, you can't protect us if other people know what you're capable of?"

"It does have its benefits," he concedes.

"Is there *anything* you've thought of that I can do to jar my memories loose?"

"Not that I've been able to find yet. Every version of you is different. I'm always starting from scratch. I don't know how many different variables there are, nor do I know what's different about you. Do I do the same things and hope that you're different or do things differently and hope the outcome changes? I always pick changing it up. I can't afford to keep making the same mistakes. Some of the things are the same, by default. Like the blueprints for this house. You wrote me a note asking to build it secretly. That's not something I can change, ever."

My heart breaks for him again. He's built this house thirteen times and killed the builder thirteen times. What toll must that have placed on him? I don't think I'm a nice person.

To put my own soul mate through several circles of torture, to condemn him to giving up a piece of his soul over and over and to relive the pain of losing me is too much. There's no excuse. I'm an asshole.

"Maybe we should talk about what you've done?" I stop at the negative shake.

"That's a waste of time. Nothing I've done is right. If we were to repeat it, it wouldn't change anything, and I can't risk it turning out the same."

"But everything you've said before pointed to me being different this time around, right?"

"Well, yes. You've never known this much, all of it really, without diving off the deep end. I don't know why you're able to handle it now." He frowns. His hand runs through his hair and down his neck.

"Thirteen!"

"What?" he asks, confused.

"Thirteen. It's my lucky number. Don't lots of myths refer to things like that? Was my lucky number thirteen then too?"

Excitement weaves onto his face, making him seem less

tired. "Yes! Maybe this is it? This version is the one I'm supposed to have found?"

Thank the fates my lucky number wasn't seventy.

"Can you think of anything that also is the same before and now, that wasn't in the other Delaneys?" It's so weird to think of myself in the third person.

He rubs his neck, turning it red from the friction and the pressure. If he could rip the information from himself, he would. I know.

"The only other thing I can think of is, I noticed just over your towel, you have a tattoo on your ribcage. It's the same place mine is."

He gets up and goes to the alcohol cabinet. He pulls out the never-ending bottle of amber liquid. How many bottles does he go through?

"Do you want any?"

"Thank you, no. I'm not a huge fan of bourbon."

"Ah, but this isn't a bourbon. Try it." He pours me a couple of inches or so into a glass and hands it over. "Smell it."

I bring the glass to my nose and inhale. "Apple pie?" I bring the glass to my lips and tilt my head back.

"Don't...drink that in one shot."

"Holy shit!" I sputter, gasping in air. "Damn that's strong." Tears stream from eyes, as I valiantly battle the alcohol currently burning a trail down my esophagus.

"You just downed several shots of Tennessee's best, Ole Smoky Apple Pie Moonshine, like it was water. Here." He hands me a piece of cheese.

I chew the cheddar cube and sip some of my water until my eyes stop watering. The moonshine has now pooled in my stomach similarly to the way I feel when I'm touching Drew. It simmers.

"Next time, sip it." He pours me an inch. Just in case, I'm sure.

I sip the smallest sip. When it's not trying to set my throat afire, it's surprisingly smooth and flavorful. "It's good. But I think I'm done with the alcohol for today." I giggle, slightly woozy.

"With what you drank, give it a couple of minutes. It'll no longer be in your bloodstream."

He sounds sad. How awful that he can't even rely on alcohol to numb him. Now I realize the snide judgments I made were extremely privileged. I had no idea of the pain, yet, that he must feel.

"Anyway. The tattoo is one you made me promise to get. After one of your nightmares, before...you died. I kept my promise as soon as I could. You had gotten one as well, though I don't know how that was possible. You never left the house and yet, you had one on your body when you died. I don't know if the one you have is the one you had. What does yours say?"

"It says, 'Wait for me.'"

He closes his eyes and exhales. "That's what it said then, too." He sits in silence for a moment. "How is it you got those words tattooed?"

I laugh. "On a dare one day, my friend and I went to the tattoo shop. We were supposed to get anything the tattoo guy recommended. We snuck out of the house and lied about our ages. My friend flirted hard core with him and we ended up with free tats. The only thing I said was I didn't want any flowers. And this is what he tattooed on me.

"At the time, I thought it was ridiculous, but then I thought it was kind of poetic. And it was better than my friend's tattoo which ended up being the overdone butterfly. I saw when we were lying together yours says, 'And time goes by so slowly. And time can do so much.' I guess I can see how prophetic that is now."

His eyes widen. "You don't know the words?"

I shake my head. "Am I supposed to?"

"It's a line from 'Unchained Melody.'"

"I've never heard it."

"You should listen to it when you get a chance. You loved that song. It's considered old-fashioned, but you loved it regardless."

"That's two things, I think. So, we go on the assumption that I'm it. This...this version of me."

Shit.

The fate of the world, of Drew, of Katrina are in my hands.

I want to cry. Instead, I scream as the house rattles from a blast. Drew leaps over the table and throws me back, chair and all on the floor.

"Stay low and get to the bookcases. The windows should hold, as long as they aren't using rocket launchers." He pushes me and we stand up, bent over double, racing out of the room. He's already on his phone, yelling to someone to get into the war room. I straighten as we pass the staircase and run to the bookcase.

I hate wasting precious seconds being scanned, but at the same time glad that anyone can't just stroll in and get to Katrina. I run down the stairs to the next level. Liza's holding her in her arms and stares with eyes wide. "Everything ok?"

I nod, quickly running up to them and giving Kat a hug and a kiss. My arms tighten around her fiercely. I want to stand here, plant myself in front of her door armed to the teeth and mow down anyone who even thinks about harming her. "You stay here and play with Ms. Liza, all right, darling? I'll be back soon."

"Momma, stay with me."

Her words etch themselves in my head and fear lances through me. I feel like I'm going to get sick, but I can't. I have to be the strong one. For her.

"I'll be back soon, baby. I promise." Should I be making such promises? What if I can't keep them? The bile burns in my throat. No. I *have* to do this.

I lean in and whisper in Liza's ear. "I think we may be under attack. You should probably be safe here."

I scan the room. Would Liza need a weapon if something happened to allow a breach? I turn to ask her and nearly laugh. Liza's pressing numbers into her cell phone and a mirror on the wall swings open revealing a large safe. I don't know why I expected anything else. She puts Kat down and whispers something to her. My baby skips to the play area and pulls out some dolls from a cabinet. While she's occupied, Liza briskly walks over and punches a number into the keypad of the safe.

It opens, revealing a small arsenal of weaponry. Several handguns are mounted to the door and knives lay on what looks like velvet. There's probably more, but I'm sure it's sufficient. Liza pulls out a handgun, puts a magazine in and tucks it into her pants.

"I'll make sure no one gets to her."

Her chin raises, and I wonder if I've met another Guardian member. Drew seems to have surrounded himself with them.

"Thank you." I run out of Katrina's room and call Drew. "Where do you want me?"

"I'd rather you stay behind the bookcase, but I'm guessing that's too much to ask you to do. If you want to be here, meet us in the war room."

The sound of silence rings in my ear. He never told me where it is.

Since he never came in with me, it must be on the main side. As I head to the front of the house and notice a door next to the stairs, I open it and step into what's unequivocally a war room.

Monitors line the entire room. A console in the middle serves as the cockpit. A long counter stretches out next to it. I watch in horror as the screens show a vast number of people running through the woods outside. Some are getting shot, some convulsing with some unseen force before falling over. One thing is clear.

They just keep coming.

Mark's talking into a cellphone to somebody else, Charlie's on a walkie-talkie, and Drew's standing, slowly turning and surveying each monitor, over and over. I don't know how he had the time to strap weapons to his body, but all of them are armed and prepared for an invasion.

It's here.

I walk over and, panicked, slip my hand into his. He doesn't acknowledge me other than a tightening of his grip. The warmth that runs through me does manage to calm me down enough that I don't hyperventilate. I find myself turning slowly with him. I'm near dizzy with the constant revolutions, but I'm not willing to let go on my grip of comfort.

"Are we going to make it?" I'm petrified of what he'll say.

"We'll be fine. Nothing we can't handle. I'll want you to stay in here though, if we must go out again. Promise me you won't leave."

"I can't promise you without knowing what's going to happen, but I promise to stay here, if you don't need me."

"I *need* you to stay here and remain safe."

"I know. And I want to stay here for Kat, too. But I can't promise you if something isn't happening to you that I won't help." I turn my head and he stops.

We're standing shoulder to shoulder, like a wide shield. Both of us sure of our footing and where we stand on things. He nods. "Fair enough."

I release my breath. I expected to fight for what I want. Too many habits to break from everything I've known. But he treats me like I'm his equal, even though I don't remember if I am.

"Don't get yourself in a situation where I have to assist."

He squeezes my hand and lets it go, the warmth rudely leaving me to the sick feeling of panic. He walks to the counter and presses a hand to the palm reader. It opens a long drawer. In it are various weapons. He waves, indicating I should partake of whatever I'd like as his gaze remains on the monitors, constantly assessing.

"Charlie. Some men should go around the side of the garage and see if they can draw some away and over to the shack." I look up as he relays Drew's message to someone on the other end of the walkie-talkie.

Charlie moves over to a monitor, and we observe three men shooting their guns in a random area and run to the east. My eyes narrow. They look unprofessional as they run out into the open and make no move to be stealthy. My eyes track Charlie as he moves over to another set of monitors and we both see the men enter a shack-like building.

Dread fills me as a dozen men surround the building, and I gasp as realization finally strikes. This is a suicide mission for our three guys. The intruders open fire on the shack, riddling it with bullets. I'm horrified when it erupts in a blast, taking out all twelve men. I turn my head toward Drew willing him to look at me. To acknowledge what I just witnessed. He continues to watch another screen, and the muscle at his jaw jumps several times before he responds.

"It's them or you and Katrina. I'll pick them every time."

My stomach churns and tears prick my eyes. What do I even say to that? I can't very well say pick me or Kat. My hands shake, and I'm not sure my legs can keep me up. I hate that I want to agree with him.

After a minute of silence, he finally looks at me. His eyes are sad, but also flat and predatory. There's no doubt he'll do *whatever* it takes to keep me safe. The responsibility of his actions weighs heavily on my conscience. How much guilt can my shoulders stand before I break?

Mark yells over. "Several have made it to the courtyard. They're yelling for us."

"Turn on the audio."

"...bring her out and we won't burn down the building. I repeat. This is Guardianship business. Bring out Delaney Naasgoo and her child and you'll be free of Guardianship penalties. No harm shall befall you. If you don't bring her out, we'll burn down the building and smoke you out. Everyone except for her and her child will be shot and killed."

I jerk at my maiden name. The Guardianship doesn't consider me married since I never was. I hadn't been referred to it in years.

"I'd like them to try. Bring it. This place is fireproof." Mark scoffs, ready to tackle them all. The idea that the men I've gotten to know and like would be shot because of me sits like a stone around my neck.

"Delaney!" My head jerks up at the familiar voice and my heart pounds erratically. *No.*

"Delaney, I know you're in there. Do you want the death of everyone protecting you to be your fault?"

"Tyson." I breathe out his name, the blood draining from my face. I *hadn't* imagined I'd seen him on that footage. He's alive. Grief and rage war within me. I want to hug him fiercely and ask him how it's possible and I want to hit him for everything he did in the past. For what he's doing now.

"I'll kill him." Drew's body is wired tight, and if I thought he could get angry before, I underestimated him. The man standing before me isn't the Drew I know. *This* man is a killer. A weapon without the capability of understanding mercy.

Fear bubbles up to add to my mix of emotions. "No. He's Kat's father. No matter what he did, why he lied, he's still the father of my *child*. I can't let you kill him." Hurt him, maybe, but now's not the right time.

There's a manic look in his eyes. I step forward, knowing I'm risking being shoved aside. I put my hand on his arm.

"Please." The crazed look leaves like a slow tide out. "I need to talk to him."

"No." The steel is back in his eyes. Like metal, he's unyielding.

"Maybe he'll give me information. We can find out something. It's a risk, but I trust you not to let me get hurt."

He's quiet for a few seconds, his jaw clenching and unclenching. "You stay behind me the whole time."

"I will." Panic bubbles inside me and my stomach rolls with a sick feeling. I don't know why I'm feeling all these things. I want to hate Ty, but strangely, I don't. "Don't kill him. No matter what. Please don't." I swallow hard. I'm desperate and I don't understand it. I should want to hurt him. "For me." Drew sighs deeply. I'm asking a lot of him, I know. "Please. Promise me."

"I can't promise I won't hurt him. But I'll promise to not kill him."

Chapter Twenty-Six
DELANEY

Some of the sickness eases from my throat. Relationships are all about compromise. Some are worse than others. I'll take it. "Thank you."

Drew barks out orders. "Charlie, I need you on the rooftop as sniper. Mark, call in however many we have left alive and have them circle around to the back of Tyson's men. We'll have Delaney in between us."

Charlie's answer is to slap a palm onto the reader next to the door and yank out a rifle from the gun rack that opens behind the wall of monitors. He races out the door and his footsteps pound up the staircase. Mark speaks briefly into his cell to a faceless person on the other end. How many more innocents must die because of me and Kat?

"Let's go. Delaney, I want you armed and your weapons drawn. Don't relax." I don't bother to answer either. I pull two handguns from the open drawer and check them.

The three of us head to the front door. Both men hold a gun in each hand. Drew cracks the door open slowly, giving time for Charlie to get on the roof and the men heading for their death sentence to convene.

"Tyson!" Drew shouts. "We're coming through the door. If I so much as feel someone intent on shooting me, I will kill you. You know by now who I am and what I'm capable of. I'll hunt you down and tear you apart limb by limb." The coldness in his voice has several of the hardened assassins shifting their feet out in the yard.

"Stand down," Tyson orders his men.

He opens the door wider, and I look out over his shoulder. The men have lowered their weapons, though they still have their fingers on the trigger. It wouldn't take much effort to raise an arm and shoot.

"I want you to turn her and the kid over, Drew. This is Guardianship business. You do remember what it is to be carrying out Guardianship responsibilities right?"

There's something in the way he says this. An inflection I can't put my finger on. What does he mean? Maybe I'm just trying to find something redeeming in Tyson being alive. Maybe it's just simply a jab at Drew and I'm plucking at whimsies. Honestly, I can't trust any of my feelings right now.

"Yeah, I know what is like to be blindly following orders. Not a chance. They stay with me, Opmerker."

"Laney, honey. It's so good to see you. You need to be with me. Get Katrina and come out. I promise you won't be hurt," Tyson says instead.

How dare he!

"Don't you honey me, Ty! All these years? All these lies? I thought you were dead! I grieved for you! You've no right to call me honey!" I shriek over Drew's shoulder, itching to shoot Tyson at his feet. He'll squirm and wonder if I'll hurt him, and a small part of me wants to do it, to make him piss himself in fear. "And I don't believe you. I wonder why that is. Oh, I know, because someone came here for our child! And you want me to believe nothing will happen to her? Fuck you!"

"I'm not going to explain to you here right now, but you

have to trust me. You've known me for years! You know I'd never hurt you or Kat. I'd never order anyone to kill any of you, especially not her." He sounds earnest, but then again, the man lied for years. He pretended to be dead. I can't believe a single thing he says, no matter what he sounds like.

"We're at an impasse, Opmerker." Drew's arms remain up, guns pointed. I marvel that there isn't the slightest sense of fatigue in them. Mark's the same, right behind me. I'm set in the middle of a trap of two male bodies, who might as well have an invisible forcefield. Nobody would be able to get to me. My own two hands are out by their sides, guns pointed willy-nilly. We must look like a squid with pistols for tentacles.

"Delaney? Please."

"No. I'm not coming with you. And if you burn this house, with me and Katrina in it, well, I guess I have your idea of trust then, don't I?"

The sound of guns cocking loudly behind Tyson and his men spurs him to retreat. "This isn't over yet. You know the Guardianship won't stop."

There's a slight sound of desperation in Tyson's voice, but I can't trust myself to believe it.

Drew snorts. "Oh, I'm sure it's not, but it is for today. My men will relieve you of your weapons and escort you off the property as a show of good faith. Take your dead with you. And tell the Guardianship counsel to shove their responsibilities up their ass."

As one, we slowly back into the house, guns still raised. My arms feel like they're going to fall off, but if Drew and Mark are going to keep their arms up, then I will too.

I'm nervous the entire time the door shuts. We watch on the monitors as Tyson's team is corralled by Drew's men, and picking up bodies off the ground, they leave piles of weapons everywhere and make their way to the gates at the driveway. It's obvious there are far more dead men than live men to carry them, and I swallow hard at the thought of more bodies being burned in the incinerator. I try hard to remove the look of disgust from my face.

"There's not much else we can do. Most will be for hire. They never carry identification. No one will collect them, and we can't bury them all. It's practical."

The bile rises into my throat again. "I'm not sure what you were like before, but I sincerely hope you weren't always so callous." I hate the words that spill out, but I can't seem to stop them. I've always considered myself a levelheaded, pragmatic person. But ever since I've met Drew, emotions I don't recognize bubble inside me and spew without warning. I frown.

"It's not callousness, it's efficiency. We don't have the time or the luxury. Do you want dead bodies rotting everywhere? Should we leave them outside the gates so the general population and police must deal with it? Tell me you have a better idea. I'll listen to it."

I'm at a loss. I don't have a better idea, but that doesn't mean I like this one. "No, I don't," I say quietly. I hate that I don't have a solution. I hate everything about this.

"If it could be different, I'd make it so. It's not like I want it to be this way. You have to understand that."

I do, but nothing is right about any of this. I know there are casualties to war. To any fight. It's wrong on a different level, and everything seems to rebel inside me.

"Besides, we have bigger problems," he continues. Yeah. Like my pseudo-husband being alive.

"First, there are not one, but two groups coming here after you and Katrina. The first attack was run by someone else. They were here to get Katrina, and you would have been a side bonus. This group today was Guardianship orchestrated."

My heart races at the possibility. The idea of the Guardianship coming after me is scary enough. The thought of an unknown entity additionally trying to kill me is the stuff of nightmares.

"What's the second part of that statement?" I don't want to hear it. I don't. Deep down, I already know what he's going to say.

"They're both after Katrina. She's the mark." The words paralyze my lungs, keeping the breath from my body as surely as a noose tight on my esophagus. Anger flexes my hands. She's not a fucking mark. She's an innocent kid.

"Fuck!" He slams his palm down on the counter. "I didn't see this coming at all. I thought the Guardianship was coming for you. I was protecting you. Now, they're coming for Katrina, which will place you in their direct path, and I've no idea why. Fuck!"

He yells again, pounding his fist on the console table of the war room. I'm numb. It's even more important we keep Kat safe. And it's no longer just about keeping her safe. It's about keeping her alive. An even worse thought occurs to me.

"I won't let you give her to them. I won't let anyone take her or hurt her. Over my dead body, you hear me?" I shove myself into his personal space, fury rolling off me in waves. I poke him in the chest several times.

"I won't let you take her because your only focus is me. I. Will. Not. Allow. It." My brain nudges me there's something there. For once, my soul is quiet. If there are any tendrils of warmth with each touch, I don't feel it.

"What do you take me for? I've already told you I know she's important to you, and you don't think I know you'd lay your life down for her? That means I'll protect her, in order to protect you. Damn."

Drew sounds frustrated and offended. There's a flicker of regret in his eyes. But he only has himself to thank for my assumptions.

"I just want to make sure we're on the same page here.

That's all." I step back. "I can't tell you how scared I am right now. You aren't a parent, so you don't understand."

"No, I'm not. But I am one-half of a soul mate. I understand sheer terror. I understand that you'll do whatever it takes, even if that means sending men on a suicide mission and putting bodies in an incinerator."

Chagrined, I acknowledge the well-deserved rebuke. "Touché."

I need to do better. This version of me can't succeed until I can control myself and stop being so volatile. I can't seem to help myself, and the frustration of it makes me want to stomp my foot. Or hit something.

Drew steps forward and pulls me into his arms. I barely resist before I melt into him. The warmth circles lazily through me once more. Maybe I don't need violence, after all.

"There are lots of new things that I'll have to learn to accommodate. As will you. But we can do this together. We'll be stronger for it," he murmurs into my hair.

I happen to agree with him. I step back out of his embrace, slightly cold from the lack of warmth.

"I'd like it if we could have dinner with Kat. I'd like you to really get to know her. You ought to know who you're protecting."

"That's a great idea. I'll let Charlie know we'll be eating in her room. If you'd like, after we eat, we can go for a swim in the pool. It'll let you relax a bit." He reaches out and taps my tense shoulders.

I focus on releasing some of the tension in them. "Why am I not surprised that there's a pool in here?" This entire house and the complete house on the other side of the bookcase literally have everything in it. Apparently, I'd planned for every conceivable scenario.

My brain nudges me at the oddest moments, and this is no exception. I just wish it would stop nudging me like quick hints and let me know the entire thing. It would be helpful right about now. We head up the stairs to our rooms.

Drew laughs. "Because you've always been a planner. You should know better. I'll meet you in Katrina's room, and I'll bring the towels too. There's a bathing suit somewhere in your closet or dresser," he adds, anticipating my question. I'm not surprised with that information either.

I should probably worry about how quickly we move from terror, tension, and deadly fighting to talk of swimming and eating a leisurely dinner. I suspect Drew and I are extremely adept at compartmentalization and going with the flow of things. Must come with the territory.

Like chameleons, we can adapt at a moment's notice. Is it the ability to do so that keeps us sane? That allows us to find happiness in the small spaces of time we're able to? Have we always been this way, our inherent traits?

Or is it because of so much loss and pain we've experienced? For it's obvious now, my previous self knew all of this would happen. I can't imagine how I must've felt knowing how much I was placing on Drew. How much he'd suffer, how much I'd suffer knowing he suffered. The detritus of our minds must sweep away constantly with moments of joy or we'd become insane.

An autonomous self-healing.

I hurry through my room, searching for and finding my bathing suit. I'm happy it's a one-piece. I briefly worried it would be a skimpy little bikini, but I should've known better. Drew has never, not one time, behaved in the kind of manner I would've expected from a man who's in love with his soul mate. He never uses it to his advantage. He's simply there.

I'd need only to reach out and accept. He'd wait forever if that's what it took, even if there was no happily ever after. I love that about him. I imagine my other selves loved him wholeheartedly. I have no doubt it'll eventually happen again.

The attraction is there, the familiarity is there. It won't take much, and I'm not sure how I feel about that. About it kind of being a done deal.

I head to Kat's room and intercept Charlie, who's pushing a cart full of food.

"Here, I'll bring it in. I'm sure whatever you've made is delicious. I didn't get a chance to thank you earlier. For being observant. You've saved my life. That's a debt I can't ever repay."

Charlie's cheeks pinken slightly. "It was nothing. It's my job to keep everyone healthy and alive here. You enjoy your swim."

As I push the cart into Kat's room, Drew's right behind me and uncharacteristically waits quietly by the door. I gesture for him as I set the plates of food on the table. He silently takes over as I'm bombarded with Kat and her exuberant hugs.

"Momma! I'm so happy to see you. Ms. Liza and I were watching a movie about dinosaurs. It was scary."

"Aww. Well, you know dinosaurs are extinct, and they can't hurt you. Remember how we talked about how movies aren't real?"

"I know, Momma, but they look so real!"

"All right, well, go wash your hands. We're going to eat dinner with Mr. Drew. As you know, this is his house, and he has been busy making sure you're safe here."

Katrina turns shyly toward him. "Thank you, Mr. Drew, for keeping us safe."

Drew dips his head in acknowledgment but doesn't say anything at all. Katrina runs to the bathroom to wash her hands and I turn, bemused.

I find it funny he doesn't know how to act around children. The unflappable Drew can be brought to his knees by a child.

I grin. Dinner and swimming ought to be fun.

Chapter Twenty-Seven

DELANEY

I don't tell Katrina we're going swimming until after we've eaten. I know better than to give her news that will have her squirming in her seat throughout our meal. Drew continues to be quiet during most of dinner, letting Katrina and I get caught up on what her and 'Ms. Liza' have been doing the last couple of days.

There's something soothing about innocent chatter from children. A normalcy to my meal. Not so much Drew's.

"Mr. Drew, is the rest of your house as nice as this room? I love all the stuff you have here for me to play with."

"I like to think so. I'm glad you like it. We wanted to make sure you have plenty to do here so you don't ever need to leave it."

I laugh and shake my head at Kat's wide eyes. "You make it sound like she's going to be imprisoned here."

"Oh. No. I'm sorry, that's not what I meant."

I find it funny that he doesn't know how to talk to her. His utter lack of confidence in this area gives him a vulnerability that is unbelievably attractive. "Don't worry about it.

She's already moved on to something else. The joy of having the attention span of a five-year-old."

I turn to her. "Guess what we can do after dinner? We can go swimming!"

Kat's face lights up enough to blind me and guilt robs me of the pleasure I should be experiencing. I should be spending time with her, but it's imperative I uncover my memories. How many times have parents sacrificed to do what needs to be done for their kids? Countless times, but that doesn't make me feel any better.

"Really?" At Drew's nod, she says, "This is so cool! Thank you!" She runs over and throws her arms around him, her head resting on his shoulder, and my entire body turns to mush.

"Uh, you're welcome." He pats her on the back with one hand, the other one laying uselessly in his lap, crushed into place by a bouncy little girl.

I thought his vulnerability was sexy before, but the light-red growing up his cheeks puts that thought to rest. There's nothing like a strong, sexy man flushing at the exuberant thanks your child plasters him with.

"Go look in the closet, baby. I'm positive there will be a bathing suit in your size there. You can go change while we finish up eating."

She immediately runs off, chattering to herself, and I catch a smile on Drew's lips. I briefly wonder what Drew had thought when the house plans had a child's room, clothes and toys as part of the schematics. Had he wondered whose child it was? Had he hoped it would be ours? A flush hits my chest and spreads happily. I can picture a little boy with green eyes and floppy, dark hair sitting on my lap. I swallow hard and focus on the present. I can't even spend time with my own daughter.

"You just made her entire day."

"It's no problem. We can all use a break. Nothing like

floating in a pool of water to make your problems disappear for a while."

The pool room is gorgeous. Water flows from the rock in the mountain. I don't know if it's coming from a spring or just hidden in the walls, and it doesn't matter. It's idyllic and relaxing, with warmth pumping in from vents. Drew swims in the pool and then heads to the hot tub nearby, while Kat and I have our fun. We frolic and splash. We float and throw a beach ball around. We giggle and pretend nothing is wrong. I pretend nothing is coming for her and that nothing will harm her. When she starts rubbing her eyes and becoming a little whiny, I know it's bedtime. I leave Kat in the capable hands of Liza, say good night, and make my way to my room.

There's a covered tray with a plate of food on the table. Another sandwich, chicken salad with crunchy bits in it, a pickle, chips and more fruit. A bottle of water and a bottle of apple juice as well. Now I understand the juice at every meal. The instant sugar is a balm to my blood levels. I'm famished, so I sit on the chair, hoping I'm not dripping pool water all over the rug. I scarf down the food and hop in the shower again. I've had more showers, both cold and hot, than I have in a long time, but it's kind of rejuvenating. I've run a gamut of emotions from panic and terror, rage, to fun and laughter. Underlying it all is the very real emotional tie to Drew. I can't deny it. My soul recognizes the other half of itself and is happiest when we're near each other. I'm getting addicted, besides wanting him. The water sliding off his abs earlier had me focusing far more intently on Kat than I needed to so that I'd stop staring.

I've started touching him in various little ways, just to get a quick hit. A brush of my fingers when I'm passing the salt, a hand on his arm when I'm pointing out something. My unconscious need to be in his personal space, stepping in when I need to make a point. Trusting him to soothe me, like when my knee was touching the back of his when we stood outside with Tyson.

I need him just as badly as he needs me. After this morning's kiss, the sexual tension hovers over us, enveloping us in an invisible blanket that caresses my nerves and continues to keep them ablaze.

I want him. I need him as simply as I need to breathe. My soul can never be without him. In the last twenty-four hours, I saw him weak and dying. I saw him dead. I saw him alive. I saw him full of need. I saw him angry. I saw him laughing. His entire being, imprinted on mine. And tonight? Tonight, I need to feel safe. I need to feel like myself. Whoever that may be. I just need.

I dry off and put on a T-shirt. One that barely covers my ass. I'd lament the lack of lingerie, but I've no need for seduction. He'd want me regardless of what I'm wearing. I could wear nothing at all. But I don't think anyone wants to see me walk naked to his room, so a T-shirt it is.

I knock on his door. There's no response. I knock again then huff out a breath.

Nothing like wanting something only to be denied. Just as I move to head back to my room, Drew opens the door and my mouth dries up.

I see why he didn't respond immediately. He, too, was in the shower. And now he's standing in the doorway, dripping wet with only a towel wrapped around his waist. Earlier, I saw him dripping wet from the pool in only swim trunks. Same scenario, different mood.

Now, there's a half-naked man and the heat rising between us, slamming us together like magnets. Energy coils in my gut. His green eyes darken. I barely make it two steps toward him when he grabs me by the arm and pulls me into his room. He shuts the door and leans back against it. I whirl around, steps away from him. His breathing is shorter, quicker. Desire, evidenced by the towel rising. Drew's gaze drops down my body and hungrily travels back up again.

"Are you sure this is what you want? I don't, *we don't*, have to do this. We can be a unit without sex." His voice is raspy, quiet and strong.

He wants me, badly. I can see it. He knows I want him, that I only came here for one thing. And he still gives me the choice to leave. Ever the Protector.

"I showered. I dried off. Yet I'm still wet." I step closer with each word.

His body visibly tightens, the muscles contracting, the towel twitches. He's in danger of losing it completely.

I move another half step. The slightest bit of fabric grazes my thigh, and I watch in fascination as his jaw clenches. I cock my head to the side. "Do I need to give you permission to touch me?"

He swallows hard. "No. I want to make sure that this is what you want and that this isn't the after-effects of fighting and fear. Of Tyson."

"This is the after-effects of the kiss you gave me today. It's the after-effects of thinking of you all day."

"I want the words."

"I want you."

And with them, I unleash a storm.

He reaches out and twirls me around, my back slamming against the door. One hand on the door by my head. I remember the last time this happened. How badly I wanted him then. I was an idiot. He reaches for the doorknob and my heart stutters for a split second. Is he going to shove me out again?

The lock clicks and his hand returns to my peripheral vision. His head dips, bringing his lips millimeters from mine. I want them on me.

"No matter how far we go, if you have any doubts or you

want to stop for any reason. Tell me. It might kill me to stop, but tell me. I won't have you regretting this tomorrow."

"Shut up and kiss me." I wrap my arms around his torso and slide them up his back before pulling on his shoulders. I can't get close enough. He cradles my face, his eyes searching mine before finally succumbing to a need to kiss me. When his lips slant over mine, the warmth from his breath teases me, and our tongues circle and slide. Drew yanks me against his body—every inch of his hardness pulses against my skin, and impossibly, I'm hotter. And wetter.

He picks me up and, swinging my legs around his waist, carries me to his bed. His lips never break contact with mine. Drew lowers me to the bed, kissing my mouth, my jaw, my neck, and yanks up my shirt. My hands roam over his body, desperate to know every inch. My fingers trail down his back and encounter his bare ass. The towel finally loses the fight.

Drew's hands, rough with calluses, roam over my breasts, my nipples hard against his palms, stoking a fire inside me. My fingernails scratch their way up his back as the heat continues to grow. My soul is an inferno. Frantic, I beg him. "Drew, please."

He stills, panting hard. "You want me to stop?" The tip of his dick, hot and silky, twitches against me. Oh, so close to what I want.

I gasp and my eyelids fly open. Sweat beads on his forehead as he waits. "Don't you dare stop."

And he slams into me. We both still, my body adapting to his.

"Fuck. Give me a second."

He kisses me deeply. My body rages on. The need to finish in a primitive rhythm has me moving, but he grips my hip to stop me and moves ever so slowly.

In. Out. His thumb circles my clit sinuously with soft insistence.

My vision clouds as the pressure builds. The warmth of my body echoes the warmth penetrating my soul. I *sense* his soul reaching out to mine as they do a ritual of their own.

The slow, silky movements of our bodies, meeting and separating, drawing time out causes a tear to slip from my eyes. Pure joy and ecstasy invade my senses.

The room disappears. We might as well be on top of a volcano, the heat pumping out, both burning and oddly comfortable. The pressure builds in me with each thrust of our hips. My heart races and my nails dig into his back.

My soul *burns*.

The orgasm rips a scream from my throat, and Drew growls in response, head thrown back. He collapses on me and quickly props himself up on his elbows, dropping little kisses on my forehead and cheeks. His eyes are half closed, blinded by lust, as he shudders in after-shocks. He leans his forehead on mine, and the sweat on our brows melts together. Two become one in every way.

"I love you."

I stiffen in response. Does he want me to say it back? I can't. I barely know him. And my love isn't worth much anyway. Tyson hadn't wanted it. Anxiety has me wrapped up. What do I say? What do I do? My stomach clenches and my body stiffens.

"Don't say anything. I know you don't. But I do. I've missed you, and I've missed saying it. I've missed saying it casually, I've missed saying it in amusement. I've missed telling you every damn day. I want to tell you that I do. I never, ever take the opportunity for granted."

He withdraws from me, and for a moment I want to cry out. Not in pain—in loss. It's momentary, as my soul adapts to being without close proximity to his. But the effects of sex with Drew drown out everything else and my own previous thoughts quiet.

I'm invincible. My body doesn't ache anywhere. It's rejuvenated and refreshed. I know if I look at myself right now, I'd look like a perfect model. Something beyond contentment whips through me and silences the anxiousness I felt. I'm having my own aftershocks, it seems.

Without saying anything else, Drew gets up and walks over to the shower and gets in. I sit up. I have two choices. I could walk out of his room and never let this happen again. He'd let me. He'd never say another word about it. I'd see his desire for me every day, and he'd shut it down so that he doesn't hurt me. The idea brings tears to my eyes.

Or I could join him and let him know that, though I can't offer him those same words, I'm willing to grow into that, if that's where it goes. My soul stills, my brain nudges me. Together we are stronger. Together we can do anything.

I have no choice at all.

I get up and join him in the shower. The joy on his face rivals the joy I felt when our souls touched.

I pour everything into the kiss I give him and hope it's enough.

Stamina isn't a problem either one of us has. After a trip to the kitchens, and Drew's insistence we eat, we have our own sex marathon. We're both learning what we like, what brings us the most pleasure. I learn the contours of his body; he learns what sighs mean I'm pleasured.

After a couple of hours, we lay spent, and I marvel over the smoothness of his chest, nary a scar.

Not even the one I'd given him years ago.

It's truly a medical miracle. If I hadn't seen it with my own eyes, I'd never have believed it had ever been there.

My fingers follow where it would've been. The pain I must have caused him. He catches my hand in his and raises it to his lips, kissing the knuckles. I look into his eyes, knowing my tears shimmer there, but not knowing the words to convey the sorrow in my heart for his pain. Pain that I caused.

"You don't have to say anything. Every moment of everything I've ever felt mean nothing to me when I have you. Truly."

"I'm sorry. I'm glad you trusted me and came for me. Even though I don't know what it is you've done for me, I still am in awe of your commitment to me." I tug my hand out of his grasp. I trace the words of his tattoo, my brain murmuring, a whispered crescendo building.

"Do you have a copy of the song you said was my favorite?" It's an asinine question, I'm sure.

"Yeah."

He gets up and softly walks over to a radio system. He picks up his cell and scrolls for several seconds. After plopping it into the speaker box, he hits play.

"Woah, myyyyy love, my darling, I've hungered for, your touch." The deep voice comes out of the speakers like vocal velvet. I close my eyes and listen to the words, the smooth melody.

It's an incredibly romantic song, and I see right away why it was my favorite. I imagine, given time, it'll become a favorite again.

"I wonder why I wanted lines of it tattooed on us."

"I don't know."

"Can you play it again?"

"Sure." He sets the song on repeat and returns to bed. We both listen to the weepy chords and the sad words, and enveloped in his warmth both on the outside and internally, I drift off to sleep.

Chapter Twenty-Eight

DELANEY

I'm in a house I don't recognize. A very young Drew sleeps in front of a door. I stare at the lady who draws out her hands in the universal sign of 'I'm not here to hurt you.' The woman, hauntingly pale, speaks.

"Delaney, I'm Moira of the Magicals."

"Is this a hallucination?" My younger self asks, sitting up in bed.

"You're not hallucinating. Most of you in the Guardianship have no idea we still exist. We prefer to keep it that way. I've asked my Dreamer sisters to help me come to you now."

I look down and see my current self, sleeping. Legs wrapped around Drew's, his body heat warming me. What the fuck? Is this a dream? My head swivels between the ghostly lady and young Drew on the floor. No. Somehow, I'm seeing what happened years ago. Finally. My brain has let me in on the secrets.

"I'm coming to you to warn you of what will happen if you don't help me," Moira continues.

"You want me to help you? With what?"

I listen carefully to the words coming out of fourteen-year-old me. I need to know everything.

"To save my race. You're our only hope. There's a dark energy in the Guardianship. They've hunted us and killed us one by one. See?" Moira swirls her hands, beckoning to someone I can't see.

And the brief scenes she shows to a young Delaney, (and me by default) are horrific. Men hunted down like beasts, with swords and spikes, tortured to reveal the whereabouts of their loved ones. Women weeping and screaming, their hair ripped out, knives carving symbols into their skin that glow from within. The convulsions rip out the location of their children.

Their secret children that would never see the light of the next dawn. No amount of forced and endured agony revealed the location of a Stone.

They were all tormented and murdered callously with rivers of blood left in their wake, mouths wordless, tears in their eyes, physically unable to speak the words that could set them free. They didn't know the secretive whereabouts.

I watch as I scream for hours, young Drew fading in and out of my vision with furrowed brows and clenched fists—worried—the torment of thinking hallucinations gripped me. But my heart cried out, my throat screamed at the injustice of murder of an innocent race, hunted for greed, for power. They had not been hallucinations.

They were visions.

I scream along with my younger self. The horror is enough to bring a voice to my sleeping body.

Drew wakes and grasps my shoulders. I can't hear what he's saying, and I can't help him now. I'm sorry to worry him. But something is happening. And I need to know what happened long ago.

I can't pull out of this vision.

Moira is visiting a young Delaney again.

"I'm sorry I couldn't stay long. My power is too strong to stay for too long. Showing you what was, *will bring them to your door."*

"I understand. I'm sorry for what my people are doing to yours. What can I do," I say simply.

"I was hoping you could help save us all," the pale lady replies. "The Guardians have no idea the powerful magics that spellbind the location. None of those tortured, consciously or subconsciously, knew it. All that death, for nothing." A dark tear spills down her face.

"But what is it that I can do? I'm a Destiny, but I'm also just a child."

"I want you to see the possibility of what will be first. You'll need to open yourself up to the future and see for yourself. Only then, can you help. I warn you, young one, it won't be pretty. But you must see for yourself what will be. Or you won't be willing."

I nod my head.

Knowledge slams into me as my brain unlocks another secret. My younger self didn't tell Moira that most of the futures were horrible. It's why I am. To set them right. I'd grown a thick skin, seeing what humans were capable of doing to each other. Without it, I'd have succumbed to visions years ago. My shoulders stiffen as I refocus on my dream.

"I'll need to meditate, and it will take some time. Can you return tomorrow?" I ask her. Moira inclines her regal head, with blue eyes so pale they're white. Her skin, her hair completely devoid of color, leached of melanin.

She is beautiful.

I empty my mind of thoughts and cut off my connection to Drew, knowing it'll be better if he doesn't feel my terror.

I open my mind and scatter my senses to the winds. They travel the air, looking into the universe for a vison of what is to come.

I gasp as the vision I had then hits me now. The smell of burning flesh brings bile to my throat.

The world is on fire. Humans killing humans, the streets run with a black liquid. The dark shifts and swirls and becomes an entity of its own. It becomes the ruler of the Earth. Terror grips me. People enslaved, wrapped in chains so heavy they stifle any emotion. They labor to feed the dark. The maiming and feeding upon innocents is revolting.

I cry tears of blood, my heart pumping out its life. I wipe my eyes to see crimson on my skin. Fourteen-year-old Drew's hovering over me, begging me to hold onto him. I shove him and turn away. He'd feel the cut connection and question why.

He'd see the blood on my skin, flowing out of my eyes, and worry.

The nightmares are unceasing.

They ruthlessly devour my oblivion until I no longer have peace. My body is a giant bruise, battered with helplessness. Moira returns the next night.

I have only one question.

"*What's the dark?*"

"*It's evil in its purest form. My people, your people, the races of the Earth, we all work together to protect us from it. If one of us shall fail, we will eventually all topple, one after another, until the evil comes to be. Until it becomes a form that can control everything and everyone. It can't be allowed to happen.*"

I agreed then and still do. Never would I allow this to happen. My emotions had been raw, but now, they're ravaged beyond repair.

"*What do you need me to do?*" *I asked.*

"*I'll show you an alternate vision. We work together. With help from my Dreamer sister, you'll see what you need to do. Just remember, young Destiny, all you've seen that will happen. And what can happen. Ultimately, you must make the choice to help us or not.*

But you have to choose. We can't force you into it. It will require much sacrifice from you and your soul mate."

A shadow moves near the edge of the bed and, at first, I think it's the evil from the scene shown to a young Delaney. My heart pounds blood through my veins in an angry rhythm and fury rips a roar from my throat. But the inky skin reveals itself to be a devastatingly beautiful woman.

Moira's opposite.

Here, the melanin converges, even her voice reminds me of a dark abyss. From the tips of her hair to her toes, she's varying shades of the night sky.

"I am Nirvana, young one." She holds out her hand. "You must accept my invitation to this dream and remember it when the sun bleeds in the sky."

With the screams of children echoing in my ears, I place my hand in hers. "I accept."

Impossibly, I'm thrown into a state of flotation. Like a cloud, but not really. Completely in my head. I watch my young self look at myself on the bed. My soul inside my body struggles frantically for me. It's a living being, I can see it. It's beautiful, golden and shiny.

I remember that I had felt...nothing. Not numbness. Not cold or hot. Nothing at all. It had been strangely pleasant. Little did I know it was the balm before the agony.

I scream out loud as I scream then, in pain. I'm walked through, again as I was then, everything that would happen if I helped Moira and the Magicals.

I relive the pain that I'd cause Drew. Tears flow down my cheeks. The pain when, time after time, I'm ripped from this world and Drew is cast aside, wandering the world searching for clues. My shoulders hunch under the emotions. The anguish rips me to shreds.

I'm mentally on my knees. The pain of watching the world end because of me, watching the pieces of Drew's soul being torn away from him as he makes the choices to save the world from my actions. Again.

I scream. The guttural sound pours out between my lips.

I'd relived it once. And I'm reliving it again. The tears on my cheeks feel thick, and I know if I wipe them away, they'll be a dark blood red.

I grieve when Drew wants to die, time and time again. I grieve when I'm lost to him and with another. I grieve when I bear a child. The tears fall faster. I grieve when I'm told I must give up the child. Tears continue on. How much blood can I lose?

I fall from the sky, my soul soundlessly screaming for me.

I tumble back into my body and sob with the knowledge of consigning myself and Drew to living in torment.

"Wake up, hey, hey, you're ok. Della. Please wake up."

I revolt from the clutches of the dreamworld and grip onto a young Drew, sobbing rivers of tears. Drew rocks me back and forth.

"I'm sorry, baby, it was just a dream. You're okay, I promise."

I gulp in air, my throat closed from the emotion that's been wrung from me.

I grip him so hard, I think he might break. It's the only thing to grab onto.

And then I collapse into oblivion, my young body barely able to survive the pain.

The tears carry over from my dream to reality. They don't stop as my entire life pours back into me. The knowledge of years of training soaks into my pores, reaching the recesses of my brain.

Memories flood my body, the storm battering any defenses I have. I scream with pain. Drew is here and doesn't let me go.

He anchors me. Again.

Hours pass, a lifetime crammed into a small space. The

visions, the gifts of knowledge from extra races, inundate me. A token of their appreciation for *me*.

Little did I know the crushing weight of it would press into me until there was no room for anything else. My body curls into a ball and tries to remold itself, to open crevices within my brain, floodgates built to control the flow.

My soul shrinks into a corner, protecting itself. Then it expands into twice itself as pieces of Drew's soul slam back into me and reunite. A token of *their* appreciation for him.

My body isn't meant for more than it was born with.

My brain fractures. It can't process the information, the extra *everything* that's there.

My body eventually gives out and I pass out.

Moira is there. And Nirvana. Their hands linked as they watch over me. Their lips move, but I can't hear anything

I gasp, waking up in my own bed, and glance over. Drew had moved me to my room, and for a moment, I'm sad that I can't reach over and touch where we had lain, smell his scent mixed with mine and the peculiar aroma of sex. A tray filled with food is beside me along with my cell and a note that I pick up and read.

Call me. Eat while you're calling me.

I smile. Last night was cathartic. I'm glad I went to him, my soul calling to his when I still didn't remember. Proving that love and soul mates will win every time. I pick up an already peeled egg and bite, chewing slowly. I don't know how to tell him everything that happened.

I'm afraid that he'll be pissed. That he'll be angry that I'd gambled on his soul, on his love for me. That I chose to consign him to the depths of torture. He'd still love me, I know. Whether he'd forgive me is something that I don't.

I feel different, body and mind. No longer nudging me, my brain is running at full capacity. Impossibly, it's running at more than that. My body vibrates with energy and something...more.

I think about what I've done. Each branch is different. I don't know much more about the Magicals and Dreamers than I had then. Guardians have long thought themselves superior. How wrong they were.

We're all equal, with powers both terrifying and awesome. It's up to those of us with a conscience to keep the rest of the world in check. Not the leaders, those on counsels. But those with heart, with the determination, with the will of what's right.

Fairness. Diplomacy. None of that matters when it's up against Humanity. Compassion. Life. And that's what we had done.

Moira, Nirvana, and me. A Magical, A Dreamer, and a Guardian. We pooled our resources together, figured out what we needed to do and did it, no matter the cost to ourselves. But the time was coming when I'd have to pay the final price.

I jump out of bed and stretch, my muscles moving with renewed energy. The sex last night with Drew was incredible. And probably the only thing that stopped me from breaking down completely. From my mind fracturing from all the information crammed into my head. The then, the now, the future. The bits that weren't Guardian

Not everyone has a soul mate. They're *so* getting the short end of the stick. I'm renewed, reunited, and my memory returned. I'm in love with someone in love enough with me to hurt himself because I asked him to. There's probably a therapy session that has our name all over it, but that's for another time.

I shove another egg in my mouth and gulp down juice as I throw on leggings and a tank top. I'm going to need to be able to move today, unhampered by shirts that might fly up. Drew and I have work to do to get ready for the fight that's coming.

I bounce on the ball of my heels as I force myself to finish my breakfast. I need the fuel. The energy zipping around my body needs an outlet, and I know just how to do that.

I've been waiting for this for a long, long time.

DREW

Last night started out as the best night of my life. I've had sex with a version of Delaney once before, so I knew what to expect as far as our souls touching. But that version of her wasn't the right one. The mind had already fragmented and was on the verge of chaos and destruction.

The sex had only put her over the edge and cemented the rage. I hadn't made that mistake again, no matter how badly I wanted her. I allowed Delaney to talk me into believing this version of herself was the one. I wanted so badly for it to be true. I dread each turn of time, the pain that racks my body for obvious reasons.

But I also always miss her. The missing part of me brings me a little closer to the brink of insanity each time. My humanity disappears little by little. I know it. Yet, I continue this mission because Delaney asked me to. Not to do so is like denying my very essence. I just can't not do it, no matter how it kills me.

The sex was wonderful. As intense as I remembered it. This time I'm lucky I got to experience it several times. That was a first for us. My soul is content. I haven't felt like that since before Delaney died. I know it's not possible, but for once, I feel almost whole again.

Lying in bed with Delaney as she fell asleep, our bodies languid from the flood of endorphins, the crooning strains of the Righteous Brothers in the background, was the epitome of romance. I held her tight. Whispered how much I loved her. Told her how much I'd missed her. And I'd felt the fake optimism saturate my mind and body.

But then she started thrashing. The moaning and whimpering as dreams descended. My reality came crashing down on me. What had I done in my life that the Fates kept fucking me? What had I done to deserve the pain of her death over and over?

To have my soul willingly torn from me piece by piece? Despair descends for a moment. And the reality of what I have to do forces me to get up. I can keep her contained here. Maybe this time she won't be able to rain chaos on unsuspecting humans. Would I keep her chained up like a rabid pet? I don't know. But first I need to get everyone here to safety.

I pick her up gently and carry her to her room. Quickly getting dressed, I run downstairs and grab food from the kitchen. Our physical sessions will have depleted her blood sugar, even though I made us stop to eat. When I return, she's still tossing and turning. Sweat beading on her skin. The bloody tears on her cheeks causes my heart to stutter. It's like the night I lost her all over again. Defeat burns through me.

Fuck.

I gently kiss her forehead, knowing this may be the last time I can do so. I linger, pressing my lips against her skin, inhaling her scent and desperately wishing our time wasn't up. Sadness and resignation force my shoulders in, and a heaviness I wish I could forget drops over me. I've failed. I've failed her and myself and suddenly, for one moment, I wonder what would happen if I just left it as it is. Left the world up to her shattered mind's whim. Tired doesn't even begin to describe my weariness, but I can't. It's just not in me to let the world go to shit, nor let Dela create that havoc. She's better than this—I'm better than this.

I straighten and leave a note for her and her cell, hoping that she gives me a heads-up before she destroys everything. Maybe I can stop her from doing so...maybe there's a third option.

I run downstairs to warn Mark and Charlie to prep the house for lockdown. We'll need to move Liza and Katrina to another room and gather supplies for them to be locked in for a number of hours. I call Mark and Charlie and tell them to meet me in the war room.

"So, she's not the one?" Mark asks. "Damn man. I liked her, too." He kicks the wall.

"Are you sure? What prompted you to think that?" Charlie's the one who will think strategically first. I'm not going to tell them what the two of us did last night. That was between Delaney and me.

"It's a gut feeling. You're going to have to trust me. I hope I'm wrong, but I highly doubt it." My phone pings and my heart drops to my stomach. I'm not wrong then. She didn't call me like I asked her to. I look up at the men.

"It's time. I'll head her off, and you, lock down the house."

We scatter like three seeds in the wind. I stalk quietly down the hall. She isn't anywhere on the landing or the staircase. She wouldn't have had time to get to the bookcase. The alarm I'd set was meant to trip when she opened the door to her room. I race back upstairs, looking first in her room and mine. Both are empty. I pull up the system on my cell.

"Where's Delaney?" I'm already running back down the hallway.

"She's in the room assigned to Katrina."

Shit! How did I miss her? I jump the railing of the staircase, landing in the hallway, and run to the bookcase scanners. I barely wait for the door to slide back and I'm squeezing my way in. I race to the sublevel, taking the stairs two at a time.

I skid around the corner and run at a breakneck speed to Katrina's room. "Pull up the live camera in Katrina's room," I yell into the phone. I stop at the door and look at my screen.

And stare at it in confusion.

Delaney's sitting next to Katrina's bed, rubbing her daughter's hand. Liza's at the table, eating. I pull up the audio.

"So there I am, covered in flour, only my eyes showing circles free of the dust, and only because I managed to scrunch them shut right as a cloud billows down. I looked like a ghost. And Kat's entire backside is white since she'd been walking away. From the back, she looked like a little old grandmother! What a sight we made!"

Liza laughs along with Kat.

What fuckery is this?

"Drew's here, baby. I'll be back soon."

My palms dampen. How does she know I'm here? Is her connection working that well?

She stands up. "I love you so much. Bye, sweetheart."

Saying a good-bye? Was she sane only with Katrina? Was her daughter the key?

Delaney walks toward the door. I back away, putting several feet between her and me. I don't know what to expect, and I'm out of possible scenarios. And damn it, I only want to kiss her, hold her only one more time before she's gone again.

She exits the room, slowly. But there's an energy around her. Like a faded light outlining her skin.

This is new.

She walks toward me, barely placing her weight on her feet. She glides. I retreat. With each step she takes forward, I step back, determined to draw her away from Katrina and Liza.

She slows and stops. I slowly step backward. She takes a cautious step forward. I take another step back, and she finally lets out an exasperated sigh.

"I promise I'm not going to destroy the world."

She gives me a big grin and breaks into a run, jumping into my arms.

Chapter Twenty-Nine
DELANEY

It takes me a moment to realize he's drawing me away from Kat. If I didn't love him before, his protection of her would have made me fall in love with him now.

I leap into his arms. I'm happy to have my connection back and so thrilled to have him that I can't describe the joy pouring out of me. It oozes out of my pores. With my legs wrapped around his waist, he has no choice but to hold me, to support me up. I grab his face with my hands and let my whisper disappear into the kiss. "I remember everything."

He pulls his face away from me, slowly, and I hope, reluctantly breaking contact.

"What?" He doesn't believe me. Or maybe his wide eyes mean he's hopeful.

"I remember everything. I'm back. We did it. You did it. You amazing, wonderful man." I pepper his face with kisses. And pull back as he stands there, slack-jawed.

"Really? Are you for real? I'm dreaming. I must be." He slides me down his body, holding me close. He doesn't believe it, yet he doesn't want to let me go. I know because I feel the same way.

"Try me."

I back a few paces away and put my fists on my hips, standing in the middle of the hallway, an open invitation. "Bet you I can put you on your ass." I wink.

Drew stands frozen. Then he moves toward me. I run a few steps and, using the wall, I run up it and placing one hand on his shoulder and with a crooked elbow wrapped around his neck, I ricochet myself around him and, using the momentum to jump off, I flip him onto his stomach. He lands on the ground and rolls over. I land lightly on my feet at his head. I smirk. "I bet it's been a while since you've been down there."

I give him my hand. He tugs me down and, anticipating it, I go with it, jerking my hand out at the last millisecond, landing in a handstand, my hands on either side of his head. I lower myself to kiss his lips, and with a burst of strength, I push myself up, an acrobatic maneuver into a standing position at his feet. I turn.

He quickly rolls to his feet and stalks toward me slowly. Deliberately. I back away. His body pushes me against the wall, and I allow it. His face is inches from mine. He reaches up, touching my face and hair. The sense of wonder in his earnest expression, the tightness around his eyes betraying his reserved disappointment, breaks me. He leans and kisses me hard, his tongue plunging into my mouth, seeking the truth.

I let him probe and plunder. There's coffee on his tongue, and the spicy scent of him, like oakmoss and vetiver. I open all my senses and let my soul touch his. The warmth rushes into both of us, slamming us with its intensity. He pulls away. His eyes bore into mine. And he thought that could only happen with sex.

I smile, remembering how great it is for our souls to be united. Each time they do, I'll be giving back a piece of his, until we're equal again. The smile slides from my face as quickly as he slides down my body, dropping to his knees. He buries his head into my stomach, holding me tightly. His shoulder shakes lightly.

This strong man, who withstood years of pain, just broke because he found me.

I slide down to join him, on my knees. "I'm so sorry. If there was a different way of doing things, I would have. Please believe me. Once I catch you up on the why, I hope you can forgive me for all that you've been through."

The tears on his lashes shimmer like crystals. "It doesn't matter why. I'd do it again. And again. I can't believe you're back."

With a whoop, he stands up and pulls me back into his arms, twirling me around and around until we're both dizzy and laughing.

Charlie and Mark walk into the hallway, guns drawn, confusion written all over their faces.

"What the fuck is going on?" Mark's gun is level with my chest.

"It's okay, man." Drew walks toward him and pushes the barrel down.

Mark's eyes never waver from mine. "Are you sure?" he whispers.

"I'm positive. She remembers everything." Drew nods at Charlie.

"Well, okay then." Mark holsters his sidearm.

Charlie's eyes are wide. "So you...you are you." He sounds awestruck. Mark jerks his head back, eyes narrowed, reassessing. He backtracks a few steps, and my stomach clenches.

I'm no celebrity and don't want to be treated like one.

I remember the days that other children, and even adults, from the Guardianship would tiptoe around me. Some were fearful, some starstruck. It was hard when you held so much power in your hands. I hoped adults would be different when I was an adult. I guess that's too much to ask.

"I do. And I'm the same person I was before."

He nods, not knowing what to say. I take pity on him, remembering his kindness to me and to Kat. I walk over, ignoring the stiffening of his muscles, and kiss him on the cheek. It immediately turns a ruddy shade of pink.

"There you go, we're back where we were." I smile, hoping he remembers me as I was.

I wink at Mark when passing him and grab Drew's hand. "Let's go. We have catching up to do. I need to hit the training room. On second thought." I turn back and throw over my shoulder. "Mark, if you want to see him get put on his ass, join us too."

His eyes widen, and I laugh. It's so good to laugh. I grin. Damn it's good to have my memories. Mark and Charlie disperse to whatever responsibilities they have, but I'd bet my next meal that Mark's going to be checking the cameras to see his idol knocked down.

As we walk to the training room, I tell as much as I can to Drew while retaining secrecy.

"I'll have to tell you more in my room, but I do want to tell you that you were right. All of this is about her, not me. I've so much to tell you, but I need to explore my returned memories and what I'm capable of. I don't want to falter on the battlefield. And there will be a battle. Soon."

"You lead, I'll follow. Honestly, right now, I can't think past that I have you back. Also, I'd like to know how you did that move earlier." He laughs with pure joy.

"Some of my memories are...extra. Courtesy of a few friends."

We head to the middle of the mat and spar, meeting each other blow for blow. I've a few new tricks up my sleeve, and several times, I hand Drew a bodily throwdown. But he also has a few moves he's learned and picked up since I've last known him, and he returns the favor just as often.

Through grunts and slaps, the kicks and twirls, we both work up a sweat, and an appetite. Of both the food and sexual variety. We barely make it from the training room to his room. He pushes me onto his bed, and we tear the remaining clothes off. Our bodies meet just as violently as they did in the training room, each of us giving as much as we take. It's over in minutes, both of us shuddering.

My heart feels like it's going to burst from my chest. "Damn. Thank the fates we didn't know this is what it would be like when we were young."

He chuckles. "I've missed you. More than words can ever convey."

I link our hands together and look deep into his eyes, make sure he's focused on me. "I've missed you."

I lean over to kiss him. I'd sent another piece of his soul to him during sex, and I'm hoping he starts to feel it some. I know I feel lighter knowing he's regaining it. The process itself is beautiful enough to bring a tear to my eyes. Like letting myself go in my night-sky trips with Nirvana, I could release it —anchor it—with my love for Drew. We really were two halves and having more of his was...too much.

"I need you to make this room secure."

Drew doesn't question me. He uses his cell, turning on the security measures that amazed me before. I quickly catch him up on what happened with Moira and Nirvana. Tears trickle out of my eyes when I tell him of the atrocities I'd witnessed in a dream that prompted me to gamble our lives. I'm desperate to let him know just how bad it was.

Not so that he knows what was at stake, but so that he understands that I didn't make the decision lightly. I tell him how each night, Moira and Nirvana and I came up with a plan, altered it, pulled threads in different directions until we could force the eventual outcome that was needed.

Ultimately, we needed to save the Magicals and expose the

ones in the Guardianship that thought clandestinely killing off a race was okay. It wasn't all Guardians, and we women agreed simple exposure would not be enough.

Guardians had to die and had to have a personal stake. Guardians would have to have no choice but to face the detriment of their actions in unforeseeable futures. Not everyone could see past their own noses, even if they had my abilities.

The hardest revelation was telling him how I had to hurt him. Physically, mentally. After all, he too had to choose. He had to choose when he didn't know he had a choice.

We tried being able to tell him. We tried so many different ways to spare him the least amount of anguish, but nothing worked and they never ended well in the visions. The results were far too catastrophic. He had to choose me, *us*, repeatedly.

He squeezes me. "I can't tell you how happy I am that I did."

"Me too. Believe me, me too."

I'm relieved he sees only the good we did. The benefits of sharing a soul, I suppose. We're alike in many ways, in the ones we're not, we complement each other. The perfect unit.

"We need to eat."

I jump out of bed. I still have energy. Too much energy to burn off.

Drew laughs. "You've no idea how good it is for me to hear you say that."

"I do, actually. I remember everything I did in this version of my life, too. It's...conflicting." I grab a clean pair of jeans and shirt. "I keep meaning to thank you for all of my clothes. I appreciate them."

"Every version of you had a wardrobe. I'd write it down and I'd buy it in each lifetime." There's an odd tone to his voice.

Puzzled, I wonder what's wrong. "I'm sorry you had to do that. You've no idea how sorry I am." I mean to console him and move forward. Instead, he backs away. I tip my head. Something is wrong here.

"So does that mean you still love Tyson? Now that he's alive?" Drew's face draws in, the jaw tight. I imagine the pain he must feel thinking I don't love him, still. I walk over and cradle his face in my hands.

"First, I should've said it. I know the words are important. I love you. Only you, Drew. *You* are my heart, my soul, my life. *You* are my anchor, my rock, what keeps me grounded in visions. *You* are what I come back to every minute of every day. Always."

I kiss him on the lips softly, my soul reaching out and adding another piece of his into him. This is the only thing I can do for him that will make him whole. That will restore his own humanity.

"Second, I never loved Tyson. Ever. And it hurt me so badly, knowing I had to do it. It hurt knowing it would hurt you. Part of the plan required me to overcome my own soul's inherent need to be with itself.

"Every year, we went to The Coveted Pearl on our anniversary. This was important. There, someone from the Magicals would feed us a potent solution. At its basic concept, a love spell.

"We needed it knowing neither one of us loved each other but needing to keep up pretenses for the Guardianship. Tyson, undercover as a Guardian, needed to be given the assignment of watching over me, and I...I needed to be in love with him. But none of it was real."

The resulting relief on Drew's face makes my heart ache. "You never loved him."

"No. My brain had to believe it enough to override my soul." The next part was the hardest for me to reveal. "I *had* to have a child with him."

It was, without a doubt, the hardest part of this. Pain, I could deal with. The inevitability of Katrina's future is not.

"Knowing everything that was going to happen, I..." My heart stutters. Even though she was born out of a loveless union, I love her dearly. More so when I knew that I'd have to give her up as a child. Looking back, the clinginess I thought was her trait wasn't; it had always been mine. Subconsciously reveling in every moment, every hug we would share, storing the memories for later.

Drew holds me tight. "It's my turn to say I'm so sorry. I know it's inadequate."

"It's part of the price Nature demanded." I bury my head into his chest. It's the only thing I'm ashamed of.

"Why was there a price?"

"Because I made a bargain for Katrina's immunity."

"What?" Drew draws back from me. "Fuck. Why would you do that?"

"She's a Time-Turner and she's going to save the Magicals. But...she's my daughter—*my child*—and I can't see her death and not do everything I can to stop it." I drop my head to his chest.

Drew holds me tightly. "Well, I certainly didn't see that coming."

I don't move from his arms. I don't want to see judgment in his face. I can't live with condemnation from him.

He moves back enough to be able to see into my face. "You did what you should do. I believe that everything that happened was the best possible scenario because it's not in you to do otherwise."

I drop my head onto his chest again. "How do you know that? We had so little time. I was overwhelmed, and it was way beyond anything I'd done before. I was so young."

"Look at me."

I pick up my head, and he steps out of my arms circling

him. He holds me shoulder length away from himself, his palms warm on my shoulders, and shakes me lightly.

"Because I know you. Because you always have been and always will be fair. You're levelheaded, logical, and have an insanely deep streak of what's right. If there'd been a better way, you would've found it. I know it, and the fact that you're beating yourself up and Monday morning quarterbacking this entire thing proves it."

Relief flows through me. I close my eyes. I don't think I understood how much his belief in me meant. Without the loss of souls, without the possibility of death. Just him believing in me.

I give him a dazzling smile. "I love you so much." Now we need to seriously eat and prepare. "Let's go downstairs. I'm famished."

Drew's answering laugh is music to my ears, the balm to my conscience.

After refueling our bodies, we convene in the war room. We're anticipating all the different scenarios and waves of attack when Drew suddenly says, "So you're telling me that Tyson is a good guy. That I can't hurt him?"

I laugh. "Yes, he's a good guy. He's an integral part to this entire thing. He was a double agent. And remember, he's Katrina's father."

He glowers. "I don't need a reminder of that, thank you. I'm thinking of paying him back for two years of torment."

He's referring to the fact that one of the main reasons for Drew's wandering the earth for clues from me had to do with the simple fact that Tyson hadn't been born yet. You can't alter a path when one of the main players doesn't exist yet. But it killed two birds with one stone. We needed Tyson alive for obvious reasons, but Drew really did need to make sure that if anyone was following him, they'd get lost in the twists and turns of different locations. Nothing familiar, nothing that could be anticipated. If anyone from the Guardianship had caught on or the wrong Guardians got involved, it would have been disastrous. And though Moira, Nirvana, and I planned and mapped out the best we could, the outcomes were never set in stone.

"It's not his fault. You can't hold him accountable to that."

Drew's response is a growl.

"Jealousy isn't becoming," a blonde woman says as she steps into the war room. Drew's arm is out sideways, a gun pointed at her heart almost immediately. "Please put that thing away." He whips out a second gun and aims it at the person framing the doorway.

"How the fuck did you get in here?" Drew roars.

At the same time, I say, "Lydia?"

Behind the woman in the war room, a friend who worked with me during the visions and planning stands in the doorway, wearing a long, sleeveless, leather coat and multiple weapons strapped to her thighs. "Delaney, Drew." She nods her head at each of us and turns back, preventing anyone from entering the room.

The lady pats Lydia on the shoulder and walks farther into the room, ignoring Drew's hiss. "I walked in through the front door. You should probably start locking it. Depending on technology might kill you. And Lydia is *my* Protector."

She's as pale and as beautiful as I remember her. The Magicals tend to have some otherworldly physical traits. The Time-Turner that stands in the war room like a regal queen is no exception.

As a fourteen-year-old, my dreams were haunted by the lady leached of all color. Today, she still does. Until I make payment, she'll always be here. A vivid reminder of the past, of the future.

Drew isn't putting his weapons down. "How did you both get past all the scanners?"

I clear my throat. "Drew, meet Moira. Moira, Drew." Drew reluctantly lowers his weapons, but his trigger finger is still engaged.

"I'd say nice to meet you, but you still haven't told me how the fuck you got into my house."

"Easy, young Protector. Your need to see Delaney safe is admirable. I'll remove the device that allowed me to do so off your person as a show of good faith. Please turn around."

"What the fuck?"

He stands his ground. I know damn well that to turn his back on someone who just barged into the house unannounced, bypassing all security measures, isn't something he's going to do.

"Moira? What do you mean? I've not seen a device on him."

"It's there. The assassin, Astrid, put it there. She's a Magical. I'm sorry. I didn't know until Lydia and I were able to walk in here and pick up on her signature."

"Shit. She could've strolled in here at any time?"

Drew's pissed and his trigger finger twitches. I place a calming hand low on his back.

"Not just her, unfortunately. Any Magical. Unless you trust someone, I'd refrain from letting people bite you."

Drew reaches up and rubs the back of his neck. "I didn't *let* her bite me. She just did." He glances at me with sorrowful eyes. "It was one time."

"Don't look at me. I wasn't here. No judgment at all." I knew it would happen. Had seen it. Fourteen-year-old me wanted to kill her. Adult me understands. But my heart stops for a second anyway and red hazes my vision. I close my eyes, take a deep breath, and open them again. He's all mine now, and that's all that matters. And it's not as if I hadn't slept with

Tyson and had a child, no less. Tit for tat and all that. Karma had had her say too.

"What did she implant in me?" Drew asks Moira.

"Her saliva. That's all that's needed is for her saliva to be in you. Anywhere you go, any Magical can go, within so much distance. The only thing they can't penetrate is lead."

Drew looks over and I wink. Now he knows why lead was imperative behind the bookcase.

"I'd appreciate it if you would remove it now, please." He holsters his weapons and stiffly turns his back to Moira, every muscle tensed and poised to move.

She walks to him and, running her hand over his neck, slowly coaxes out a silver liquid from his skin. It's such a small amount. The total size of half of a grain of rice. Moira plucks it out and places it in a vial pulled from her jacket.

"Thank you," Drew says stiffly. I can't imagine how betrayed he feels right now. "What can we do for you?"

"I was dropping in to see how our girl is doing. How is she?"

She pointedly never says Kat's name. I know that Moira's branch is of the belief that to speak their name is to call attention to it. She doesn't want to ever utter her name, and I understand. She'll be their savior. But I don't want her to leave yet. There's no need.

I shake my head. "She's fine."

Moira closes her eyes and lifts her hands in a great circle, her hands meeting in front of her, palm to palm. She stands still, but her pants and jacket flutter lightly, moving from her feet to her hair, the pale strands lifting in a strange breeze in a room without windows. The hair stands on the back of my neck.

She opens her eyes and blinks back tears that shimmer opaque. "One day soon. Not today, but soon."

The breath hisses out of me, and I lean into Drew. My rock. Always there. "Thank you, Moira."

Moira dips her head regally. "It's the least I can do. My plan is to send someone here to train her. She'll need her mother's help."

My heart stutters again, but this time rage has no place where fear resides, and I tamp it down.

Moira continues, "If anything goes awry, we'll bring her with us and conceal her. You know what to do if they come for her."

"Yes. Plan B." Sadness tinges my voice, and Drew automatically reaches for me, intertwining my fingers with his. Calm washes over me.

Moira nods and she glances speculatively over at Drew.

"Thank you for the sacrifices you've made for my people. We won't ever forget it. If you should ever need anything, please ask."

He acknowledges her thanks with a nod of his head. I need to remember to tell him that they gave me his soul to give back for them.

"Be well, Moira."

I know this is the last time I'll ever see her. Impulsively, I give her a hug. At the contact, a fine dust flies up all around us. A shimmery concoction of particles, swirling in the air. I look around, delighted, and smile at Moira. She grins back.

"Be well, young Destiny."

She puts out her hand, and Lydia steps back into the room, linking arms. She dips her head at us as they both disappear into thin air. Drew pulls me hard and yanks me away from the dust.

"What is that stuff?"

"A gift, I suspect. We'll have to see what it solidifies into. The Magicals know about Guardians. The Dreamers know about Guardians. And now, we're of the few Guardians, not out to destroy them, that know about them. There are more branches. We've never discussed it, pressing matters and all. But I imagine that's the first time in a long time a Guardian has hugged a Magical, accepting them for who they are."

I sigh deeply. There shouldn't be such hate, distrust, and secrecy between us. The particles of gold collect on the floor. We watch, entranced, as the particles move toward each other. They collect into what looks like a figurine and a small ball the size of a pearl. Both shimmer with the pale version of pink, gold, silver, and white. The challenge of being leached of color, I suspect.

The figurine opens her mouth and swallows the pearl. I can see it drop into the figurine's stomach where it glows briefly. Instantly, it turns into a simple, all-white statue of a young girl. I pick it up delicately. I imagine this is supposed to represent Katrina. In awe, I look at Drew.

"I have a feeling this is more powerful than it looks."

We look at each other wide-eyed. The burden of protecting it now falls to us. Gifts from the other branches have been wonderful, but there's always a price.

"Are we going to get any more drop-in visitors?"

I laugh. "I hope not. I don't think you could survive another one. Particularly since she likes bedrooms."

I squeal when he picks me up and carries me out.

"There will be no one else in our bedroom."

I agree. We head to Drew's room to collapse for a couple of hours. Of course, there's the never-ending tray of food and we eat first.

While we do, I tell Drew of his gift from Moira.

Chapter Thirty

DELANEY

"I'm getting pieces of my soul back?"

The huge smile transforms his face into boyish charm.

"Well, you were kind of forced into helping out. You chose to give up pieces of your soul to save me. You took a chance each time, on a whim, a delicate thread of an idea that I was able to come back to you.

"That's a steep price and completely justified. However, you were doing it to save their race, though you had no idea of course. It was the only way to get this to work. You had to choose, each time. Because you were choosing me and it saved them, they gifted you your soul back.

"But they can't just give it to you. So they gifted it to me so that I can return it to you. It's too big for me to pass on at once so I can only give you pieces at a time. I'm not sure how it all works. But I've been giving you pieces back every chance I can. It's like a weird conscious effort."

It's Drew's turn to look like a fish out of water. I laugh at how the tables have turned.

"What's so funny?"

"Just that our roles are reversed. Mere hours ago, everything you told me was indescribable. Incomprehensible. Now it's your turn to look stupefied at the things I tell you."

"So now what?"

"Now we must train. I have to work the kinks out of my muscles. And there's so much to show you. Part of my gift was information. I was specifically given combat knowledge, and I've been dying to try it out."

My grin falters and my face sets. Tension radiates through me and settles in the pit of my stomach.

"There will be a battle. It's coming. I no longer have the playbook, because as you know, it can change. We'll be flying blind. They'll come for her. And come for her. Over and over. Until she learns enough she can't be accessible for anyone to pluck her out of thin air and manipulate her."

"And what happens after she learns enough?" Drew's muscles tighten in his forearm, the only indication that he's worried.

"She'll go with her people. They'll teach her things that I never can. She'll learn to be all that she's meant to be."

My voice breaks on the sentence. Drew's eyes narrow, taking in my slumped shoulders and the tears in my eyes.

"And you're okay with them taking her?"

"She was never mine. I knew before I was old enough to have a child of my own. I knew that she'd never be allowed to stay with me."

"That doesn't make it any easier."

I snort. "No, it doesn't miraculously make it a better tasting pill to swallow. But I agreed to it. My eyes were wide open when I made the choice. That's my price to pay."

"You're an amazing Destiny. You know that?"

"Yeah. We all make sacrifices for the greater good, right?"

I hang my head for a moment. A million memories of my daughter flit across my brain. I've been given years with her.

And hopefully will have several more. "She's going to have to make a sacrifice too. She's going to lose the only person she's ever known as her mother."

"Surely, she won't lose you?"

"Not in that sense, no. But I won't be with her anymore. They start training them young, just like we do. But my destiny is here, and hers is with them. We won't be together.

"I don't want to think too much about this anymore. I want to protect her and train her. If it's the last thing I ever do, I'll make sure she gets to her destiny."

My purpose was chosen years ago. It solidifies in my head.

"We'll keep her safe." Drew squeezes my hand.

"Let's go get some sleep. We need to start early."

We head downstairs and through the bookcase and I tug on him. "I want to check in on Kat, first."

Liza looks up from the book she's reading. "Morning!"

"Morning, Liza. Kat still sleeping?"

"She sure is. I think the swimming wore her out. I'll let you know when she wakes up."

I nod, and Liza sips her water and starts reading again. Drew's leaning against the doorway. If I'd been blind, I'd still be able to tell how handsome he is. The goodness in him shines out of him. The man is truly something. I'm forever grateful that the Universe gifted the other half of my soul to him because I'd be devastated without him. But it's more than that.

He's the glue that holds me together. He won't let me falter, and there's a strength in that knowledge. He'll prop me up time after time, pick me up, give me a good kick when I need it. I can always rely on him.

"Let's go to the training room. I've a need to get sweaty." I walk through the door and head down the hall, Drew matching me step for step.

We work on training exercises till my muscles scream with

fatigue. We run maneuvers in tandem and separately. I force my muscles beyond their breaking point. And then I push them some more. I don't have time for relaxation. I don't have time to spend with Katrina.

I don't have any time at all. I push myself until I'm shaking with the need for calories, and only then do I stop, reluctantly.

"You're in quite a frenzy." Drew hands me a towel and a bottle. I plop myself on the mat and gulp down a sports drink, allowing the electrolytes to temporarily give me the strength to get up and find food. "Charlie brought a tray while you were whipping yourself." He nods to the table. I swear softly.

"I never heard him bringing it in."

"Yeah, well, I'm not sure you would've noticed much." His brows scrunch together. "Is there a reason that you're trying to kill yourself on the mat?"

I grunt with the effort to bring myself to my feet. My muscles are shaking from the exertion I've forced on them. They're desperately trying to defy me. Years of not training, coming to a head. I wobble onto my feet when the sugar hits my system. Thankful for the extra oomph, I stand tall and walk to the table fairly straight.

"I'm trying to cram as much training time as I can in as little time as possible." For added emphasis, I shove a forkful of baked potato in my mouth.

"They'll come here. They'll try to take her." I talk around a mouthful of chicken.

"Who exactly is coming?"

"Guardians. Magicals. And probably some of the Dreamers." I shrug. "I'm not sure. Each time I've gotten a vision, it's been different."

"They're *all* coming here? Fuck!" He slams a fist on the tabletop, rattling the plates. "How the hell am I supposed to protect you and her from things that I know nothing about? Dammit."

He shoves his hand through his hair. I look fondly at the action. It's something he's picked up since my death, but I find it comforting. Something I remember from this time that reminds me how much he worries for me.

"You're not doing it alone, first of all. I'm here. I'm capable of helping to protect myself. We've got Charlie and Mark, too." I put my hand on his fist in a show of support.

He turns his fist over and laces his fingers with mine and nods. "We're stronger together. I've been doing this without our connection for so long, I've forgotten we're capable of so much." His face hardens with conviction. "We will be ready. And I want you to tell me what you know of the different branches."

We get up and square off on the mat. We walk through techniques and combinations I can easily pluck from my brain that I've barely visualized, let alone physically attempted. There are so many we have to talk through and figure out. By the time we need to eat again, we're confident in a handful of maneuvers and partially in a dozen more. Without discussing it, we end for the day and walk to our rooms for showers.

"I can't believe some of these techniques. They're incredible. You know that we'd be able to wipe out any Guardians with this." I swipe at a rivulet of sweat on my neck.

"More than likely. It's the other branches I'm concerned with." As always, Drew's running calculations in his head. The odds of winning, the odds of others joining in. By the frown on his face, he doesn't like the odds. At all.

"Hey." We're standing in front of his door when I pause and put my hands on his face, forcing him to look at me. "I know that it's going to be hard. It's going to be brutal and bloody. But we will win. I've seen her destiny. She's the Magicals' salvation." I lean in and kiss him, deeply, reuniting another small piece of his soul.

He breaks our kiss and, taking my hands from his face, he

leans his forehead against mine and stares at our linked fingers.

"You know it's not always set in stone. And at what cost?" He releases my hands and turning, walks into his room.

The door shuts behind him, leaving me staring at it. I know he needs more time to process everything that's been revealed in the last twenty-four hours, but he doesn't have the luxury. I don't have the luxury. And Katrina damn well doesn't have the luxury of time.

Pissed, I pound on the door. "Dammit, Drew!" I pound on it again.

He opens it, and my anger deflates at the sight of him with a drink. The vivid reminder that that was his only solace for years. Maybe we can afford to take some time, after all.

"I'm sorry. I wish the information that came with my memories was different. I wish things were different. But they aren't, and that's the kicker. I know." I step forward, hoping that he invites me in.

Instead, he moves the door, effectively shutting off any idea that I'd be allowed to enter.

"I'm sorry, too. I'm overjoyed, believe me, that you have your memories back. I just, I don't know."

He sighs deeply and closes his eyes. The hand around the glass tightens. A sick feeling coats my stomach. Drew says nothing for several seconds, and the blood drains from my face. I force away any semblance of sadness. He won't want my pity or fear, and I'm not going to shove it on him.

"I need some time to wrap my brain around all of this. And I need to do so by myself. I can't believe I'm saying this."

He grips the glass harder. His eyes implore me to understand. And I do, no matter how it hurts. Turnaround is always fair play. It was never going to be that easy.

I nod in silent understanding and step back. "I'll see you later."

My soul is heavy with the knowledge that we didn't escape

unscathed, in more ways than one.

And it's always been my fault.

I don't see Drew at dinner, and the next morning the breakfast table is devoid of his presence, too. Hoping that a night of solitude would be enough time is foolish. My brain understands it, but my soul weeps for him. My heart, the illogical organ that it is, berates me. I'm the one who set us on this path, after all. If only it was just about us, I could let it go. But it's not. This is far bigger than us, far bigger than even Katrina.

This is an entire branch of people that will be resuscitated, literally on the brink of its death.

I workout in the training room alone. I again push myself to the edge of collapse. I've no choice. Charlie once again brings me lunch. I crawl toward the table and inhale the food on the tray without tasting it. Waiting until the sugar hit my blood stream. I know my body is processing the calories by the spike in energy. I hit the mats again.

Over and over, I run combinations. I run up walls, I pull myself up ropes. I run sprints. I perform calisthenic maneuvers on the bars. I pause only to chug gallons of liquid electrolytes and to inevitably pee. I despise the breaks.

They're a weakness that will hold me back.

Someone grabs me from behind, pinning my arms, while someone else rips off the VR goggles, ruthlessly bringing me back to reality. Mark shoves his face into mine.

"Are you trying to kill yourself? Lady, you need to stop and eat."

Charlie releases me. Breathing heavily, I mentally remove myself from the bloodlust I was battling in another reality. I shake my head, trying to clear the world the goggles spun for me out of my focus.

My hands are shaking, and my knees give out. Thankfully, Charlie's still right behind me, and putting his arms under my armpits, he half drags me to the chair.

He hands me a bottle of apple juice and a straw, and I gulp at it, my literal lifeline right now. I'm furious with myself for not realizing how dangerously close I was to passing out. I lash out on the first handy person.

"No, I'm not. I'm training hard. I know that you don't know what that is, but that's what I'm doing here." I wave my hand vaguely. "I've already killed myself once, believe me. If I wanted to do it, I know damn well how to get the job done. Or have you forgotten who I am?"

Mark backs up, his face frozen in fear. "I...didn't." He stutters and stops.

I'm already ashamed of my response when Charlie steps into my personal space.

"Now, look here." He pokes a trembling finger into my chest. "You can't just go around threatening people. We're trying to save you from collapsing and bringing heartache to Drew again. You've no idea what that man's been through. What you've put him through. Every time you go and fuck the world, he's there to clean it up. He pays the price every time. Have you no sympathy? No empathy? No remorse? No respect?"

He pokes me with each question. A man poking a slumbering bear in her cave. Aware he's probably making a grave mistake, but intent on it.

Loyal to a fault. I commend him.

"I'm sorry." My mercurial mood has showed itself again. Another weakness. "I'm sorry." I look both in the face. "I didn't mean to lash out at you at all. I'm so mad at myself for forgetting to eat. I knew I needed to stop but pushed myself anyway. I'm truly sorry. Mark, I'd never, ever, use my abilities out of petty vengeance, no matter what my previous versions have done. Please believe me."

He nods his acceptance of my apology, but there's a shadow of fear in his eyes. I've put that there, and it'll take more than an apology to remove it. He leaves the room rather quickly. I'm an idiot. I sigh and look at Charlie.

"I'm an idiot," I repeat out loud.

He chuckles softly. "No. Just emotional. We all get that way. I understand. Just be more careful of people's natural fear of you. Exploiting it is wrong," he gently rebukes.

"I know. I'll make it up to him somehow. I'll try to be more normal. Do you know where Drew is?" I've purposely severed our connection to give him privacy.

"No. He said he wanted to be alone. If you're worried, you can always look it up on the monitors."

I slump in my chair. "No. I'll give him his time for reflection." I pick at my dinner. Random bites go into my mouth. I'm just surviving at this point.

Charlie sits with me, thoughtful. "Is it going to be that bad?"

"Worse than you can imagine. I don't know what Drew's told you." I stop at the negative shake. "He hasn't said anything?" It's unlike him, and the fear that maybe I'd pushed him too far sits stubbornly in me.

"No. Just that the four of us will get together when he gets back—"

"He went out?" I interrupt him, panicking at the idea of him being out there by himself.

"He probably went up to the lake."

My heart stutters back into its regular rhythm with relief.

"I haven't seen him since yesterday, but you need to be prepared. This is worse than anything you've ever encountered." I lay a hand on his arm. "I'll need the SEAL and the Healer."

There's a seriousness I've not seen before. "You'll have both at your back."

"Thank you."

As Charlie leaves, he calls over his shoulder. "Drew will

come around. He just needs to wrap his brain around everything. That man will do anything for you."

I watch him leave, the former soldier turned chef, who'll stand up to anyone threatening his friends, even if he too is afraid. That kind of courage is what will turn this fight in our favor.

Those willing to sacrifice the most, those loyal enough to blindly battle at our sides, are those who come out winners. The losses may be great, but the win will be greater. It must be.

I contemplate training some more. But my muscles are already crying foul, and I desperately need a shower. I head to my room. After showering and changing, I knock on Drew's door. No answer.

I should go visit Kat. I've been seeing her for only a few moments at a time. Seeing her and knowing the battle is coming, one that we must win or else I'll lose her much too early, gives me such an incredible sense of urgency I can't breathe. The panic floods through me, squeezes my throat dry. My time is better spent preparing. I should go back to training. Fourteen-year-old me had no idea what guilt would hang around my neck. My heart squeezes hard, lancing pain through my chest. The pain of few to save many is a common Destiny mantra, but it's fucking shitty.

The pain Drew has been in, the things I've put him through, eat at me. Yes, it's for the greater good. But he's been there, over and over. Taking care of me, and now Kat. And I've put even more on him like 'Here, you'll have an army coming for us. Won't it be fun?' I should have taken him into consideration more.

Old Delaney was right. I'm not a nice person. I need to find Drew. He shouldn't be alone dealing with everything I've thrown at him. And I need to apologize because being a Destiny doesn't mean being a heartless bitch.

Chapter Thirty-One
DREW

Fuck. Fuck. Fuck.

Years of protecting the world from Delaney has not prepared me for protecting her from *unknown branches of people*. I down the moonshine and let it trace a path of fire down my throat. It settles in my stomach, but it doesn't soothe me. Instead, it burns.

I have to protect her. I can't live without her. And I damn well can't do this all over again. If I fail her, I fail myself. I fail the world.

Fuck.

I love Delaney. I can and have walked through several rings of torture for her, without even knowing what I was getting into. But this might be asking way too much, even from me.

I throw on a jacket and pull out my knapsack. In it are things I'd need to rough it overnight outside: a temporary pop-up tent, a solar blanket, rope, shears, knife, some matches, a high-power flashlight, a pen light, and some duct tape. I shove in a fully charged battery block and a cord and check to make sure my nine-millimeter has a full magazine.

Downstairs, I stop in the kitchen to pack a few bottles of

water and food. Charlie eyes the knapsack and raises his brow. This isn't the first time I've taken off to contemplate shit, but I'm sure he didn't think I'd be doing it now. Me neither, Charlie. Me neither.

He wipes his hands on his apron and pulls items out of the fridge to make sandwiches. "How long you going to be gone?"

"A day or two at the most. I'll be up at the lake and only a phone call away. You'll keep an eye on things here just fine."

Charlie nods, and for the first time in our relationship, he intrudes in my personal life without invitation. "Everything okay? Want to talk about it?"

My throat constricts and my shoulders hunch down. This isn't something I can talk out. He can't help me fight a battalion of people we don't know anything about. And he can't fucking take care of everything like I should be doing.

"It's fine. I just need a few days." The excuse will work. I've used it plenty of times in the past.

He nods and hands me a couple of sandwiches. I bag a few apples and cram some of the freeze-dried fruits into my pack. If I need anything else, I can hunt and cook it myself. I head out and up the trails to the side of the house.

Nobody knows what I've needed to do in my time alone. To talk myself into continuing, to open myself to the pain, to rail against the Fates. And ultimately, to remember why I was doing this and reorganize my thoughts and recharge my faith in us.

Love trumps Fate, and Karma can kiss my ass. Delaney's smarter and better than all of them and we were one. And it had worked.

Here we are, whole again, a unit with a bond so strong it can kill. And this time, I think it just might. Because I'm afraid I'm no longer strong enough on my own.

Once the tent is set up, I gather firewood and start a fire in the ring of stones where old ashes remain from previous trips

I've taken. The water on the lake ripples with fish jumping for their evening meal as the sun slowly sets.

I move long enough to shove some food in my system and add more wood to the pile I've already dwindled down. Stars spread out across the sky.

There's no better place to contemplate how shitty your life is than outside in the night air while watching a raging fire consume everything you place in it and while the nocturnal creatures mercilessly hunt their prey.

How the fuck am I supposed to protect Delaney and her child? How am I supposed to orchestrate a three-man army while listening to the beat of death?

I lay back and stare up through the canopy of trees and watch as the sky lightens from the dark. I only move when I need to fuel my body and the fire.

I watch as the sun rises. It never wavers and never fails to do its job. It just rises over and over to fight another day. And do I have any other choice? I can't run. It's not in me. And Delaney won't run because it's not in her.

I was born a Protector and she was born a Destiny. And our soul split in half and settled in each of us. We are one. Always will be.

Delaney won't waver, and I won't waver. We're like the sun—always doing its job.

But I still can't fight blindfolded.

Shit.

My hands curl into tight fists, and I get up and cram the last sandwich into my mouth. I strip off my shirt and work maneuvers over and over, using the Mook Jong I installed here. An outside training room is just as good as an inside one.

Shit.

I strip, and running off the pier, I dive into the still cold lake. I swim back and forth until my arms no longer cut through the water with precision and the tips of my fingers turn blue.

I dry off in front of the fire and crack a can of soup from the bottom of my knapsack. Bleh. Cold soup. Not the best meal, but it'll get me by.

Shit.

I'm a master strategist. Capable of analyzing data at an incredible rate of speed, and no matter how I look at it, I still can't fight the unknown with just us.

Shit.

I already know what I need to do. And I fucking hate it. My hands curl into fists again.

Shit.

I need to call Astrid and get a hold of Tyson. The only two Magicals I didn't know I knew. I'm going to need them, and both of them owe me and Delaney.

Because fuck if I'll just hand over *our* soul to Death.

DELANEY

I run out of the house and let my soul guide me to his. The sick feeling in my stomach grows. What if he doesn't forgive me for the things I've put him through? Sure, we're soul mates. But that didn't mean we had to live as a couple. What if he decided to go that route?

I'm an idiot.

When I get to the clearing, I don't see Drew. The fire barely smolders in the ring, covered up by ashes. I feel him but don't see him.

Suddenly, the leaves part and he steps out of a tent. It's so well camouflaged I would've walked right into before I saw it.

His eyes are sad, and the flutter in my chest pours panic through me. I put my hand up as his mouth opens.

"Before you say anything, I want to say I'm sorry. I'm so

sorry for everything I've put you through. I know I apologized before, but it took me a little longer than it should have to realize that it was so much more than I thought it was."

His expression hasn't changed at all. The pressure builds inside of me. How could I have been so stupid?

"I never should have assumed that you would help me. It's an awesome responsibility, and I used our love and took it for granted that you would simply follow along with my plans. It was an awful thing to do, and I wish I had talked about it with you instead of just telling you. And I understand if you don't want to pursue this. I can't expect you to join up in every Destiny calculation. I didn't treat you like the other half of my soul and therefore equal, and I'm sorry."

Drew shoves his hands into his pockets and his jaw clenches. Is he mad or just waiting me out? Am I too late? I clasp my hands in front of me. Fourteen-year-old me had been too naive to the compromise required of relationships. Non-Destiny Delaney knew what it took to make a partnership work. And I fucked it up.

"I never even asked you if you wanted to be with me. I just assumed you did and jumped your bones. I...I'm sorry. I mean, I'm not sorry I jumped your bones, but that I didn't talk it all over with you. Can you forgive me?"

Drew doesn't move. The dread rises up and joins the guilt. Both tighten my throat until I'm afraid I can't breathe.

I turn and stare at the lake. "I don't know what I should be doing. I'm afraid I'm doing everything wrong, yet there's a need to get it all done yesterday. Unfortunately, yesterday is already gone. I'm afraid I'm not preparing fast enough or hard enough. I can't breathe, I'm so terrified. But none of it terrifies me as much as you not wanting to be by my side."

I open my eyes and stare into Drew's. I beg him with my own to understand.

"I love you. There's nothing to forgive. You should never

have to ask." His rough voice calms my chaotic thoughts. Soothes me instantly. The knot that's been pulled tighter and tighter in my stomach relaxes for the first time in hours.

"Yes, I should. We're partners and equals, and if I want or need to include you in any manipulations, I need to ask. And I promise I'll never make the same mistake again."

He puts his hand out and, grabbing mine, pulls me straight into his arms. They cage around me, bands of steel. Instead of trapping me, they protect me. As usual, the comfort coming from him calms me, the warmth curls into my blood. I close my eyes and inhale his scent. My heart rate slows and the panic melts away. This is why soul mates are meant to be together. Two souls joined for a brief contact, like a hit from a drug. Maybe there isn't euphoria, but each time there's something close to bliss. The peace, the comfort, is something that can't be replicated. What one needs the other gives. I sigh. He makes everything right just by being.

"I forgive you. I'm sorry to have left you alone. I needed to think. I can't think clearly around you. I've been without you for so long, I can't think about anything but you when we're together. I don't know how to adjust yet. To know *you* are here for good."

"I'm the same. I want to spend time with Kat, cherishing my moments with her. I want to spend time with you. I missed you so much. Even though I wasn't consciously aware of it, my soul was. And believe me, it missed you dreadfully. But I have to put that aside. I must focus on training, prepping for combat. This is huge. Bigger than you and me, bigger than Kat and me. I don't know what else I can do. This urgency builds in me, and I'm all wrapped up in it."

"I feel it, too. That's why I needed some time. I've been without you for so long, I don't want to care about anything else that's happening. At the same time, I need to care, because it puts you in danger. And nothing is going to take you away from me again. Do you hear me? I forbid you killing yourself or putting me on a wild goose chase or anything else ever again. I can't lose you. Ever. I don't think I'd be strong enough a second time."

His forehead rests against mine. We both close our eyes, wrapped up in the moment. Simply feeling.

"I won't leave you again. I wouldn't have left you the first time either, if we could have helped it. It was the only way. I love you. Thank you for forgiving me, for being you." Reluctantly, I step out of the protective warmth of his embrace. "We need to sit down with Charlie and Mark. We need to warn them."

"All right. Let's go then."

We convene in the war room. The two of them stand gravely, listening as we tell them what's coming and why it's so important we win this battle. No more secrets.

Mark's jaw drops. "She's a Time-Turner? I thought they didn't exist?" Shock colors every word he utters.

Drew responds. "You're not the only one."

We decided beforehand not to mention the stone Drew has hidden in a secret spot in the house. We must continue to guard it. If Mark or Charlie wonder if Time-Turning is what brings me back, that's on them; we won't be confirming it. The dangers of being in possession of it would bring a different kind of army to the house we couldn't possibly fend off.

"I knew that little girl was special." Charlie beams as if he had a personal hand in her uniqueness.

Getting over his shock, Mark asks, "So what's the plan?"

"We guard against an invasion. We protect the house. We protect each other, and we protect Katrina," I respond.

"Mark, I want to get together later with you. I have some ideas for the grounds that we need to go over."

"Sure thing." Mark turns toward me. "We won't let

anything happen to her. I promise."

Loyalty, even when I threatened him earlier. I don't deserve it, but Katrina does, and I'll gladly accept on her behalf.

"Thank you. I can't tell you how much I appreciate it."

"Anything for a pretty lady." At Drew's growl, Mark drops a wink.

I laugh, relieved. He's forgiven me, too. My heart soars and feels a little lighter. I smile and put my hand in Drew's. Rising on tiptoes, I whisper in Drew's ear. "I only have eyes for you." He squeezes my hand in silent reply.

With a strong sense of foreboding, we wrap up our planning session. I look at each person in turn. Nothing comes in the form of a vision, and to search, I'll have to meditate. It's been so long since I've done it, but the rhythm of it'll be the same.

I'll do it tonight in the hopes of seeing happy futures all around.

But first, Drew and I need to ride into town and visit a few people who will need to be part of our inner circle in this greater scheme of things.

The dark SUV idles at the front door. Mark parked it there but remained in the vehicle. Drew and I run out of the house and into the car, switching with Mark, and take off at a high speed, gravel and dust spewing out behind us.

Drew's eyes are everywhere, searching for an attack. One thing I hadn't been able to foresee was how seriously he would take my protection now that he has me back.

"I told you they won't be here for this trip. It's safe enough."

A huff is the only response I get. The GPS is set up for a club called Ferraro's, a short twenty-minute ride from the house.

"Why is it that we need to go to this club?"

"I told you. I need to meet up with the owner. He's a Guardian that's doing some things for Magicals. I really don't know what's going to come of it because some of my vision was obscured. And fourteen-year-old me didn't really know how to keep looking. I'd probably been overwhelmed as it was."

"Clubs have people in them. Lots of them." His fingers tighten on the steering wheel, and I reach over, laying my hand over his.

"You've got to relax. It will be fine. Trust me."

Drew turns his head, his green eyes piercing mine. "You know I do. But I'm never going to lose you. And this whole trip is a hazard to that plan."

I don't respond because nothing but time will change his actions.

We pull into the back parking lot in time to see a woman with dark hair, dressed all in black with a pair of lethal looking blades strapped to her back kick down the door.

I glance over at Drew, whose thunderous expression practically screams, I told you so. "I've seen her before. She's a friend."

A man's body flies out of the open door and lands with a thud several feet away.

"Reeeeally?" Drew's exaggerated drawl makes me laugh.

"Yes, now come on."

"Who. The. Fuck. Are. You." The low, gravelly voice floating out through the door sounds furious.

"Exactly what I'm thinking," Drew murmurs. I smack him playfully on the arm as I sidestep the body in front of me.

"I'm Arnica." Her voice embodies a no-nonsense, fuck around and find out tone, and I one hundred percent approve. I can't wait to meet her in person.

We step through the doorway behind her and without a second passing, a weapon materializes in her hand, the tip inches from my face. I don't flinch, knowing she'd take it as a sign of weakness. Besides, Drew's gun isn't far from Arnica's head. None of this is how I envisioned us all meeting.

I glance around at the bodies of well-trained Guardians lying in various states of blood and moans around the kitchen and can't help being impressed. I'd just managed to catch a glimpse of her black attire when she opened the door to walk through. She's fast.

I stare up at the couple on a landing above us.

"And I'm Delaney and this is Drew. We need to talk to you. All of you."

We're all seated around a massive conference table, and if this meeting had been under different circumstances, it would be comical. But the tension fills the room rapidly, and I know I need to diffuse it quickly. Too many egos in a small space is a problem. Too many trained fighters with egos in a small space is a mistake.

"We need your help. I'm a Destiny and Drew is my Protector." There's an inhalation from the man named Dexter. His dark eyes and dark brows don't give off any friendliness in the chiseled face. Power emanates from him in a silent way that makes him even more formidable. The scent of salt hits my nostrils, and I put out my hand, catching his sleeve and giving it a yank before he's back in his seat. "Satisfied?" I put my other hand on Drew's lap, effectively holding him in his chair. "He was just testing me," I murmur.

Drew speaks to Dex softly. "Testing is fine. Touch her and I'll kill you."

Dex nods and Drew nods and suddenly the tension isn't nearly as palpable. Arnica leans back just enough that her blades touch the chair. "Now that you're done swinging your dicks around, anyone want to tell me what the fuck we're meeting about?"

"Magicals, Dreamers, and Guardians. And what that

means to all of us."

There isn't much information that can be shared as of yet because this is all new to us. But we ultimately decide that Dex is going to coordinate a quarterly meeting. Our very own secret club. I nearly snort at the name, but I know none of the people here except for Drew would get my humor. The blonde, Cassie, who seems to be bonded to Dexter, keeps staring at me. I've forgotten how unnerving it can be for people to do it so blatantly, and I'm itching to get home.

As I'm getting up, a fleeting vision shadows me, and I stop Arnica from leaving the room. "Watch the moon."

"Excuse me?" she hisses, her dark eyebrows angry slashes in a much too pale face. I shake my head because telling her anything else could mess up everything I'd seen. But her indecision had been so great that the ramifications would have rippled for eons. I had to try to help her without telling her what to choose. "That's all I can say."

"For Fuck's sake, keep your destiny shit to yourself then. That's all I need is to twist it round and round and figure it out. Like I don't have enough shit on my brain." She continues to mutter to herself as she walks out the door.

Cassie side-eyes me, but it looks like Dexter is keeping her in place. Suddenly, none of them seem very friendly, and I wish it didn't matter what people thought of me.

"Let's go home."

Drew rushes me through the place and has me in the car before I can do much more than nod at the owner of Ferraro's. "I swear to Karma, if one more dirty look had been sent your way, I'd beat them all to a bloody pulp."

I sigh because I had kinda felt the same. But I know better. People fear what they don't understand. "I'm used to it. Even though it hurts sometimes. You forget, I've been the object of such looks my whole life."

He growls softly again, but his hand moves off the steering

wheel and grips mine in my lap, his thumb rubbing circles and heat coursing through us both. Our own method of relaxation.

When we get home, I spend an hour with Kat and meet back with Drew for dinner. "I'm going to the pool room for a meditation session if that's good with you?" I ask him.

He nods, chewing the last of his steak and potatoes. "I've got a meeting of my own."

Drew's still with Mark and Charlie concocting some devious plans as killing traps for the grounds when I head down. I'd worry how ruthless and bloodthirsty he is if I didn't know his soul is pure gold. That I'm also not going to turn away from all the ruthlessness I need to protect Katrina doesn't play into it all. I snort.

Nobody is kidding anyone here. I've taken a life or two. Nowhere near as much as Drew. But I've lived them through him. It never gets easier. You can only beg for something so pure that it cleanses the taint of death. And hope it won't cling to you.

I turn into the pool room. There's a natural hot spring that feeds into a stone water fountain. Eventually, it trickles into the pool, creating a warmth much like a heated pool.

Vipassana is a Buddhist meditation practice that I'd learned from the moment I was able to comprehend the idea of sitting still. Ideally, I'd be in the forest surrounded by the very nature I'm calling on. But this will do.

With the sound of tinkling water and the warmth of the heavy air, I gently roll through the meditative maneuvers of Tai Chi. Breathing through the combinations, I hood my eyes, working to relax my body and mind.

Once my tense muscles are loose, I sit cross-legged in front of the stone statue of Buddha, my back straight. Closing my eyes, breathing in and out, my abdomen rising and falling, I focus on my soul. It's my anchor, the other half firmly rooted in Drew. If anything should happen during my meditation or my visions, no harm can befall me. The other half isn't in danger and therefore capable of reeling me in. It's one of the reasons soul mates exist. To protect itself, the soul needs a haven.

I open my senses and let them wash over me. Until I'm blinded by nothing.

I search then, for the destiny of my friends. I won't see much of the coming battle. It's been obscured by Nirvana and Karma. Those two have worked hard to conceal bits of the future in an attempt to keep anyone else meddling in things we've worked too hard for, risked too much for.

I smile at the image of Mark. He's wrapped around an unknown woman. The smile fades when I witness the heartbreak. Let's just see what I can do about that. A mental tug here, letting the line slack there. The heartbreak returns tenfold. In the end, I leave it be. There's nothing I can do for now. I'm sorry for it, but I know that any prize he ends up with will be that much sweeter having gone through the pain. And it's better that I don't change anything.

I look at Liza next. The knowledge that she lives to a ripe old age, content, makes me happy. Nothing to change here.

I can't look into mine and Drew's. We're on a path, blind. I've done too much to ours. It's the price I pay when I meddle too much. I don't look into Moira's either. I know how that will end. And she's made her peace with it a long time ago. It doesn't stop her from her path. She's already chosen.

I'm saddened by the dark when I look into Lydia. Any attempt to fix it won't change a thing. Fate has already been here.

I mentally stumble hard when I see nothing for Charlie.

NO.

No matter how I change things, the outcome remains the same. A dark nothing. I can't touch this one either. Fate isn't just a bitch. She's hard and ruthless, ripping one of my favorite people from my side. I stutter in my thoughts, and breaking the connection, it jerks me out of my landscape. I open my eyes to stare into Buddha's. And I weep for what I can't change.

I wash away the signs of tears. My knowledge is my burden alone to shoulder. I can't share this with anyone; it's simply not fair. Nobody should know when they're going to die, or what they're going to do or make of themselves.

Once I'm dressed, I search the house for Drew and food. My stomach is rumbling with hunger, and I'm sure his is too. I catch up right outside my room.

He reaches for me, grabs me, and in a fierce movement sweeps me up into his arms for a kiss. The storm that's always right behind our passion unleashes and our lips fuse. Tasting the desperation in his kiss does nothing but make my soul struggle to reach his, to soothe. I'm not sure which one of us tugs the other into the bedroom. The desperation spills over from mouths to hands and frantic, we tug at each other's clothing, rushing, fueling the need to reassure.

The wall is sturdy enough to withstand my body. He picks me up and slips me over and on to him. With my back against the wall, I grab the molding of the doorframe. I need something for leverage, to hold on to. Drew holds me up, guiding his penetration, but I've never been one to be a bystander. I want full participation. Using the doorknob to brace my foot on, I hold on to the slim molding with one hand. The other is wrapped in his hair, guiding him to my breasts.

Desperation colors every movement. Need coats it.

Our souls slam together in their own ritual. I send him the last of his soul I'm carrying. The force of it hits him, the fullness from being equal again causes his orgasm to explode and draws out mine. Drew turns and weekly slides down the wall, and we settle on the floor.

"Are you okay?" I ask, catching my breath.

"There was a minute, after working out some of the plans, that wrapped a moment in my brain where I lost you again. I needed to make sure you were here still."

"Here I am." I grin.

"Yes. Yes, you are. You have no idea how happy that makes me."

I look pointedly at his crotch. "I can tell."

He laughs. "I'll never get enough you."

"I hope not."

We barely manage to rise, both of us on shaky knees. I look at him and we both say, "Food!" I giggle. I can't help myself. I'm beyond giddy to be back with him.

Afterward, we spend some time with Katrina. Drew looks at her with new eyes. He may not understand children, but he does understand Guardians. And Kat being half of one is enough for him. He's in his element chatting her up. Kat has never been one to put up with childish language and cooing and she's always been wise beyond her years.

Maybe that's what made her and I a good team and why I never seriously considered any boyfriends during our time together. They didn't understand what Guardians are and how we operate day to day.

And with all that's happened in her life, I know she's aged. She may be almost six, but soon she'll be learning her craft, honing her abilities. Learning defense and offense. Learning whatever it is that Time-Turners need to learn. The days of her being treated like a child, by anyone, are over.

Briefly, I despise her childhood being cut short. The emotion doesn't last. Guardians have long been training children at a young age. It's not just required but necessary. The world is hard. It's dark. But there are great big pockets of light, too. In order to stay in the light, you need to be able to navigate the dark. And be a survivor.

Chapter Thirty-Two

DELANEY

As the morning sun rises, a sensor trips. We roll out of the bed, fully dressed. It's the way we go to sleep now. There's no time to make sure you aren't butt naked when the fighting starts. Drew pulls up the audio for the speaker at the gate.

"Identify yourself."

"I'm Lucinda. I was sent by Moira," replies a stilted voice.

When the video pops up on the monitor, I jerk minutely. It's enough for Drew to notice.

Drew looks over at me. "Do you know this Lucinda?"

"I don't. But she was in my visions yesterday when I was looking. So, she's definitely here. I just don't know what her role is."

Drew knows better than to ask anyway, but I wanted to clarify it. We're on new ground here. The face up close and personal is the one that causes Mark's heartbreak. The hard part for me is always pretending I don't know anything.

"State your purpose." He pulls out his cell and scrolls until he gets to Mark's name. I keep my lips clamped closed.

"I'm here in the capacity of teacher. And that's all I'm

prepared to say while out in the street," she huffs. She's got balls, I'll admit.

"I'm going to send a man to escort you. I'm sure you don't have a problem being scanned."

"That's fine. I'll wait here. But please don't leave me hanging for too long. I've already observed a patrol rolling through." Her voice sounds prim and proper.

Drew doesn't bother to answer her. He calls Mark and asks him to go down. I bite my lip hard to stop myself from asking him to send someone else. It won't change anything.

Noticing the bitten lip, he leans over and places a kiss on it. "I don't know what you've seen, but you know you can count on me treating her fairly."

That's what I'm afraid of.

None of the sensors trip as Mark drives Lucinda up. Drew and I head to the front yard to confront her. He'll never let anyone in the house without vetting them first.

Mark drives up in a golf cart with Lucinda sitting stiffly on the chair. I can't hide the smirk that drifts over my lips before I catch myself. Mark has a gun laying on his lap, one finger on the trigger, pointing in her direction. Lucinda, it seems, isn't too thrilled with the notion.

When they stop, Drew draws his own weapon, pointing toward her. She steps out of the cart, bravely staring at Drew as if she didn't have steel pointed at her back and chest.

"I'm Lucinda. Moira sent me to teach Katrina some of the things she needs to learn. You can call her if you'd like."

"Why didn't she send word before you got here?" I hate her glorious, fiery curls.

"She was preoccupied at the time she gave me my orders. I've no idea," Lucinda responds with a shrug.

Pulling my cell out, I call Moira. No response. At Drew's silent question, I shake my head.

"You will have to leave until we can verify that you are who you say you are," Drew says.

"Excuse me? You're asking me to leave? A Magical who's helping a Guardian?" She draws herself up to her full five feet.

"I'm a highly prized teacher to young Magicals. You can't be serious." The diminutive woman looks outraged. It's easy for me to picture her as an English governess of old.

"I don't care how prized you are. Until we verify you're who you say you are, you won't be coming in."

Drew pulls his own phone out, and holstering his gun, he taps into the Guardianship database. He lifts his phone to snap a picture of her, presumably to scan in.

I shove my hand in front of the lens just as he snaps the picture.

"No. We can't risk letting others know what's going on here."

"Damn. Try Moira again." He's frustrated with it all. He doesn't like people he doesn't know here. I can't say I blame him.

I call again, and this time Moira answers. The peculiar sounds of a fist hitting flesh is loud in the background.

"Moira, you okay?"

"Yes." Her reply is short, and worrisome. But I know she can handle whatever is coming her way.

"I'm staring at someone claiming to be a teacher. Do you know anything about that?"

"Damn, I forgot to call you. Yes, Lucinda. Tiny little thing with fiery hair. Might need an attitude adjustment, but she's the best we've got, and she's there to teach the youngest one."

I snort. "Just wanted to be safe." At the slap of skin against skin, I double check *her*. "Are you sure you're ok?"

"Yes, I'll be fine. Keep her safe." She clicks off, and I stare at the phone, bothered by something, but I don't know what it is. I turn to Drew.

"She confirms she's here to teach Kat."

Drew scrutinizes my face. I know he's picking up on my consternation and worry.

He looks over at Mark and nods his head. Mark holsters his weapon. "Welcome, Lucinda. I'll show you to a room."

Lucinda slowly releases an annoyed hiss.

"Fine." She picks up her bag and walks by us to enter the home. Drew throws his arm out in front of her, effectively stopping her. She turns her head, her green eyes somehow shooting flames.

"If I find out you're anything but what you say you are or something happens to anyone in this house, I'll kill you."

Lucinda looks Drew up and down, insolently. "You can try."

Drew's body tenses, and I put an arm on his shoulder.

Outrage stiffens his body, but he puts his arm down. "Watch yourself."

Mark ushers Lucinda inside and puts her in a bedroom on the first floor where she'll be monitored.

"Until we're hundred percent sure, I think we should bring Kat to her, not the other way around."

"I agree," he murmurs. His brain is already preoccupied, analyzing the information he's got.

The meeting with Lucinda and Kat goes surprisingly well. Lucinda has a totally different demeanor when she isn't held at gunpoint. No surprise there. I see nothing wrong with the way she is around Kat.

She wraps Lucinda around her finger, as she does everyone else. It's not long before our house falls into a rhythm. Drew and I train in every spare minute. I peek at the monitors at times to see what Katrina's learning. I'm curious how different Guardians are from Magicals. There are things I don't know, and Drew takes notes constantly, looking for information.

Time-Turners are apparently also taught meditation, and I use the opportunity to do my own meditation with her. Another way of spending what little precious time we have together. Drew joins us on occasion, but he fidgets worse than she does, and when the giggling starts, I shoo him out of the workout room.

In the short time I've talked to Kat and broke the news of what she is, what I am, she's blossomed. Like Guardian children, she quickly adapts to the lifestyle and learns faster than the average child.

The household slowly accepts Lucinda, who prefers to go by Lucy. Her prickliness dissipates once she gets to know someone. I'm sure it's hard for her. Magicals don't have a high regard for Guardians. Understandable, given that Guardians are trying to kill their people.

I'm chagrined by the knowledge that Mark and Lucy spend a great deal of time together. Mark can usually be found by her side when he isn't busy with his own duties, and I stay away knowing I might not be able to keep my mouth shut. Unfortunately, I, too, find myself liking her.

Weeks go by with little but hard work on all our ends. Lucy is allowed to teach behind the bookcase but still needs to be scanned in with one of us. Drew isn't taking any chances. This irritates Lucy to no end and she simply ignores him, as if he is an abomination to her.

And then one day, the madness begins.

Drew and I've just gone to bed. As I'm falling asleep, I sense someone in the room. I sit up, wild-eyed, and glance at Drew, who's also sitting up and has a weapon in both hands. There's nothing there. But I continue to peer around the room.

Slowly, the inky shape of a woman separates from the shadows. I put my hand on Drew's gun, drawing it down.

"Nirvana. How nice to see you." I smile. The gorgeous

woman carrying all the colors of the night hasn't changed a bit.

"Yeah, real nice," Drew grumbles. "Why do they insist on popping up into my home?"

Nirvana smiles. She's as serene as ever, the dark to Moira's light.

"I'm not really here, Guardians." Her deep, molten voice is as soothing as a lullaby. "May I take you through the night sky?" She extends her arm and I nod.

Drew throws out a hand. "Wait. You're going to go with her?"

"Yes, kind of. Don't freak out, my body and soul will be right here."

Drew furrows his brows.

"It's more of a transient mental thing." He doesn't like it, but it's the only way.

I put my hand in Nirvana's outstretched one. I'm immediately thrown into a floating state. Time hasn't dulled the shock of it. It's exactly as I remember. I look down to see my body on the bed, Drew hovering over me. Then he's pacing, the poor man. With gun drawn. Nothing will happen to my body. He'll make certain of it. Something else he has to go through because of me. My chest aches with remembrance.

"You are well, Nirvana?" It's been years since I've seen her, and though I've grown from a gangly fourteen-year-old to an adult, I've aged, and she hasn't. She looks exactly as she did, her face unlined.

"I am well, Guardian. I need to show you what's coming. Are you prepared?" I swallow hard. I hope to all the fates that it isn't as bad a vision as last time.

"Yes." I'm thrown into the bowels of a war yet to come. Fires and screams, guns and blood. Again. But I relax at the absence of evil. And then, the black cloud rolls in. It covers everything, including the sun. The world is plunged into darkness. Screams echo in the night trailed by the wails of pain.

I drag in a long breath of air and sit straight up in bed. Drew wipes my bloody tears.

"What the fuck is this?" He whirls on Nirvana, but I reach out a hand, grabbing his shirt, stopping him from flexing his hands around her throat.

"It's okay, Drew." He doesn't retreat, but hangs his hands down, flexing and unflexing with the need to squeeze.

"What is that, Nirvana? Everything we've done is for nothing?" Drew tenses at my question.

"No. Not for nothing, Guardian. But I'm afraid that's from the Dreamers that have sided with the Guardians. They think they'll be spared if they side with them. It won't happen." She shakes her head. Her own eyes leak bloody tears. "I am saddened to send them to their death." She sets her shoulders. "But they have chosen."

"I'm here to tell you how you can defeat them. As I do, they'll arrive and attack you in your sleep."

Drew's body jerks. The rage rolls off him at the knowledge yet more unwanted visitors will breach his defenses like they're nothing. "How do we kill them?" he grinds out between clenched teeth. Nirvana turns blood-stained eyes to him.

"It pains me to tell you this. I consign them to death." She bows her head and is silent. She looks up at him. "You'll need to cut off their head with a sword of our making. They can't be killed with anything of yours."

"Where can I get this sword?"

"I will place it in your dreams. You will have it when you need it."

Drew scoffs, but I quickly cover his sounds. "Thank you, Nirvana. I know how this must hurt you."

She lifts her hand, palm up. "They've made their choice, and I've made mine. I have a gift for you."

I shudder at the thought of their gifts. They mean well, but Guardians were never meant to house their knowledge.

"You will need to find the flowers with the blue petals. In the most peculiar place, they will grow on top of the trees and bloom only in the moonlight. You must harvest them and prepare a tea for its use. Keep this flower with you, for one day, you will need it. This is my gift to you. It will give you life when there is otherwise death."

She glides over, a dream on the night wind, and places a hand on Drew's shoulder. He stiffens but doesn't move.

"I'm grateful to you for all that you've been through. I can remove the memory of your pain if you want."

Drew steps back quickly. "No. Thank you."

Nirvana tilts her head. "Very well. I can give you knowledge if you'd like, instead."

He glances at me and then back to her. "Is there a way for it to be written? I'd prefer not to have anything added that can scramble my brains."

She pauses, thoughtful. "No. We don't have tangible things like books. But I can give you a miniscule amount of knowledge by touch. This will not cause your mind to fracture. I promise it."

Drew looks at me and I shrug. Taking a gamble, he accepts and steps forward. Nirvana moves toward him, and with the barest touch of skin to skin, transfers whatever information she's given him. Drew's body shakes and convulses, and every muscle in my body tightens in order to not move to his side. I know enough to know interference isn't wise.

"Be brave, my Guardians. I wish you nothing but the most pleasant of dreams."

Nirvana disappears, and I run to Drew's side. "Are you okay?"

His body is rigid, the muscles throughout, tensed. "I think so. Fuck. No wonder you've lost your shit before." He blows out a wheezy breath and forces himself to relax. The muscles still bunch and quiver.

"I think I need a drink." Walking to the cabinet, he pulls out a bottle of alcohol and doesn't bother with a cup. He swallows several times and recaps it.

"I don't know how you managed to do all that at fourteen." He gathers me up in his arms and holds me tight. "You're an amazing woman."

I don't ask him what Nirvana gave him. He'll share it in time. In the meantime, my body aches and I'm exhausted.

I kiss him softly. "We need sleep."

We get back into bed, making sure our weapons are, once again, within reach.

"Drew? Why didn't you want the memory of your pain removed?"

"Because without it, I can't fully appreciate you." He puts his arm around me, and I snuggle into his side, a smile on my face.

Chapter Thirty-Three

DELANEY

I wake to sirens blaring. Drew and I race out of bed, grabbing our weapons and holstering them before we've even swiped at our bleary eyes. We rush out of the room. Down the hallway, Drew's pulling up the house system on his cell. I'm running side-by-side without any idea where we're going and why.

He leaps the banister of the stairs and lands on the first floor. In awe, I hurry down the stairs and meet him at the bookcase as it opens.

"It's coming from Katrina's room!" he yells.

Panic makes me pick up my pace, and we dash for her room. Katrina's in the middle of the room crying by a pile of ashes. An acrid smell dances on the air. She looks up, shock on her face.

"Momma?" She runs over, wrapping her arms around my torso.

"Baby, are you okay? What happened?" I pull her away from me and visually check her, every inch.

"I'm fine Momma, but it's Lucy. I don't know what happened."

Liza's staring at the pile of ashes. The whites of her eyes echo her horror. "She just...caught fire," she whispers.

"What?" I say at the same time Drew says, "Are you sure?"

He pulls up the monitor and rewinds the footage. Sure enough, we watch Lucy wake up and frantically get dressed. She makes a mad dash for the door but doesn't make it. The fire starts at her ankle, the orange and green flames licking at her clothes. It's over in seconds when she bursts into flame and showers ash into a pile.

"What the?" Drew and I glance at each other. We have no idea what to do.

"Well, I guess I'll just clean that up and..." He trails off, staring in wonder at the silvery pile. We stand transfixed as ashes rise and swirl, twirling round and round, a cyclone, until it takes shape in the form of a woman.

"I'll be damned," Drew whispers. "She's a Phoenix."

Lucy stares at us, as we watch her fully reform. "I'm so sorry. I didn't realize this was going to happen here or I'd have left earlier. I never meant for anyone to witness this."

Katrina slowly walks over to her and reaches up, patting her cheeks carefully. "You're alive?"

Lucy chuckles. "Yes, I am. I hope I didn't frighten you."

"No, that was so cool!" Katrina jumps up and down.

Lucy laughs and looks at us. Her laughter dies off. "I think I need to talk give some explanations right now, okay?"

"Okay." Kat hops back into her bed and covers up. Liza gently sits with her, whispering.

Lucy, Drew, and I walk out into the hallway. Drew crosses his arms.

"Talk," he demands.

"You're right. I'm a Phoenix. I can't always control when it happens or I would've never burnt up in front of her."

"Why didn't you tell us?"

"Well, it's not really your business is it?"

"Aren't Phoenixes supposed to be reborn?"

"Yeah well, I'm kinda operating under a curse."

"What?" Drew yelps. "What do you mean a curse?" He's already skeptical of Lucy. The fact she's cursed isn't helping his view of her. Or me, for that matter.

"That doesn't pertain to you at all. It's my business. It affects nothing here, except for the fact that I can't control when I catch fire and rise up from the ashes." She shows us the ink tattoo at her wrist of a Phoenix. "This disappears when I'm ready to go up in flames. But I was sleeping and didn't realize it until I felt the burn. I wasn't fast enough. Next time, I will be, and no one will need to witness it."

Suddenly, I feel sorry for her. I guess we all have our pain.

"It's okay. Do you need anything?" It's been hard to not like Lucy, and if it wasn't for Mark's future, I'd have enjoyed being friends. She's got a dry wit that borders on sarcasm—my kind of person.

"No, I'll be fine. Thank you."

Saying good night to Kat, Drew and I leave the room. "A freaking Phoenix. I never thought I'd see one."

"I guess everything we've been taught has been false. I wonder who in the Guardianship keeps falsifying documents. Someone is doing it. But why? Why can't the branches be equal?"

"Because they're erasing the trail of Magicals."

Unanimously, we decide to grab something to eat instead of going back to sleep. It would be hard with the excitement anyway.

Once we finish eating, Drew asks, "Want to go for a run?"

"Sure, I'll grab my sneakers." I race up to my room and nearly decapitate someone. I sheath my knife.

I don't normally expect someone in my room that's uninvited. "Lucy. Damn. You can't do that. I nearly killed you."

"I'd only rise back up. I want to talk to you. About

Katrina. She's ready to begin learning some of how to turn time. I assume you want to be there for it?"

"Absolutely! When do you start?"

"This morning after breakfast. We're going to work in the training room. I just came to grab my staff. Could you let me back in through the scanners."

"Sure thing." I lead her through the bookcase. I'm so excited. I can't wait to see some of Katrina's training.

After our run, we head to the training room. Katrina and Lucy are already there. Lucy, holding a large staff, is all business.

"Good, we can begin. The first thing I'm going to tell you is to keep quiet. It will be easy for Katrina to break her concentration. And that can have devastating effects.

"Second is that I'll be placing her in a sort of protective bubble, and you won't be able to reach her."

I open my mouth, but Drew beats me to it. "Why must she be in a bubble?"

"It's for the protection of the world," Lucy snaps. "You of all people want to protect the world, right? She needs to concentrate, but if she were to break concentration, it won't affect the outside world."

I shake my head.

"It's not negotiable. I won't teach her without it." Lucy is being uncharacteristically rude.

"Fine. But how do we break the bubble if we need to."

"You don't." Lucy grins. "You have to be a Magical." Her sense of superiority is grating on my nerves this morning. I have my misgivings, but I'm sure my parents did when I was young and in training too. I finally nod my consent.

"Good. So, it begins."

She thumps the staff on the floor and a polygonal half-sphere made of a shimmery gold substance forms over Katrina.

It reaches down to the floor. Katrina looks at us. I can't blame the slightly terrified look in her eyes.

"Oh, that was too easy." Lucy claps her hands in delight. She points her staff at the two of us, and Drew and I dive for the floor, missing a stream of energy. It burns a hole in the floor. We both duck and roll, running toward Lucy, who's running to the back of the room.

Another beam of energy flies out at our head, hitting the wall behind us. It blows a hole in the wall, and I see mountainous rock behind it. She runs out into the hallway, Drew and I hot on her heels. Damn Magicals, they certainly don't fight fair. Drew's already yelling at the house system, calling for Mark and Charlie, and arming the scanner. Realizing she won't be able to go through the bookcase, she dashes into the stairwell. We're right behind her with Mark on our tails.

We slow down, looking around the corner. "Where the hell is she?"

Mark seems dazed. "I can't believe she's a traitor. She, she," he stutters and trails off, and remembering his vision, my heart breaks for him. So, he's in love with her already. Damn.

Creeping carefully into the hallway, we spot her at the opposite end. There's no escape.

Mark hollers out. "Lucy, stand down or so help me, I'll shoot you where you stand."

"Oh, that's rich! The pathetic housekeeper will attempt to prove he's a man?" Lucy taunts. We all know it for what it is, but the red stains on his cheeks show the barb hit home. I'll kill her myself for hurting him. I can't believe I let my guard down. I *knew* this would happen.

Drew picks up on my fury and doesn't bother to offer a warning. He pulls out his Beretta and shoots. Lucy throws up her hand and a wall of gold shimmer rises, protecting her. The bullets bounce off as if made of rubber.

An impotent growl spills out of Drew's throat. Or is that mine?

Lucy laughs and slams her staff down on the ground. She herself shimmers, becoming opaque and then solidifies again. With a scream of frustration, she points her staff and sends a blast at the ceiling. Drew dives for me, rolling me to the ground. The hallway goes dark. There's a whisper of sound near my head and someone reaches out, grabbing blindly. There's a brief struggle. And then silence.

"Damn it. I almost had her," Drew says angrily. "Mark, you okay?"

"Yeah, boss," his voice echoes somewhere to the left.

"You all right?"

"I'm fine. Pissed. I've got to go back to Kat." I get up, and blindly, we feel our way to the stairs. Seeing the light from above, we race back up. Charlie's just getting up from the floor when we careen around the corner.

"What the fuck happened to you?"

"I don't know how Lucy got the jump on me. I came through the bookcase just as she came from upstairs, and she clocked me with that staff of hers."

He rubs the knot that's beginning to form on his forehead. That's going to leave a mark.

"You've got him, right?" Drew nods, and I run to Katrina. She's still in the bubble in the training room.

"Kat, baby, can you hear me from inside that thing?"

"Yes, Momma."

I sink to my knees in relief. At least I can communicate with her until I can figure out how to get her out.

"I'm sorry, Momma." Tears pour down her face, and my heart squeezes in my chest. This isn't how this should be. Incompetence and frustration choke me.

"Oh, baby, it's not your fault, sweetheart. We'll find a way to get you out of there."

"I'm thirsty and I want a hug." Her face crumples. My fury soars. How dare Lucy hurt my child?

I run to the refrigerator and grab a bottle of water.

"I'm going to see if I can give this to you okay." Katrina nods, and I roll the water bottle toward the shimmer. The minute it touches it, it melts the plastic and the water sizzles away.

Katrina looks at me with wide, terrified eyes. Damn.

Don't think. Don't think.

"It'll be okay, baby. I'll figure this out. Just whatever you do, don't touch it."

"Yes, Momma." She sniffles into her sleeve.

"I have to leave you. And get help. You're strong and brave. You are a warrior. You are part Guardian, Katrina, and Guardians take care of their own. I'll be back. I love you."

"I love you." She sits on the floor, hugging her knees to her chest. It nearly breaks me to leave her, but my blood boils, and the need to force someone to fix this wins out. Wait till I get a hold of Lucy. I'll kill her. I'll tear her into pieces with my bare hands.

Running back out into the hallway, I jog to the bookcase and through it. The men are around the table in the war room, staring at the monitors. I don't have a chance to speak. Every monitor in the room shows bodies running onto the grounds. For a moment, I'm thankful Katrina's trapped. I can't get to her, but again, neither can anyone else.

The invasion has begun.

"Call in the guys. We need every able body. Charlie, I need you manning from in here. Don't let anyone get past the bookcase." Drew looks at me. "It's time."

There's an unholy gleam in his eyes. He's always loved

combat and strategy. I hate that it has to do with Kat in the middle of it.

We arm ourselves as best we can. I've got knives and guns strapped to my thighs. I've blades crisscrossing my back and guns holstered in the shoulder harness I grab from the console. I lament not having my boots as I'd stick a knife in there. Already anticipating what I need, Drew opens the panel in the console and presses a button.

One of the walls of screens opens to a closet. I grab a pair of combat boots in my size. "I didn't know that was there."

"I added some upgrades to your design." He shoots me a grin. I grin back, and then it falters. Katrina. I finish lacing my boots and sheathe knives in each one. I grab a pistol for each hand and shove clips in my back pocket. I look over at Drew. Impossibly, he looks like a walking weapons room. I don't know how he can move around without clinking. I shake my head, it doesn't matter.

The three of us stand outside in front of the front door, a pitiful shield for all that I'd seen coming. I know Drew has more men, but I've no idea where they are. Screams echo in the silence as men are killed on Drew's cleverly hidden devices. I shudder, remembering it on footage. I'll never be able to unsee that.

We wait for what seems like an eternity. Our tense, battle-prepped bodies, quiver in anticipation. Gunsmoke drifts in the air. They're coming.

I hope we're ready.

The first couple of men through the woods are easily picked off by each of us. Once we can no longer shoot at an individual, we split up. All of us fight for one thing: Katrina.

At first, it's handy to keep shooting to kill. Eventually, I empty the clips and the spares of the guns in my hand. I want the ones on my back as backup, so I switch to hand-to-hand combat. I never take my eyes off my opponent, knowing Drew and Mark are doing the same thing.

As Guardians, we're taught to never let another distract you. One of the things Drew lamented for years after letting his emotions run wild during the incident at the mall. He'd not make that mistake again. I whirl and kick, punch and slit throats. Blood sprays everywhere. I lose track of how many die at my hand. They just keep coming. We keep backing up until the three of us are fighting back-to-back. And they still keep coming.

We have no choice but to stop when we're surrounded by thirty or more men.

We dare not give up. And then, the screams arise from the group. Some of the men turn around to see what's going on. I don't care why they're distracted. With unspoken consent, we jump back into the fray, attacking people at random. The tide is turning, and between us and whoever is coming from the trees, we're surrounding the invaders.

"Took his fucking time." Drew steps closer to me. I spy Tyson, and my body jerks to a standstill. Memories of the old Delaney war with the plans of fourteen-year-old me. The love I had with him was never real, but like the VR goggles, it takes a bit to wrap my head around.

Drew asked him here? This is going to be awkward.

As Tyson's men gather those who surrender, he walks to where Drew and I are standing. They face each other, neither one wanting to talk first. What is it with testosterone?

"Thank you, Ty, for coming in and assisting. You got us out of a bind."

Tyson hasn't stopped glaring at Drew, and Drew hasn't stopped shooting daggers at Ty. He's giving a new meaning to if looks could kill.

"I'm sure you guys would've handled it." Ty doesn't

bother to look at me at all. Is there anything worse than a pissing contest between men?

I step in between them. "We're all adults here. And this was a mission we needed to work together on. Tyson and I needed to be together." I ignore Drew grumbling in my ear.

Ty steps back. "I don't want any hard feelings, Drew. I don't love Delaney. Heck I don't even find her attractive."

Drew's growl gets louder. I sigh, exasperated. He's not helping.

"Look, man," Ty says, "we did what we had to do, and we used a potion to do it. Okay? Can we just get over this thing?"

He turns. "I don't know if I'll ever get the opportunity to know the real you, but I'd like to at least thank you. For all that you've done to help save my people. I—we can't ever thank you enough."

I nod. "Of course. I'm only sorry Guardians are behind it. I don't think we're done yet."

Drew puts his arm around me and clears his throat. "I'll thank you for taking good care of Delaney for all those years. That means more than anything." He sticks a hand out for Tyson to shake. Ty hesitates a moment before shaking hands with him. I know that hoping for us all to be friends might be too much. But I do hope that Ty doesn't stay out of our lives.

"Where's Katrina?" he asks.

"She's protected in a cage that only you might be able to break." At Tyson's squawk, I hurriedly explain what happened earlier. The three of us turn to the house when we're stopped short by the sight of Kat with Lucy. I gasp.

Drew immediately draws his weapon, as do I. Tyson, not knowing what's going on, follows our lead.

"Let her go, Lucy!" I yell, rage coloring my words.

Kat throws her hands in the air. "Momma, no, this is the real Lucy. She let me out."

"What?" This must be some kind of trick.

Charlie walks up behind Lucy. "She's got a big bruise forming on her cheekbone."

Lucy steps forward. "I'm so sorry, Delaney. I didn't know what she was planning."

"Who?" I ask while Drew asks, "Planning what?"

"My sister. I'd no idea that she was on the other side. I don't know what she's thinking. I'm truly sorry."

"And how do we know that anything you're saying is the truth?" I still don't understand what's going on.

"You could talk to Moira. She'll confirm it. I can show you the picture I have of her and I on my phone." She pulls out her phone and scrolls through and hands it to Charlie. He looks over the photo.

"There's two of them."

Drew glances at me. "What do you think?"

I just don't know. There have been too many surprises.

"I'll have to text Moira." I take my own phone out and send off a question. It returns immediately with a response.

I show it to Drew.

Lucinda is an identical twin.

He lowers his weapon and Ty follows suit.

Katrina runs over, throwing her arms around me in a big hug. I lean into Drew. "Kat, baby, I think you ought to go in and find Liza, okay?" Now's not the time to introduce Kat to her father, and I don't like the way she's surrounded by dead bodies on the ground.

"Okay, Momma." She runs up the stairs and takes hold of Lucy's hand.

The sound of a gunshot rips through the air. I whip my head around and Charlie steps in front of Kat, and the bullet meant for her head embeds in his body. Numbness shoots over me, disabling my need to go to her. A second shot rings out next to me, and I stare at the wisp of smoke that emanates from Tyson's barrel. I don't know who he shot behind me and I don't care.

"Kat!" I follow Drew, already running up the steps for Charlie. Tyson runs to make sure that whoever he shot is dead. Drew shakes his head.

Tears fall silently down my face. Not now. I thought we'd have more time with him. My head bows under responsibility and the awful churning in my stomach because I couldn't save him.

Kat cries softly into my side. She looks up at me, as if wondering what has become of her life. She runs into the house before I can stop her. My heart breaks for her and the knowledge that he laid down his life to protect hers. She'll forever carry that guilt. As will I.

Drew carries Charlie's body into the house and lays him on the dining room table. Katrina runs back, but she can't be here. She shouldn't be *here*. Anywhere but where death lays. My heart stutters at the item in her hands.

NO.

She's carrying her staff, her little face screwed up with determination. "Momma, I need you. I need you to fix it, Momma."

I step forward to stop her, but she slams it down and vibrations move over me.

And she turns back time.

Chapter Thirty-Four

DELANEY

I shake my head, dazed. I'm standing with Tyson and Drew. I glance about me with a deep sense of foreboding. The front door. Wasn't Kat just there? I shake my head to clear the sudden fogginess in my brain. There's a slight movement in the doorway, and shadows move from within.

Drew and Ty are shaking hands. Lucy emerges with Kat. And I gasp as the memory slams into me. I watch as the scene plays out before me. I play my part and text Moira.

But right before a gunshot is heard, I'm already turned backward, facing the unknown gunman who means to kill my child. Ty alerted by my movement, turns with me. We watch as a gun is raised. We draw simultaneously and shoot the unknown assailant. I see the smoke wisp from his barrel.

"Nice shot," Ty says. I grin and look over to see Drew's hooded gaze. I lean over.

"I'll tell you later," I murmur softly. "But Kat has just graduated."

He processes what I told him and whips his head toward Katrina, awe scrawling along his face. I, too, stare in fascination. My five-year-old completed her first time-turn and the world didn't blow up. She smiles wide and I blow her a kiss.

Once all the surrendered men are gone and the dead bodies cleaned up and incinerated, Drew and I sit on the front porch. I tell him what happened and how Charlie had saved Katrina's life and how she took matters into her own hands and turned back time. Drew's in awe of her abilities, and I am, too, truthfully. I couldn't be prouder. But I'm also petrified. What price did she pay? She's so little, and we almost lost the battle today. If Ty hadn't shown up with his group of Magicals, things would've turned out far different. I'm sad knowing we can't protect her in the way she should be protected.

"I'll have to let her go with them. I don't want to lose her yet, but I'm not sure we can keep her protected." Sorrow drags my words until they're a whisper of themselves.

"I think we can protect her just fine. But that's your choice, as her mom, to make."

The next morning, I'm aghast to see her color change.

"Katrina?"

"I know, Momma. Lucy already explained that each time I turn time I'll turn a shade lighter."

It wouldn't be noticeable to others, but as her mother, I know her face better than my own. She's always been darker-skinned, more like her father, but now she's a shade lighter than yesterday, even her corkscrew curls. So, she'll be leached of color, too? Are all Time-Turners pale versions of themselves? My throat constricts with unshed tears.

"It's okay, Momma. One day I'll look like you, for a bit."

I gather her in a big hug and hold on tight until she squirms to go play. I release her. She needs all the fun she can get. I call Moira. Again, no answer. I hang up without leaving a message. I contact Ty instead.

"Can you find Moira? I think something is wrong. I can't get a hold of her."

"I was just at her place. She was killed last night or this morning."

I drop into the chair at his words. I knew Moira's time was going to be up soon. I'm just sorry it was this quick.

"I'm sorry," Ty continues, "I know she was your friend."

Was she? If not friends, certainly warrior partners. I didn't know her that well, but I knew her heart was in the right spot, and that's all I needed to know.

"Okay, Tyson, Plan B."

There's a silence on the other end. Did he hang up?

"Are you sure?" he finally asks.

"Yes."

"Plan B. I'll see you tomorrow."

"What's Plan B?" Drew walks into the dining room.

He drops quickly to his knees in front of me upon seeing my silent tears. "What's wrong?'

"Moira was killed," I whisper. "And yesterday...it was too close. I risk Katrina by keeping her here. With me. It's selfish."

"I'm sorry." He stands and, lifting me out of the chair, sits down and plops me into his lap.

I snuggle into his neck and breathe him in and center myself. "Plan B is Tyson taking her. He'll hide her and protect her. Only a few of us knew where."

"Let's go spend the day with her." We head to her room. Lucy lifts her eyebrow at the sadness that must show on my face.

"It's Moira."

Lucy releases a breath and leans back into the sofa she's sitting in, stunned. "Plan B?"

"Yes." I didn't know till now if she knew anything. Seems she's in the inner circle after all. There will be no lessons today.

"I want to spend all day with my girl here." I ruffle Kat's hair.

Lucy stands. "I have things I need to take care of too." She walks out, her stride purposeful.

Drew and I spend all day with Kat, playing in the pool, throwing beach balls, playing Marco Polo and aquatic basketball. Seeing Kat sitting on Drew's shoulders so she can slam dunk the ball into the water and hearing her laughter shrieking makes me gooey inside in a way I'd never thought possible. Besides Kat never having the opportunity to do such things with a dad, there's something about my soul mate and my child smiling and having fun that makes my love for them both encompass my entire being.

I snuggle in bed with her at night and break the news to her. She seems okay with it, knowing there's no choice. It helps she'll be leaving with her father. She took learning about him in stride. We giggle and laugh and reminisce. We talk and shed tears. We fall asleep wrapped in each other's arms.

In the morning, Charlie makes an elaborate breakfast in her honor. Mid-morning, Tyson arrives. I refuse to cry. This is what's best for her, for her people. And I know Tyson loves her just as much as I do, even though it's in a different way. He'll take good care of her.

"I love you, Katrina-Ballerina."

"I love you too, Momma. I promise to call every chance I get."

Drew has given Kat her own cellphone with all his tech built-in and taught her how to use it. She won't leave without a line of communication. He also gifted her her own knife made from rhodium. One in its own sheath that she can strap to her thigh. I'm not so sure I like the idea of my five-year-old with a razor-sharp, deadly dagger strapped to her little leg, but I loathe the idea of her going unarmed even more. I hug her so hard she squeals.

"I'll see you soon, Momma. I promise. It's not forever." I kiss her forehead and her little nose. And I let my baby leave.

I wait till they're all gone. Liza, Lucy, Tyson, and Kat leave before I let my emotions go. I drop into a heap on the floor at the base of the stairs and the tears flow. Drew sits down with me and holds me, his arms offering comfort and warmth, his soul soothing mine. I lean into him until the tears no longer pour out. Drew stands and pulls me up.

"You did the best thing in the entire world, Delaney."

"What's that?" I ask.

"You helped save an entire branch of people. You endured so much, made it all happen." He fingers the fourth strand of gray hair. "You changed things. For the better. Not many people can say that anything they did in life made an impact. But you did. And Katrina will. All because you have a great big heart and chose to do something with it. I love you. And I couldn't be more proud."

"Thank you." I duck my head. It doesn't feel like a win, but a defeat. I know, in time, that feeling will change, because I've seen it. The vision I had last night should pacify me, but I'm also very aware that the future can change. Time-Turners notwithstanding. Too many players. Shit, even Karma herself, can fuck with what we've all sacrificed for.

I'm grateful for what I have, for what I've been given. My privilege in helping others and Drew's love for me. In time, Kat will return—when she can hold her own—and we'll be reunited. The joy of that future moment ripples through me. There'll be battles to come, and though we'll surely lose some, there will be others we win. There's something satisfying in knowing we will kick ass another day.

Our circle of members, united in stopping the corrupt Guardians trying to wipe out branches of Infinites, is expanding. I already have plans for us to bring others into the fold and more than a few we might have to drag in kicking and screaming. Which shouldn't sound like a lot of fun. But every one of them has an important role to play.

When Drew kisses the top of my head, and I rest my head on his chest, when the warmth of our love envelopes me, and his vein pulses in time to my heartbeat, the sensation of everything being *right* flows through me. Contentment wraps itself around me like it always does with him, but at this moment, I know that everything is the way it should be. That the metaphorical axis of the world is tilted correctly.

I have my soul mate back, our soul evenly divided between us. Whatever comes, we are together and stronger for it. Our love is stronger than it's ever been.

And I've finally fulfilled my destiny...or at least this portion of it.

The End.

Arnica's Story

FALL 2023

Acknowledgments

To my Readers and Infinites Universe fans, I can't thank you enough for loving my words. So many of you have tagged me, commented, written to me about how much you adored Becoming Justice, and I can't wait for you to fall in love with Resetting Destiny. Adding characters to this universe brings me so much joy, and the interactions they'll have together has my fingers itching to type. (As I side-eye my book release timeline board.)

To my Fabulous Dev Editor, I continue to be grateful to work with you and to effusively thank you for pushing me and having faith in my abilities. Without you, my work wouldn't be half as good.

To my Amazing Husband, you make me cry with every supportive step you take. You're beyond incredible for always being proud of me, for wanting to shout to the rooftops that I'm an author, and for every text telling me that I've got another great review because you stalk Amazon lol. The universe knew what it was doing when it decided we were soul mates, and I'm beyond thrilled that I didn't have to wait long for us to find each other. Love you so much.

To my Wonderful Kids, thank you for loving me and putting up with free-for-all dinners and less movie nights. You're my world and I love you infinity-infinites.

To my #PitSquirrels, thank you always for your unwavering support and friendship. Writing has never been lonely since we got together. We are ALL going to slay.

To my Best Friend, thank you for endless coffee talks since

the beginning of time (Time together, that is. We're not THAT fucking old!) and for always listening. Love you!

To my Friend who always wants to announce that I'm an author, thank you for all the talking and laughter—and coffee and window shopping—we can handle. And by window shopping, I mean going to our favorite store with the intention of not buying, but dammit, always leaving with something!

To all of my found family and friends, I can't imagine a universe without you in it.

To my copy editor, I CANNOT seem to exist without having a tight deadline and I promise I'll work on it! Thank you for always being flexible and hitting the impossibilities I throw at you. (And also polishing my words till they shine!)

To my newest additions to team Liv, my miracle working personal assistant, and my fabulous promotions and marketing genius, thank you for believing in my books (and me!) enough to want to work with me day in and day out. I appreciate you both more than you know!

About the Author

Liv Macy is a debut author in the adult paranormal romance genre. Becoming Justice is the first novel in the Infinites Universe.

A mother, chef, taxi driver, maid, referee, teacher, shopper, wife, and advice-giver by trade, Liv spends her free moments dreaming of characters that refuse to keep their story to themselves.

With a lifetime passion for reading and writing that infused every spare moment, it was only natural that Liv took her love of words to the next level. When there are leftover moments, she loves to cook and hang out with her family and friends—and if there's time remaining after THAT...well, Liv likes to sit in a cozy chair with a blanket and a cup of coffee and contemplate life.

Learn more about Liv Macy by visiting her website and sign up for her newsletter.

www.LivMacy.com

facebook.com/LivMacyAuthor

instagram.com/livmacyauthor

tiktok.com/@livmacyauthor

bookbub.com/authors/liv-macy

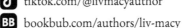
twitter.com/LivMacyAuthor